Aliens, Campers, and Coffee

Karen Bruno

Published by Jesus is the way, the truth, the life., 2024.

With endless gratitude, I dedicate my life and my work to the Holy Trinity: God of Heaven, Jesus Christ, and the Holy Spirit.

"You are the light of the world. A town built on a hill cannot be hidden. Neither do people light a lamp and put it under a bowl. Instead they put it on its stand, and it gives light to everyone in the house. In the same way, let your light shine before others, that they may see your good deeds and glorify your Father in heaven." Matthew 5:14-16 NIV

Additional Clauses: No Generative AI Training Use. For avoidance of doubt, Karen Bruno Young the Author and Publisher of *Aliens, Campers, and Coffee* reserves the rights worldwide and no other person, platform, company or agency has no rights to, reproduce and/or otherwise use *Aliens, Campers, and Coffee* the Work and Literary Property in any manner for purposes of training artificial intelligence technologies to generate text, including without limitation, technologies that are capable of generating works and literary property in the same style or genre as *Aliens, Campers, and Coffee* the Work and Literary Property unless the person, platform, company or agency obtains from Karen Bruno Young the Author's specific and express written permission to do so. Nor does any person, platform, company or agency have the right to sublicense others to reproduce and/or otherwise use *Aliens, Campers, and Coffee* the Work and Literary Property in any manner for purposes of training artificial intelligence technologies to generate text without obtaining from Karen Bruno Young the Author's specific and express written permission. Furthermore, the scanning, uploading, and/or distribution of my writing and my photographs and including all material from *Aliens, Campers, and Coffee* my Work and Literary Property whether in a print, audio, or electronic format without the specific and express written permission from Karen Bruno Young the Author and Publisher of *Aliens, Campers, and Coffee* this Work and Literary Property, is a theft of the Author's Work and Literary Property and Intellectual Property. I do not allow and I do not give my permission for any of my writing, my photographs, and including all other material from *Aliens, Campers, and Coffee* my Work and Literary Property to be used for Generative AI Training or to be harvested by AI technology, computer programs, or computer software, and including by any other means and by any person, platform, company or agency including any person, platform, company or agency that engages in piracy and theft of Works and Literary Property and Intellectual Property theft. I do not give permission to use my writing, my photographs, and including all material from *Aliens, Campers, and Coffee* my Work and Literary Property for any other purposes or by any other means. Thank you for your respect and support of this Author's rights. Karen Bruno Young is the only Author and Publisher of *Aliens, Campers, and Coffee* this Work and Literary Property, and is not responsible for websites (or their content) that are not owned directly by the

Author's Note

I started writing *Aliens, Campers, and Coffee* on April 4, 2020 which was the twelfth birthday of my horse Windy. It was during the Covid-19 Pandemic lock down. I wanted to amuse myself and to get more brain exercise. I enjoyed learning the creative writing process. I wrote a plot outline of my story to use as my road map. My early writing was awkward but at least I had all of my characters' identities firmly established. I kept trying and as I continued working my brain was flooded with new ideas and my creativity and my story flourished together. It was an enjoyable process. Except for editing and formatting, which were very challenging for me.

I take my work seriously but it also became very entertaining. I laughed aloud frequently while writing this novel and the characters feel like friends after all this time. Most of my characters are named after my animal companions. While proofreading, I read *Aliens, Campers, and Coffee* aloud to my dogs Sedona and Sam. They decided that it's a fun story and I hope you do too. Full disclosure here, Sedona and Sam may be slightly biased because they are the story's main characters. Additionally, as loyal friends they love me unconditionally and are very supportive of me. Plus, I shamelessly bribed them with dog treats until they finally proclaimed *Aliens, Campers, and Coffee* is the best novel they have ever heard.

Each chapter has a theme song that enhances the action and emotion of the story. If you're interested, please spend a few minutes and listen to the songs so you can experience the full emotional impact of the journey. It's wonderful music and you'll have fun along the way. My thanks to all of the song writers, musicians, and singers whose song titles are mentioned in my story as the chapter titles. I enjoy your music and listen to it every day. Your dedication and talent for sharing God's message through your inspirational music brings blessedness. These are the musical artists that I listen to every day: Anne Wilson, Carly Pearce, Cheyenne Mitchell, Katy Nichole, Zach Williams, Crowder, Maverick City Gospel Choir, Bart Millard and MercyMe, Sam Wesley, Walker Hayes, Casting Crowns, Matthew West, TobyMac, Rhett Walker, Jeremy Camp, I AM THEY, Big Daddy Weave, Third Day, Chris Tomlin, Ryan Stevenson, Gabe Real, Newsboys, Mac Powell, Brandon Lake, Pastor Steven Furtick, and Elevation Worship among many others.

I'm fond of my fictional characters and their adventures. I created my characters and their personality traits and experiences from my own authentic creative process. None of my characters are based on actual people. However, like most writers, I'm inspired by many of my own personal life experiences and they are used fictitiously in my novel. Naturally, I utilized creative ideas from my own biological brain. I unleashed my imagination to suit my creative vision. During my writing process, I worked hard to create my own specific style, mood, and my own authentic voice as a creative writer. I attest and I certify that truthfully every part of *Aliens, Campers, and Coffee* (with the exception of the cover art, *Holy Bible* Scriptures, song titles, names of singers, and album titles) is entirely created by my own creative writing and authentic creative process, that I dredged up from my own memory, and that I created it by myself using my own biological brain, and that I physically typed every single word with my own hands. I'm a practitioner of authentic 100% human-created writing, 100% human-authorship, and genuine 100% human-powered creativity. The book cover art is designed by Richard Ljoenes and is protected by copyright ©2024.

The trash throwing scene in chapter two is based on an experience I had in high school. There was a tropical storm that day and P.E. activities were cancelled. We were gathered in a concrete amphitheater with all the other P.E. classes to ride out the stormy weather. I was sitting alone on the concrete steps working on my homework. Two boys seated higher up the steps were throwing things at me. They were lobbing spit balls into my hair, throwing pebbles at my back, and rolling empty soda cans down the steps into my backside. I tried to ignore them for a long time, then I finally went to get help from my teacher. Surprisingly, my teacher refused to protect me when I went to him and asked for help in dealing with the two bullies. Disappointed, I went back to my books and tried to concentrate on my work.

Why didn't it occur to me to find another place to sit? I wish I had but it was just so crowded with several classes in the amphitheater. Anyway, the boys kept throwing things at me and I finally had an Incredible Hulk moment. I might have roared with anger. I may have grabbed a trash can. It really was the Hulk's fault for taking over. The good news is that no one was hurt and the can held mostly paper cups and candy bar wrappers. My teacher actually laughed at me with disbelief at my audacity. After the incident, the two boys were repentant and whenever they saw me, they would smile and rush to hold doors open for me. I bet they never tried to bully another girl. All is forgiven. Here's the disclaimer: This happened way back in the mid-1980s when you could still get away with a few shenanigans. Kids never try this at school or anywhere else!

While my novel is a work of Christian Fiction, I believe that every word in the *Holy Bible* is true and is truly God's message for humanity. I tried to share the Good News about the Kingdom of God with accuracy and respect. I spent years diligently studying the *Holy Bible*, New International Version and the Common English Bible translation. I studied for four years at church with several serious, in-depth classes led by pastors. It was a wonderful experience of Christian fellowship and it helped me grow spiritually. I'm forever grateful to my friends from the Disciple Bible Study courses. I also use the YouVersion Bible app on my smartphone. It has guided Bible study plans and includes a large number of Bible translations to choose from. I also enjoy listening to the audio Bible feature on YouVersion. I believe that seriously studying the *Holy Bible* helped me to be as accurate as possible with sharing Christian theology.

All of the *Holy Bible* Scripture verses quoted in my novel are from the *Holy Bible* (NIV) New International Version, unless specifically noted as NRSV. The NRSV is the *Holy Bible* New Revised Standard Version. All *Holy Bible* Scriptures quoted in *Aliens, Campers, and Coffee* are used in accordance with the publishers' gratis use permission guidelines.

I'm inspired by countless talented authors and their wonderful books. Reading has been one of my favorite hobbies since I was in third grade. It was at our school book fair that I first discovered *The Black Stallion* series by Walter Farley. His exciting horse stories were a joyful way for me to experience amazing adventures through reading. As a child, I was obsessed with horses and Walter Farley's books captivated me and allowed my imagination to roam freely. I'm grateful that my teachers and librarians and our school book fairs encouraged reading. What a wonderful gift. My heartfelt thanks to all teachers, librarians, and public libraries. Thank you for encouraging reading and for providing access to books. In high school I was a skinny and socially awkward girl who loved dogs, horses, and reading novels. I was almost an artist, almost an athlete, almost a musician, and almost a great student. My favorite subjects were art class, team sports, band class, language arts, and lunch. I'm very happy that reading novels became a healthy life-long habit.

During high school, I distinctly recall the exciting feeling of being immersed in the dramatic novels of Danielle Steel. Her novels quickly became my favorite companions and reading them really helped me get through the growing pains of my high school years. I remember sitting on the concrete steps outside of the art building during lunch breaks and reading *Palomino* and *Wanderlust* along with many other novels. As an adult, I still enjoy reading Danielle Steel's novels. I've also discovered the works of James A. Michener. I love his epic historical novels. I'm fascinated by the innovative novels of Michael Crichton. His exciting novels have captured my attention for many years. I'm still perched on the edge of my seat, happily reading novels today.

To all of my fellow human beings: Please understand that I acknowledge and I agree that each person has free will and every person should make their own choices in life and especially about the religion they choose to follow. I sincerely respect human cultures and religions. I sincerely respect your right to make your own personal choices about your own individual lifestyle. Travel your own unique path in life. Whatever you choose to believe in: I wish you peace, love, and blessings. I also believe in the rights to freedom of speech, the freedom to choose your own religion and to practice religion, and the freedom of expression. In creating and writing my own Christian Fiction novel, I simply choose to share my own personal beliefs at the heart of what I hope is an inspirational, humorous, adventurous, and positively entertaining work of literature.

Chapter 1

Theme song: "-[DASH]" by Crowder featuring TobyMac from the album The Exile

"Hey Sedona! Take out the trash, now!" Kaya, our unhinged cook, bellows at me with unreasonable rage.

My coworkers, like a herd of startled deer, quickly leap into action. They collect the waiting dinner plates which are piled full of the house special and like a panicked herd, they fearfully scamper out of the kitchen and into the dining room. *Cowards!*

Kaya looms over the grill, a belligerent hairy giant wrapped in a ridiculously tiny grease-stained apron. With his towering height and barrel belly, barely contained under the apron, he looks like a disgruntled cave bear. He wields a spatula in each hairy bear paw hand. He grunts wildly at me like a neanderthal. With extreme annoyance, he impatiently gestures with a greasy spatula to the overflowing trash cans.

"Okay Kaya. I'll take care of it right away." I hustle over to the smelly cans.

I glance back to be sure he stays at the grill. Kaya is glaring at me with a hostile glint in his eyes. The overhead LED lights make the drops of sweat clinging precariously to the tip of his nose appear to sparkle like diamonds. *Ew, gross.*

I look down at the floor and grimace at the fetid mess in front of me. My nose hairs curl at the disgusting stench. *This is an offensive and malodorous stink and it's physically painful.* Someone on the morning shift failed to place new bags inside the trash cans and they clearly never considered emptying them either. As a result, by the start of the dinner rush there's an avalanche of raw and rancid kitchen waste spilling down onto the floor in a slimy, smelly trash dump. *Well, I'm going to need some music to get through this nasty chore.*

I pull my smartphone from my apron pocket and tap my Pandora app. I turn up the volume on the Zach Williams station and get to work. The song "Slave to Nothing" by Zach Williams from the album Rescue Story Deluxe Edition starts playing. *Yup, it's the perfect song for this unhappy chore.*

My worn-out shoes hydroplane in slippery raw egg yolks, pools of melted butter, spilled mayonnaise, mustard, ketchup, slimy melted cheese goo, and decades of slick grease residue covering the filthy diner floor. Like an Olympic ice skater, I gracefully glide my way over to the storage shelf to collect trash bags. As I cruise smoothly past the shelf, I make a desperate grab for the industrial strength long rubber gloves as I slide quickly across the greasy floor.

Wearing my fashionable opera-length gloves, I kneel pathetically on the floor like a real-life Cinderella. I gag as I scoop the reeking moist mess into the trash bags. When I finish my distasteful chore, my blue jeans are stained with goo and cling wetly to my legs. I have three bulging bags tied securely to prevent another hazardous waste spill.

I commandeer the mop and bucket. I frown unhappily at the filthy water swirling inside it. I lug the bucket to the sink and dump it. After refilling it, I pour in a bottle of cleaning fluid. Working up a sweat, I strenuously scrub the floor until it's perfectly clean for the first time in decades. With a sigh of relief, I inhale the clean scent of citrus.

I wrestle with the heavy trash bags and awkwardly drag them to the back door. I step outside the EZ to be a Pro Diner and stumble with my burden toward the dumpster. I peer into the inky night. There is only one bare bulb blinking feebly over the door and the light doesn't reach far into the back alley.

Cautiously, I make my way further into the alley, struggling with my odoriferous load of trash. I hear loud grunting and moaning and I startle in surprise at the unexpected sounds. My arms and hands sweat profusely, still safely encased in my classy, opera length rubber gloves. My poor fingers are wrinkled up from soaking in tiny hot tubs of perspiration pooling in the fingertips of my sweaty gloves. *What's going on out here? No one's supposed to be loitering in the alley.* I hear loud metallic thumping reverberating in the grim darkness.

"Oh, oh! Yes, yes, yes!" Someone is screaming passionate cries into the night.

I peer into the forbidding gloom as my eyes struggle to adjust to the dimness. I can barely make out two figures moving frantically against the dumpster. *Oh joy, will the fun never end?*

"Hey you, no one's allowed back here! This is private property! You need to leave now!"

When there is no response, I set down my load of trash. I pull my smartphone out of the pocket of my stained apron. Pandora is playing the song "Fear is a Liar (Live)" by Zach Williams from the album Survivor: Live from Harding Prison - EP. I struggle to engage the flashlight app with my sweaty, rubber-entombed fingers. Finally, it illuminates the scene before me.

I step back in shock. *Good grief!* I see the back of a tall, broad-shouldered man. *Hey, that worn blue work shirt with the denim patch looks familiar. The denim patch that I sewed onto that shirt with my own hands.* My husband Lew Dung is standing with his blue jeans lying crumpled down around his ankles. He is locked in a carnal embrace with a woman. Lew turns his head, looks over his shoulder and glares at me with annoyance. Triumphantly peering at me over his shoulder is my boss, Louanne Pooey.

Chapter 2

Theme song: "Out of my Hands" by Jeremy Camp from the album The Story's not Over

"Lew, how could you? Both of you are dirty rotten cheaters!" My smartphone is still boldly illuminating the sinful scene in front of me. Pandora cheerfully starts playing the song "I saw the Light" from the album A Collision Or (3+4=7) by David Crowder Band.

Louanne grins insolently at me. "Sugar, give us a moment of privacy to finish conducting our business."

Lew turns back to my boss and helps her rearrange her dress. He runs his hands over her hips smoothing down the slinky fabric, like a true gentleman. Her dress slides down her body and resumes its normal, modest demeanor. He whispers into Louanne's ear, then kisses her cheek.

Shaking with emotion, I shout at the top of my voice, fueled by my righteous indignation. "That's it! I'm done with both of you! Lew, you're a horrible husband and I quit our marriage! Louanne, you're a terrible boss and I quit this crappy job, too!" I seethe with anger at my cheating husband and my husband-pilfering boss.

In a wild moment of uncontrollable rage, I squat down and rip open my trash bags. I gather up ammunition of dripping handfuls of trash. With all my strength, I fire missiles of slimy rotten vegetables, lard, burnt bacon, coffee grounds, and cracked egg shells dripping with sticky goo at the couple. The diner trash is flying out of my hands and splattering all over the self-absorbed, deceitful couple.

When I finally run out of my trashy ammunition, I'm trembling with adrenaline and my rubber gloves are covered in smelly slime. The trash bags lie shredded and empty on the asphalt, mirroring my broken heart inside my chest. From the pocket of my dirty apron, Pandora merrily launches into Crowder's song "My Beloved" from the album Neon Steeple Deluxe Edition.

The three of us are standing in the near darkness locked in a stalemate of disgruntled shock. Furiously, we all stare at each other, momentarily speechless. Louanne breaks the spell of silence by loudly screeching in disgust, swiping frantically at the filthy slime clinging to her face and tangled wetly in her long hair.

With a loud, angry grunt of disapproval, Lew bends forward and reaches down to retrieve his jeans from around his ankles, mooning me in the process. There is a large gooey glob of raw egg yolk dripping off one butt cheek. *Great, that says it all. Staying in this unhappy marriage is definitely not for me.*

Crying with gut-wrenching despair, I turn away from my husband and run back inside the diner kitchen. Kaya, who is still standing in front of the grill, turns around and glares at me.

"There's no crying allowed in my kitchen! What's your problem, Sedona?"

"I quit! I just caught Louanne out by the dumpster sinning with my husband! I'm leaving now and you can't stop me!"

My timid coworkers slink out of the kitchen and back into the dining room with the hope of collecting my serving tips for the night's work.

"Oh no you don't Sedona! You're not leaving me here without enough servers on shift tonight! I don't care about your personal drama! I'll make your life miserable if you step out of this diner during our dinner rush!" Kaya shouts, spitting globs of saliva all over the hamburgers sizzling on the grill in front of him.

Gross, I'm so glad that I never eat in this disgusting dump. I hiccup as I peel off my slimy rubber gloves and dirty apron, tossing them with an audible wet splatter onto the floor.

I'm sobbing loudly in despair and a river of tears are rolling down my face in an uncontrolled torrent. Unfortunately, this causes Mount Everest, my high-altitude and distinctive Roman nose to be overcome with an unwelcome avalanche of sticky snot.

I rush into the dining room and retrieve my purse from under the cash register. I don't bother to clock out or to collect my share of the tips.

Kaya storms out of the kitchen glaring at me. "Sedona, get back in the kitchen! If you step out of this diner, you're fired!"

I toss my long hair over my shoulder. "You can't stop me, Kaya! I told you, I quit and I'm out of here!" *Staying in this unhappy job is definitely not for me.*

I shoulder the long strap of my purse as I walk through the dining room which is filled to capacity with patrons. The whole town is unabashedly staring at me over their evening meals. *Great, now I'm a public spectacle.* By this point, I'm crying loudly and gasping for breath as a panic attack seizes me. Hiccup! *Oh no, hiccups. They always accompany my panic attacks.*

Feeling dizzy now, I stop walking for a moment and leaning forward I grasp my knees trying to catch my breath. My purse strap slides down my arm and causes my heavy purse to slam into my thigh like a sledgehammer, unbalancing me. *Ow!*

With a wheezing gasp, I slide my purse strap back onto my shoulder. I'm willing myself to breathe normally again while dark spots dance across my vision. The ugly swirls and circles pattern on the greasy orange and green outdated shag carpet is swimming alarmingly before my eyes.

Feeling woozy and defeated, I collapse to the floor in a pathetic, breathless heap. My heavy purse swings violently with my movements and clocks me in the face. *Ouch, that's going to leave a bruise.*

All of the townies are still watching me in silent fascination. Not one soul steps forward to offer me assistance. *What do they think this is? Dinner and a show?* I struggle to breathe, as I weakly clamber to my hands and knees. Hiccup!

Dragging my purse by its long strap, I pathetically crawl to the front door blubbering and dripping tears onto the greasy carpet the whole way. *Come on girl! Get a hold of yourself and pull it together.*

Finally, I reach the blessed door. I grasp the long horizontal bar on the metal framed glass door, pulling myself upright I exit the building on shaky legs. I'm grateful to be on my feet again and although I'm feeling unsteady and still gasping for breath, I start running away. *Embarrassing myself in front of the entire town is definitely not for me.*

Chapter 3

Theme song: "Devil" by Anne Wilson from the album *My Jesus Anniversary Deluxe Edition*

Lew and Louanne are still standing in the dark alley behind the EZ to be a Pro Diner. They lean against the dumpster while holding hands and relishing the moment of their triumph.

"Honey, we finally did it! We got rid of my boring, goodie-two-shoes wife once and for all!" Laughing with excitement, he turns to Louanne and wraps his arms tightly around her.

"Did you see the devastated look on her face? It was priceless! That was a brilliant plan Lew, really diabolical. I loved every minute of it. Are you sure she will leave you though? She's deeply in love with you, you know. I mean the sad, clingy, sappy, unconditional kind of love. It's pathetic! She will love you no matter what you do. I think Sedona is such a devout Bible-thumper that she won't be willing to divorce you, no matter what you do to her. What if she doesn't leave town like you think she will? What will you do then?" Louanne kisses Lew passionately, melting into his strong embrace.

"Louanne, trust me we are finally rid of her. I know Sedona better than anyone in the world. Don't worry. I know how Sedona thinks and I can manipulate her mind and her emotions. I can predict her reaction with certainty. She is so deeply shocked and hurt by our betrayal, that she will pack up her pets and high-tail it out of town in her old camper. I'm sure that she is running home right this minute. She will probably be leaving Sandy Town in the next hour. She was already planning to meet her best friend for their annual girls' trip. My plan just pushed her out of town a few days earlier to serve my purposes."

"I hope you're right, Lew."

"Louanne, I guarantee she will not want to be my wife any longer after what she just witnessed. That's why I chose you, sweetheart, for my plan. She'll never be able to live with the knowledge that her husband and her boss are betraying the sanctity of her marriage vows. I'm telling you sugar, we are rid of her! Now we are free to be together for the rest of our lives. Two weeks ago, I called and scheduled an appointment for tomorrow morning with my lawyer to file divorce papers. That's how confident I am that my plan will succeed."

"Excellent. With your wife out of our way, can I come with you to your appointment in the morning? I want to be there to witness you filing for divorce. I'm so excited that I don't want to miss it. I can't wait to watch you sign the contracts selling your home and land, and the wealth of minerals buried underneath them. I want to cherish the moment we become multimillionaires! We're going to be so indecently, sinfully, filthy rich!"

"Absolutely, doll baby. I want you with me every minute. I'll move my things to your place after I sign the contracts at John's law office. Then we can begin enjoying our newfound wealth. Are you still excited about us taking that long trip through Italy for the summer? I already purchased our first-class airline tickets. I also made reservations at all of our accommodations in the most exclusive and luxurious mansions across Italy but it's still early enough that I can adjust the dates of our travel. Whatever you want babe, I'll make it happen for you." Lew kisses his mistress deeply and then solemnly slides a four-carat, oval-shaped, diamond solitaire platinum engagement ring onto Louanne's left hand.

"It's about time, Lew. I was starting to doubt your commitment to me. I've been dying to finally wear this glamorous ring that we chose together! Lew, will you still buy me the other three-carat diamond eternity ring to wear as a wedding band? You know seven is my lucky number, it has to be seven carats total, or I won't be happy! I've been waiting so long for you to dump your pathetic wife, that I think you also owe me an elegant right-hand ring. Something with platinum and overflowing in pink, yellow, and green diamonds should make me feel better. Let's go to the jewelry store tomorrow." Louanne pouts while caressing the giant rock sitting on the third finger of her left hand.

Lew sighs loudly with vexation. "Yes, Louanne! I told you already babe, whatever you want, it's yours. Just quit harping on it!"

The peaceful darkness of the cool desert night embraces me and soothes the pain in my shattered heart. I'm running in my strongest sprint with my purse rhythmically bumping against my thigh. Above me, the night sky is a limitless, dark expanse, glowing with brilliant starlight shining down upon me, guiding my path. My greasy work shoes pound the empty street as the cold breeze dries my face to a sticky mess of snot, despair, and wasted tears.

Chapter 4

Theme song: "This House" by Anne Wilson from the album *My Jesus Anniversary Deluxe Edition*

I hear my two dogs barking with excitement at the front door as I arrive home. Wearily, I stumble inside the dark and empty house. I reach for the light switch by the door and sink to the cold tile floor, desperately trying to catch my breath. My sweet boys, Blue Heelers Rex and Patch joyfully welcome me as I embrace them. They fastidiously lick my face, earnestly trying to wash away my shame and despair. I gently bury my fingers in their soft gray, black, and white speckled fur and after gratefully absorbing their consoling attention, I rise up feeling stronger.

I grab a handful of baby carrots from the fridge and the boys follow me to the backyard for a potty break. I hear a joyful bray and the drumming of small hooves rushing toward me. My sweet miniature donkey materializes out of the darkness and kisses me with her wet muzzle. Her long whiskers tickle my face and I sob a little as I laugh aloud at the prickly sensation.

"Hello Topaz, my dear. How are you? Did you miss me while I was at work?" I gently rub her sweet furry face as I sniffle.

I feed her a carrot and run my fingers along her fuzzy neck then I scratch her withers. After a run around the fenced fifty-acre property, Patch and Rex finally return to me and I hand them each a carrot.

"Guys, would the three of you like to take a long journey with me in the Tumbleweed?" I ask my companion animals with determination as an escape plan suddenly forms in my mind.

With my boys following close on my heels, I hurry back inside the house and into the kitchen to gather several large cloth shopping bags. I fill them with canned goods and glass bottles of sparkling water. From the hook on the kitchen wall, I take down my flying saucer key ring that my mom Joy gave to me many years ago. Thinking of my adventurous mom makes me smile, as I slide the keys to my Tumbleweed into the front pocket of my jeans.

I run to the bedroom and retrieve my roller suitcase from under the bed. I fetch my favorite sweater. It's a long cardigan sweater and it's a sweet butter-scotch candy color. I carefully fold it and place it inside the case. I throw in the rest of my clothing. In a moment of sentimental weakness, I grab one of Lew's decades old T-shirts from the last time he volunteered with me at va-cation Bible school. I securely tie the laces of my hiking boots onto the tele-scoping handle of my suitcase, safely securing my boots for the journey.

I make several trips ferrying my belongings out to my Tumbleweed. It's a solar powered class c motor home parked in the fenced backyard. By the time I'm done fetching my things, I have a small pile of personal belongings ready to be loaded into my camper. I'm grateful that my late dad Pasquale left me his camper, along with a small inheritance.

Because of my dad's generosity, I'm financially equipped to travel in the Tumbleweed and live in it full-time for the rest of my life. *An exciting RV ad-venture traveling in the desert wilderness of the American Southwest is definite-ly for me.*

Using the flashlight feature on my smartphone to aid me, I unlock the Tumbleweed's door. Rex and Patch jump eagerly aboard. I load my belong-ings. I start the motor and slowly back up to my small stock trailer. It takes me a few attempts in the darkness but I'm able to hitch up the trailer safely. I call for Topaz again. She gallops over and I clip a cotton rope to her rope halter. She happily steps up into her trailer which is set up for her comfort.

For the last time, I step into our home. I take one last look around then I turn off the lights and lock the door. From my jeans pocket, Pandora is play-ing MercyMe's song "Ghost" from the album Lifer. There is no need to leave a note. *Why waste paper?* I'm sure that Lew will understand the message of an empty home loud and clear when he returns later tonight. I march resolutely to my Tumbleweed and my companions who are patiently waiting aboard. I pull open the double gates in the fence and I climb up into the driver's seat and buckle my seat belt. With a feeling of excitement building within me, I slowly guide the Tumbleweed through the gates and out of the yard. I carefully pull onto the Extraterrestrial Highway and start my journey into the unknown.

A feeling of calmness descends upon me as I navigate the Tumbleweed through the dark night. Beautiful, luminous starlight shines through the windshield and guides my journey. I drive until I begin to feel fatigue. After a short search, I find a suitable scenic overlook. It has a large gravel parking area where I can park for the night and boondock in the Tumbleweed. Finally, I can get a few hours of much needed sleep.

Chapter 5

Theme song: "Holy Rollin'" by Zach Williams from the album A Hundred Highways

As bitter tears fall from my eyes, I sink into the driver's seat of my Tumbleweed. I buckle up my seat belt and sob as I put on my pink cap and pull my pony tail through the cap's opening in the back. Choking back my despair, I switch my sterling silver Sleeping Beauty turquoise wedding ring from my left to my right hand. *Lord, I can't believe I'm actually leaving my husband.* My teary, sea-green eyes squint through the sunglasses perched on Mount Everest, my distinctive Roman nose. Droplets roll down my face and splash the tattered road atlas resting on my blue jeans. I sigh, taking a gulp of my iced caffé mocha, holding my travel mug with shaking hands.

This morning, a cheerful desert sun greets me through my windshield. My Tumbleweed camper runs on solar power and I'm running away fueled on espresso. I gently lift my foot from the brake and roll the Tumbleweed slowly forward heading toward the highway entrance.

Patch and Rex curl up in their pet beds with a contented sigh, worn out from their early morning run in the desert scrublands. Topaz, the boys, and I enjoyed a long hike at sunrise this morning. I'm confident that we will adjust to our new full-time RV lifestyle. *Now all I want is to see a patch of the blue sky and a new desert landscape in my RV windshield every morning. New beginnings are definitely for me.*

I'm still having trouble adjusting to the relationship destruction that happened last night. That my husband, Lew Dung, chose to shatter our marriage vows and my heart into a million pieces. He was my high school sweetheart. Now he is a portable toilet vendor and the owner of Dung's Doody Thrones, which is a daily and very regular business in Sandy Town. *I always thought we had a good relationship and that we enjoyed spending time together. What happened to us? I wonder why he chose to have an extramarital affair?*

I know the folks in town will be talking about this romantic scandal for the next decade. *I love Sandy Town but the townies are unapologetic busybodies.* I know I'm called to forgive and forget but Lew's shocking betrayal is going to take some effort to forget. *Daringly determined to be delighted I decided to take the dangling dregs of my dignity, my dainty donkey, my dependable dogs, and depart. Ah, I admire alliteration.*

I switch on the CD player and smile when I hear the song, "My Liberty" from the album Chain Breaker Deluxe Edition by Zach Williams. I sing along with a waterfall of pitiful tears streaming down my face. I take a deep breath and try to calm the overwhelming emotions that I'm dealing with. I feel an overpowering urge to start my life over with serving God of Heaven and Jesus Christ as an essential part of my life's purpose.

I press a button on my CD player and switch songs. I choose "Freedom" also from the album Chain Breaker Deluxe Edition by Zach Williams. Grinning now, with dried tears on my face, I slowly pull the Tumbleweed out of the roadside parking lot and back onto the Extraterrestrial Highway. I'm determined to leave my troubles in Sandy Town, Nevada behind me. Loud Christian rock, iced coffee, and the open road help me start the journey into my new life.

Chapter 6

Theme song: "Good to Know" by Zach Williams from the album Rescue Story Deluxe Edition

I spy the faded teal and pink sign for the Sad Sack RV Park. As I drive slowly past the sign, I can make out peeling decals depicting flying saucers and grinning gray aliens. I carefully pull the Tumbleweed off the Extraterrestrial Highway and into the campground. It's a small, lonely place with nothing surrounding it but empty desert. However, it's perfect for stargazing. Being isolated out in the desert far away from light pollution ensures excellent sky watching.

I park the Tumbleweed in the large parking area not far from a lemon-yellow electric car. Nearly every inch of the tiny car is decorated with decals of charming cartoon witches wearing pointed hats and riding on broomsticks with cute cats. Other decals are adorable cartoon Norwegian kitchen witches grinning triumphantly and holding up perfectly baked plump fruit pies with tiny puffs of steam rising from the crusts. I walk over to the flamboyant car to study the charming artwork plastered all over it. There's also a bumper sticker proclaiming "Goodly Witch." *As Mr. Spock would say: "Fascinating."*

I also notice with a feeling of surprised joy that the car is practically a tiny library. The back seat of the little car is stuffed to overflowing with various hardback books. I'm quite impressed when I see that the books are all arranged alphabetically and with the spines out so you can read the titles clearly. *This cute and creatively decorated car is a library on wheels. I hope I get to meet the creative and unique owner of this unusual library car.* I step into the office to inquire about a night's stay at the campground.

"Hi, I'm Sedona. It's nice to meet you. I'm on my way to Fragrant Bean for the coffee festival. Do you have a campsite with full hook ups available? My motor home is thirty-two feet long with one slide out. I have three companion animals and I'm only stopping for one night."

I smile at the athletic woman with a classic runner's physique doing Tai Chi in the empty office. I notice she has tall stacks of novels taking up nearly the entire work surface of the desk in her office. *Oh, cool she's also a bibliophile. It's always fun to meet a kindred spirit. Could this be the owner of the tiny library on wheels? I hope so.*

Behind her, I spy two enormous bookshelves overflowing with mass quantities of novels and poetry books. I smile as I see that there is one shelf devoid of literature and instead there is a sweet-faced cat reclining on an elegant gold brocade cushion secured to the shelf. There is a small ornate brass name plate affixed to the bookshelf that reads: "Miss Elsa, Sad Sack's Official Librarian." The only other furniture in the office are two cozy reading chairs and a floor lamp.

"Hi, I'm Miss Information. It's nice to meet you too, Sedona." The woman smiles at me and then looks through the open ledger on her desk. "Oh, you have amazing luck. I only have one campsite left. Site thirteen and it's large enough to accommodate your camper, plus it has full hook ups. Like you, a lot of folks are on their way to Fragrant Bean. Actually, my husband and I are heading there tomorrow. You might recognize me from the coffee festival? No? I'm Miss Information and I will never give you misinformation! You've probably stopped by my festival information booth at some point. My wonderful husband David is an excellent Tai Chi instructor and he's also a very talented spiritual energy healer. His health and healing seminars and Tai Chi classes are a popular feature of the festival every year." She smiles a huge friendly grin.

"Oh, that's great. I'll take site thirteen, please. I'm sure that I've stopped by the information booth at some point. I remember picking up a few informational leaflets about the festival activities in previous years." I smile and sign the campground register and then give Miss Information a twenty-dollar bill for the night's stay.

She tucks the bill into the waist band of her stretchy exercise pants and gives me a sheepish smile. Apparently, she doesn't have a cash register in the office.

"Is that your charming and artsy electric car packed full of books out in the parking lot?"

"You noticed it? That's our Little Lemon Drop. David and I love art and books, so we decided to make our car an art piece and a tiny library. We had fun decorating it and collecting our books together."

"It's adorable, I love how you decorated it. It's very memorable. I'm sure you never lose your car in a crowded parking lot. Don't you also write the Fragrant Bean monthly newsletter? Your name is so unusual, that I would recognize it anywhere. I subscribe to the electronic version of *The Fragrant Bean Coffee Scoop* and I always look forward to reading it."

"I am indeed the author of *The Scoop*. Thanks for subscribing. It's always nice to meet a reader."

"By the way, I love your adorable librarian kitty and your overflowing bookshelves. I also love companion animals and reading novels as well. I think we have a lot in common."

"It would seem so. Miss Elsa is an excellent librarian and she takes great care of the bookshelves for me. Here's the newest copy of *The Fragrant Bean Coffee Scoop*, hot off the press. Writing and reading are my passions." Miss Information responds with a friendly grin as she retrieves the newsletter and hands it to me.

"Oh, will you please autograph this copy of *The Scoop* for me? Thanks. I hope that I'll see you and your husband at the coffee festival."

Miss Information smiles warmly and holds the door open for me. I take the newsletter from her hand and smile back then I wave as I step outside.

I slowly pull the Tumbleweed into campsite thirteen and get it level before shutting down the motor and engaging the parking brake. From the outer storage compartments, I unload small portable corral panels that I set up for Topaz. I stock it with plenty of hay and fresh water. I always fasten a large breathable tarp across one side of the corral to give her plenty of shelter from the sun and wind. I open the stock trailer and lead Topaz outside and into her corral. The first thing she does is roll on the ground joyfully scratching her back in the soft sand.

I roll out the patio awning and set out a lonely camp chair beneath it. I smile as I hang up my Milky Way galaxy wind chimes. They are tuned to the same scale and have a cathedral bell tone. Next, I hook up my fresh water line, attach the water filter, and fill my potable water tank. I get out the black water hose and hook up to the park's septic system.

Chapter 7

Theme song: "Night Like This" by Crowder from the album I Know a Ghost

As evening draws near, I feed Rex and Patch their dinner. The Blue Heelers slept most of the trip today and now they are ready for a long hike. I slide into my sweater, then gather my backpack, a travel mug of caffé mocha, and a creamy peanut butter and blackberry jam sandwich. I pick up a tiny portable camp chair upholstered with colorful images of galaxies. I sling the chair's long strap over my shoulder.

I open Pandora and select the TobyMac station. I turn up the volume on "Cornerstone" by TobyMac featuring Zach Williams. This song is from To-byMac's album Life After Death. Now that we're rocking, we head out in-to the twilight. The wind picks up as the desert slowly darkens around me. I enjoy hiking with my dogs and Topaz and I think twilight in the desert is breathtakingly beautiful.

Topaz is content hiking with me and she plods alongside me. Her tiny hooves raise little sandstorms of dust. She and the dogs have been compan-ions since babyhood and they get along very well. I'm grateful for their com-pany. I grin as I watch Patch happily mark his new territory while trying not to fall over. He has yet to master temporarily balancing on three legs.

"Patch, you're such a goof ball." I say affectionately to my cute boy.

We're walking through the blooming Joshua tree forest, also populated with Mojave yucca, and other scrubland plants. As I admire the weird trees, I see a little white yucca moth flutter past me making a beeline for the blooms. Both dogs are careful to avoid the thorns on the flowering cacti. Rex is trot-ting with his nose to the ground, snorting and sniffing in the hopes of finding dessert in the desert. I sigh and ask Rex to drop the lizard in his lips. Luckily, he sets it free and we all watch as the unharmed lizard scampers into the safety of the desert scrub plants. I spy fast moving roadrunners that dart off in search of a meal.

Gradually the desert creatures move away from the area, as they adjust to our presence. Pandora starts playing the song "Desert Road" by Casting Crowns from the album Healer Deluxe Edition. During our hike, I'm scanning for a level spot to set up my telescope while finishing my sandwich. As night settles around us, I reach the perfect patch of sand far enough from Sad Sack to allow for solitude and stargazing. I pull my telescope and its folded tripod from the backpack and get set up.

When I venture out into the desert, I keep safety a priority. I carry a GPS with me and only hike during the coolest times of the day. I stay pretty close to where my camper is parked and my backpack is always equipped with a supply of granola bars, baby carrots, sliced apples, a collapsible pet bowl, and several insulated bottles of iced water. I also carry a hydration backpack filled with fruit juice with a teaspoon of salt mixed in to prevent dehydration. For my companion animals, I set out the large water bowl. With my telescope secured onto the mount, I adjust my view finder. I enjoy a sip of delicious caffé mocha, inhaling the dark chocolate and coffee aroma.

I unfold my tiny tripod camp chair and carefully sit down, balancing myself so I don't tip over. The wind picks up and I pull my sweater around me as full dark descends over the landscape. Topaz stands near my chair and I feel the warmth emanating from her fuzzy body. I can tell she is napping, because her eyelids twitch and her long ears and fuzzy bottom lip get droopy. I smile at my comical miniature donkey. The glowing night sky above me appears limitless. I spot a shooting star and smile with wonder as I make a wish. *I wish I could fly through space and experience it up close. Sky watching is definitely for me.*

Both of my dogs return to me and they find a comfortable patch of soft sand to lie on. They have been my stargazing partners for a few years now and they faithfully guard me, keeping watch while I search the heavens. I find the night sky so mesmerizing that I started sky watching when I was a teenager and still enjoy it as a relaxing hobby. It also provides inspiration for my art that I enjoy creating with soft oil pastels. Plus, the miles of hiking keep Topaz, the dogs, and I physically fit.

Gazing into my telescope, I find the usual constellations and I watch a satellite slowly drift by as the hours pass. There's Venus, she's hard to miss. Hours later, I watch Jupiter rise. As I observe them, I'm amazed that some of the natural features on the planets' surface are clearly visible in my telescope. The luminous beauty of the night sky is overwhelming.

Pandora plays the song "Overwhelmed" by the band Big Daddy Weave from the album Love Come to Life: The Redeemed Edition. Happily, I sing along. Sometime later, I'm starting to feel a little drowsy, when suddenly the night sky lights up as bright as daylight.

Blinding bursts of white-hot lightning bolts explosively invade the tranquility of my stargazing spot, crackling and booming loudly around me. In terror, I fall off my chair and it collapses on the ground with me as I cower on the cool desert sand. I make a desperate grab for Topaz's lead rope and I miss, as she thunders off to safety. Rex and Patch scamper after her, seeking shelter in the nearby desert scrub plants. *Deserters!*

Alone now, I cover my head with both arms. I feel my hair rise up in response to the intense static electricity surrounding me. Dangerous lightning flashes continually around my stargazing spot. Suddenly, the sand in front of my face is glowing with otherworldly blue light. *Where is this strange light coming from?* I push myself up from the ground into a sitting position. I look up at the sky and there are mysterious, brilliant blue lights hovering over me.

I peer up at the sky while rapidly blinking my eyes. Hiccup! Tears of fright blur my vision. Whatever the blue lights are, they suddenly fly away, gaining altitude and changing directions very rapidly and abruptly moving with impossible angles. Unsteadily, I climb to my feet. I pick up my little chair. Blinking away the tears that obscure my vision, I stare at the unnatural lights in shock as they are zipping around too quickly and irregularly to belong to any known aircraft. *I'm witnessing something bizarre and unbelievable and I can only describe it as a UFO encounter!*

I reach for my telescope to get a detailed look at it, but then the mysterious craft flies away from me. Suddenly, the UFO turns back and flies closer to me again and then it loses altitude and drops rapidly much closer to Earth, it hovers silently above me. Now the lights on the craft change from blue to purple and they beam down like spotlights upon me. I try to get a good look at it in the telescope, but now it's too blindingly bright and much too close to use the telescope.

With shaking hands, I pull my smartphone from my back pocket and begin recording video. While it's hovering above me, I can make out the shape much better. The UFO looks exactly like an enormous purple crochet needle. *Aren't UFOs supposed to be shaped like flying saucers? Come on, give me a break. Can't I even get a UFO sighting that is somewhat normal?*

The weird craft rapidly gains altitude and then hovers. Suddenly, the lights on the UFO turn back to blue again. Now the unidentified flying object speeds up and it starts erratically zipping around and changing directions impossibly fast. Feeling a little dizzy from tracking the rapid movements so intently with my eyes, I can't help but continue staring in fascination as it speeds past me and then changes directions several times. Finally, it abruptly disappears from view. The blue lights blink out of existence. The sky above me is empty.

Eventually the freakish lightning storm fades away too. The night sky settles back into serene darkness around me. Feeling intensely woozy, I close my eyes. I lean forward a little and grasp my forehead for a minute to regain my equilibrium. As soon as I feel balanced and back to normal, I watch my smartphone video. I'm disappointed to see that it's very fuzzy and out of focus. All my phone captured is the blinding purple spotlights and they completely obscure the odd crochet needle craft. *No one will ever believe that it's a video of a genuine UFO encounter. Only I know the truth!*

"Patch and Rex! Come here! It's all over now. I can't believe that you guys deserted me in my most desperate time of need. So much for having faithful guard dogs. You cowards run away at the first sign of danger. And you, Topaz, don't you know that donkeys are supposed to be excellent guard animals as well? I'm so disappointed but I love you all no matter what. It's okay everyone, of course I forgive you. The strange crochet needle flew away and we are all safe. That was so weird! It's inconceivable but I know that I really did see an authentic UFO! Sadly, no one will ever believe me. I'm just going to forget about it and I'll pretend that it never happened. Yeah, that's exactly what I'll do. What happens in the dark desert, stays in the dark desert, forever." I pointlessly lecture my cowardly companions as they sheepishly return to me.

Patch stays close to me now, hiding between my legs and shaking with fright. Rex peers anxiously up at me and as I pet him along his back, his trembles of fear begin to subside. Topaz comes back to me as well, dragging her long lead rope through the sand behind her. When she reaches me, she lifts her head and nudges me forcefully, clearly ready to leave this place.

"Well, I'm really sorry that you were all so terrified. I was too. I'm also incredibly glad that we are all unharmed and still together. I'm completely worn out now and we still have a long hike back to the Tumbleweed."

Chapter 8

Theme song: "These Days" by Jeremy Camp from the album Deeper Waters

With a jolt of surprise and my heart pounding wildly, I wake up from a dream of flying lights speeding across the night sky. For a moment, I witness intense, pulsing blue light glowing right above me, as I lie safely tucked in bed inside my bedroom. It looks like the RV roof has disappeared and a massive, swirling, blue-lit spiral galaxy is lowering down over me. In the blink of an eye, the mysterious vision disappears.

"What is happening to me? My life is getting really weird these days." I complain to my dogs, feeling cranky as I rub my eyes and finally come fully awake.

Rex and Patch lift their heads at the sound of my voice in the darkness. I experience a sick vertigo sensation of intense spinning and I feel unpleasantly nauseated for a few moments. *The vision of the galaxy swirling above me was so vivid and it felt so real.* I rub my tired eyes and push off my comfy blanket. I cautiously roll out of bed, feeling disoriented in the early morning darkness. Patch and Rex hop off my bed and look hopefully my way. They both give me a direct cattle dog stare. *Message received. It's definitely breakfast time.*

"Give me a few minutes guys." I mumble weakly still feeling sick and unsteady.

After my dream, I'm feeling in a weird mood and it's a mixed-up sensation of doom and disbelief at my recent experiences. Sleepily, I slide into my stretchy mid-rise jeans without unbuttoning or unzipping them. I fumble clumsily in the dark, searching for my knee high, snake bite proof hiking boots hiding somewhere on the floor. While buttoning up my mint green, long-sleeved shirt I look for my pink cap. I brush my long hair and gather it into a low ponytail using a purple hair scrunchie.

I step into the bathroom to wash my hands and face and brush my teeth. *Ah, minty fresh again.* I lean into the shower stall to visit with my potted coffee plants that have taken up permanent residence inside it. I blink my eyes rapidly at the painful brightness as I switch on the grow lights hanging from the ceiling. I visually inspect the leaves and then I touch the soil with a fingertip to test the amount of moisture.

"Good morning coffee plants, my little sweethearts. How are you feeling? *Robusta*, I hope. Well, how about a lovely relaxing shower this morning?" I chat up my *Coffea canephora robusta* plants with forced cheerfulness as I take down the shower head with its long flexible hose and spray warm water onto the soil in the large round pots.

"Well, my darlings, let's see what you gals have been up to. Wow, you've been busy ripening your fruits. Good job, ladies. What good plants you are." I enthusiastically encourage my plants with good vibes. *I sincerely hope that talking to them and showering them with kindness will have a positive effect on their growth rate and productivity, because I feel extremely silly right now.*

I gently pick a handful of ripe coffee cherries from my coddled coffee plants. Once I get to Fragrant Bean, I will set the cherries out in the desert sun to dry for a few days. Once they are completely dried and shriveled, I'll remove the seeds from the cherry husk. At that point, they'll be ready for my small bean roaster. Having a supply of my own homegrown fresh coffee beans is a continuous process but growing my own coffee is a fun and interesting hobby. Plus, I feel a little less lonely with their relaxing company as a welcome addition to my animal companions. It's definitely an adjustment to be suddenly living alone after being married for so long.

I slowly stumble toward the kitchen area with the dogs excitedly nipping at my heels in anticipation of breakfast. I've heard that people sometimes refer to Australian Cattle Dogs as Velcro dogs. I agree that it's an appropriate nickname, as my dogs start pushing at the back of my legs with their noses, trying to herd me along to their food bowls.

I try not to step on puppy paws in the narrow confines of the back hallway on my way up front to the wider kitchen area. *Unfortunately, I'm well known for being very clumsy. If I ever accidentally step on my dogs' toes or bump into them with my legs, I pay them an apology tax in the form of a piece of sliced apple or carrot.*

I grind some of my roasted coffee beans from the last batch and pull one shot of espresso. The pungent aroma makes me feel connected to reality again after the disturbing vision I experienced this morning. I pour steamed almond milk and espresso into my travel mug, then I top it with milk foam and powdered cocoa. I refill the dogs' water bowl and retrieve the dog food. By now, they are both prancing excitedly around my legs.

"Patch and Rex, sit. Give me a minute. Your breakfast is coming right up." I mumble sleepily to them. I can't wait to get a sip of my latte but the boys come first.

I smile down at their happy faces, grateful for their company now more than ever before. Patch has a white exclamation mark on his forehead and a large, comma shaped black patch over his left eye. It gives him an intelligent literary expression, as if he loves reading great literature as much as I do. Rex has no black eye patches and the fur on his face is a white flecked gray-blue color with a narrow white stripe on his forehead. They are both rather dapper gentlemen.

I love my properly socialized puppies, that I raised and trained with loving care and compassion. They are great life-long companions and they are also enjoyable roommates. I always treat them with love and kindness because they are intelligent, sensitive, and extremely loyal creatures. Kindness and patience are always best. The qualities that I love best about properly trained companion dogs are that they are cheerful, loyal, and full of unconditional love and forgiveness. *Hmm, I need to work on putting these Godly attributes to good use in my own life.*

My companions enjoy their food while I eat my creamy peanut butter multigrain toast with chocolate chips sprinkled on top. After breakfast, I step outside with my caffé latte and the dogs to feed Topaz and check on her water buckets. She gives a loud snort and squeaks out a heehaw in greeting.

"Are you almost ready to go, girl?" I ask while brushing her fuzzy coat and cleaning out her hooves with a hoof pick, as she contentedly munches her breakfast.

After Topaz finishes her meal, I attach a cotton rope to her halter and I give her a carrot and a kiss. While the sun is just barely peeking above the horizon, we set out for our early morning hike before it gets too hot. I sigh loudly and take a sip of my caffé latte. I love my lattes, and I decide as long as I have lattes and my furry companions, then I don't really need lousy Lew all that much. If only I could convince my broken heart to get on board with the idea.

"I love lattes not lousy Lew." I whisper to myself as a single tear slides down my cheek.

After an enjoyable hike through the sleepy desert landscape, we find last night's stargazing spot. As the sunrise gradually begins to illuminate the sand, it casts a peachy glow over the area. I'm able to recognize it as my stargazing spot from all of my scattered hiking boot prints in the sand. My boots have a recognizable tread pattern that I'm familiar with. I can even see the indentation in the sand where I huddled on the ground in fright. Now the patch of disturbed sand is calm and lacking any strange happenings. It looks completely ordinary as if nothing unusual had ever occurred on this very spot.

I consider the otherworldly eerie lights that danced across the sky. I think they are officially referred to as nocturnal lights. I remember learning about them at the Fragrant Bean Museum of UFOs, during last year's coffee festival. Plus, something else related to UFOs called close encounters. I shudder at the frightening thought. *Is that what happened to me last night?*

I hear footsteps rhythmically swishing through the sand, coming toward me at a fast pace and I look up to see Miss Information speeding toward me. She is out for an early morning run. I wave cheerfully as she approaches.

"Hello again. It's nice to see another soul out here enjoying the tranquil beauty of this amazing landscape. Oh, and look at your furry family. They're adorable. I must say you're the first camper that I've met who travels with a donkey. How original." Miss Information trots up to me and starts jogging in place. She takes a sip of water from her hydration backpack and then she smiles broadly at me.

"Good morning, it's nice to see you again. Topaz is a miniature donkey so that makes her travel size, I guess. I'm not surprised to see that you're a runner. I thought that maybe you were because you have that classic runner's physique. What a great way to spend your morning. I really enjoy hiking but I only run when it's absolutely necessary." I smile at my new friend, feeling worn out from watching her energetically bobbing up and down while effortlessly jogging in place. "I wish I had your energy."

"Well, I had three espressos this morning! Plus, I've been a runner since I was a kid, so that also helps. My dad used to take me running with him on weekends and during summer breaks. He was a rocket scientist before he retired. Now he enjoys traveling the world. Although, I think he has finally run out of new places to visit so he bought a ticket to fly to space. He has a seat reserved for an upcoming mission on Blue Origin's New Shepard. He is already calling himself an astronaut. Isn't that wonderful? I make time for a five-mile run every morning before starting work in my office. I also like to practice Tai Chi in the afternoon, if the office isn't busy with folks checking into my campground. Are you still heading toward Fragrant Bean this morning?"

"Your dad sounds like a very adventurous character. I hope he enjoys his flight to space aboard New Shepard. I'm amazed at your fitness routine. I'm departing Sad Sack after my hike this morning. How about you? Are you and your husband still leaving for the coffee festival?" I ask, while my eyes begin to feel fatigue from watching my friend's boundless energy. *I might need to add a few more espressos to my morning routine.*

"Writing, reading, and running are my passions. David and I will be on our way after I finish my run. He's tidying up our cottage and office, then he'll load our suitcase into our Little Lemon Drop so we can head out early. We're a great team. Would you like to follow us toward Fragrant Bean? David and I know this amazing pancake eatery along the way and we can stop for breakfast together. They serve really tasty pancakes and Belgian waffles with very unusual toppings."

"I would like to meet your husband and breakfast is always a treat. Waffles with tasty toppings? Sounds yummy. I need to ask you a question, since you're Miss Information and you'll never give me misinformation. It's a really weird question but since you live here and operate the campground, you're the best person to answer it. Have you ever heard of UFO sightings in this area? I think I saw one last night when I was stargazing."

"See what I mean? I told you that you have amazing luck, remember? That's like winning the lottery! It must have been an exciting experience for you. So, to answer your question this area has a long and storied history of strange happenings and it has a reputation for mysterious lights in the night sky. Luckily, there haven't been any reports of alien abductions, so we just consider it a really good tourist magnet for our campground. Otherwise, the Sad Sack RV Park would be a pretty morose and forlorn place. After all, Nevada did name State Route 375 the Extraterrestrial Highway for a very good reason." Miss Information informs me, barely out of breath while still jogging energetically in place.

"For me the experience was terrifying and I'm pretty sure I would rather win the lottery. Funds are always welcome, UFOs and aliens not so much."

"I'm so glad we ran into each other this morning. I'm going to finish up my run and then I'll meet you back at the Sad Sack office in about an hour, okay?"

"Thanks for the chat, it's always educational and enjoyable talking with you. I think we're going to be great friends." I smile and wave as Miss Information speeds off into the brightening and warming desert.

With amusement, I watch my new friend run at top speed off toward the sunrise. *Well, she seems very comfortable with the idea of UFOs and she lives here in an active UFO zone. Maybe there is nothing to worry about or maybe she's just really brave?*

Chapter 9

Theme song: "Keep me in the Moment" by Jeremy Camp from the album The Story's not Over Deluxe Edition

Sighing loudly, I refill my companions' water bowl. I'm uncomfortable thinking about what I saw last night and I still feel extremely creeped out. I've been a stargazer for most of my life, along with my mother Joy. Until now, I've never witnessed anything unusual or frightening in the night sky. I look around and admire the brilliant beauty of the lemon-yellow and deep cranberry sunrise. I marvel at the varied earthy colors of the desert scrubland plants, the beautiful cacti, and also the stunning multihued rocks, and I finally begin to relax.

"Live in the moment." I counsel myself, as I take a deep breath and soak in the peace and natural beauty around me. I say a silent prayer to God of Heaven for strength and protection. Absentmindedly, I run my fingers over the olive wood beads and small metal crucifixes dangling from my blessed bracelets.

Rex and Patch are wandering nearby getting their energy out. I smile as I watch them run with their noses to the sand. Topaz stands near me looking very relaxed and drowsy. She slowly swishes her tail to keep away flies. I feel safe again in their company and I let out a deep breath of relaxation.

Back at the Tumbleweed, I begin preparations to depart the Sad Sack RV Park. I refill the water buckets inside the trailer and add more flakes of hay to the hay bags. Topaz loads easily and I make sure the door is securely latched. I take a few minutes to check the trailer hitch and the lights. We're good to go now and the Tumbleweed is ready to head out on the highway.

The dogs curl up in their beds as I climb into the driver's seat and buckle my seat belt. I adjust my pink cap lower over my eyes for sun protection. I place my sunglasses on Mount Everest. Slowly, I pull out of site thirteen. I drive cautiously through the gravel lane, avoiding bumps and trying not to wake the late sleepers in their campers. I park the Tumbleweed at the office parking area near the Little Lemon Drop to await my new friends.

I see a very tall man with a kind face. He is coming out of the office with a suitcase in one hand and a ginger cat walking on a leash beside him. He is dressed in Tai Chi practitioners' clothing. I smile and wave as I hop out of the Tumbleweed. He smiles and sets the suitcase on the ground. The beautiful ginger cat prances around him and then rubs itself along his silky pants while weaving around his legs.

"You must be David. I met your wife while I was out hiking this morning. I'm Sedona, it's nice to meet you. I hope it's okay with you but Miss Information invited me to follow you toward Fragrant Bean."

"Hi Sedona, it's nice to meet you as well. Of course, you are more than welcome to join us. Miss Information will be out in a minute. Have you met Miss Ginger yet?" David looks down and smiles fondly at the elegant cat who is now sitting regally beside him.

"Hello Miss Ginger. You are very beautiful. I saw Miss Elsa the librarian in the office when I checked in." I smile down at the lovely feline. "Does Miss Ginger enjoy traveling in the car? What about Miss Elsa, is she joining us for breakfast?"

"Oh, Miss Elsa absolutely refuses to leave her post as librarian. She's convinced that mice will break in and chew up our books if she leaves her bookshelf for even a minute. Our dear friend, cat whisperer Alicia will be taking care of Miss Elsa while we're in Fragrant Bean for the coffee festival. Miss Ginger feels it is her queenly right to have a personal chauffeur and quite frankly she would never tolerate being left at home. She fully expects to be included in every social outing. Miss Ginger enjoys certain privileges because she has a career as a champion show cat. She is employed as a fashion magazine model and she's also a Clio Fashion and Beauty award winner for her work as a TV commercial actress. Although, she considers herself more of a queen than a champion, I suppose." David smiles down at the celebrity kitty. "Would you like a complimentary autographed color photo of Miss Ginger? I always keep a few press kits in the frunk of the Little Lemon Drop."

"Goodness me, I'm impressed by her successful career. I'm honored by her generosity. I would love an autographed photo of Miss Ginger." I smile with genuine excitement. "I'm just a waitress from a small town and this is the first time I've met a bona fide celebrity."

While David takes the sole suitcase to the frunk and retrieves a press kit for me, I stand quietly in awe as I hold Miss Ginger's leash. I stand very still, afraid that if I move, my large feet will tread on the little queenly feline. *Don't move your feet Sedona, don't you dare step on an award-winning celebrity kitty. For once in your life, don't be clumsy.*

I spy Miss Information stepping out of the office and locking the door. She is transformed from a trail runner into a beauty queen. Miss Information has styled her hair and it frames her face in bouncy, elegant waves. She is wearing a knee length, strapless yellow dress and an elegant red hat with a silky scarf for a hat band. The flowy yellow scarf trails off the wide brim of the hat and is lifted on the breeze. I smile when I notice she is wearing red cross trainers instead of high heels. *How sensible.*

"Hey, Sedona. I see you finally met Miss Ginger and David. You look a little star struck. Don't worry most people are the first time they meet a Hollywood talent like Miss Ginger. The feeling will fade after a while and you'll see that she is just like everybody else, except with more beauty and talent. Are you ready to get rolling on the highway?"

David closes the frunk and quickly opens the car door for his lovely wife. He strides over to her and wraps her in an affectionate embrace. I stand nearby awkwardly holding Miss Ginger's leash while trying not to notice their passionate embrace as they kiss each other deeply and for an embarrassing length of time. *Aw, marital bliss is so sweet.* At this moment, I'm feeling very sorry for myself and my lost marriage.

When they finally manage to disentangle themselves from their heated kiss, Miss Information is blushing and she vigorously flaps her hand in front of her face to create a breeze to cool off. She smiles at me and takes Miss Ginger's leash.

"Sedona, I'm so glad we met. I sense a true and lasting friendship developing between us. It feels like I've known you for decades. Are you ready to go find some breakfast? Just follow the Little Lemon Drop and we'll lead you to an unusual experience at Pirate's Pancake Paradise."

The happy couple hops into the Little Lemon Drop with David at the wheel and Miss Ginger perched upon Miss Information's lap. I smile as I notice that Miss Ginger is now wearing a tiny elegant red hat and a silky yellow scarf for the journey. As I step over to the Tumbleweed, my stomach growls loudly and I realize I'm looking forward to a second breakfast.

Rolling at a snail's pace, the Tumbleweed follows the charming electric car down the driveway. I pass the sun-faded Sad Sack RV Park sign and turn onto State Route 375, the Extraterrestrial Highway. It's time to get some miles behind me.

After a pleasant drive, we're seated comfortably at a table in the outdoor patio area where leashed pets are welcomed. We are enjoying the cool shade, underneath a timber-beamed roof with large ceiling fans whirring noisily above us. Miss Ginger sits delicately on a large, gold brocade cushion in her own chair placed between Miss Information and David.

I notice there are large fan misters stationed at the four corners of the patio. It's a terracotta tiled patio that feels like a breezy tropical garden. Every inch of floor space that isn't dedicated to guest seating is overflowing with blue ceramic flower planters that are nearly waist high. They are filled with several varieties of blooming shrubs. The blooms display saturated colors in deep magenta, darkest purple, pale lavender, and brilliant bubble gum pink. The patio area is permeated with the sweet fragrance of the colorful flowers.

I wisely left Patch and Rex safely inside the air-conditioned Tumbleweed since they've never been around cats and Australian Cattle Dogs are known to have a high prey drive toward small animals, especially cats. Better safe than sorry. I'm not willing to risk the safety of any animal but I'm exercising extra caution in the case of a celebrity kitty. I can imagine sensational headlines in the newspaper proclaiming: *"Disgraced and Discarded Wife Allows her Monster Dogs to Harass the World's Most Famous and Beloved Celebrity Kitty. Miss Ginger Lawyers up and Sues for Millions!"* Not on my watch! I may be a discarded and disgraced wife but I'm a caring and responsible pet owner and also a considerate friend.

"I'm perplexed. Miss Information, can you explain to me why this restaurant is called Pirate's Pancake Paradise yet it doesn't have pirate or nautical themed decor?" I inquire while perusing the menu. It appears that this establishment only serves pancakes and waffles with a variety of toppings. The only other items listed on the menu are a selection of syrups, plus coffee and tea. There is literally nothing else on the menu.

"The owner's name is Pirate. Apparently, his father was a big movie buff and his favorite films were all of the extravagant, swashbuckling pirate and seafaring movies from the Golden Age of Hollywood. So naturally, he named his son Pirate, inspired by movies like the old black and white Errol Flynn moving pictures. Movies such as the original 1935 *Captain Blood* and the 1940 movie *The Sea Hawk* and later the 1952 movie *Against All Flags*."

"You really are an endless source of information, Miss Information. So, what do you two like to eat here? Pancakes or waffles?" I'm completely impressed by the quantity of information that my new friend stores in her capable brain.

"David often likes to get the Belgian waffles. Don't you, honey?" Miss Information takes David's hand and squeezes it affectionately and then she brings it to her lips and kisses the back of his hand. She smiles at her kind and compassionate husband. *Aw, they are the real deal: A true and lasting love match. Being with blissful people makes me feel happier.*

"Indeed, my sweetie, I love the unique waffles served here. They are battered with a sea-inspired recipe using a blend of corn meal and flour with coastal seafood seasoning and a few secret spices, then they are deep fried. It sounds weird but they're tasty, spicy, and crispy. Sometimes I order them topped with anchovies, sliced avocados, and Dijon mustard. Today I'm in the mood for waffles with smoked salmon, Reese's Pieces, A.1. Original Sauce, and I'm drowning them in the marigold flowers syrup." David leans toward his intelligent and talented wife and kisses her sweetly.

"Oh, how fun, David. You are feeling a little daring this morning, aren't you honey?" Miss Information smiles at David with twinkling eyes and a loving expression. "I often order the silver dollar pancakes topped with tofu, Sno-Caps, and pimiento cheese. Today I'm really famished, so I'm getting the waffles covered with peaches, Sour Patch Kids, and mayonnaise. I'm choosing the syrup made from green chilies. Sedona, I told you this place is an original." Miss Information smiles at me and places her menu on the table.

"Fascinating. You are both eating boldly and creatively today. I'll try to be brave too. I'm trying to decide between the waffles covered with fried green tomatoes, Moon Pie crumbles, and barbecue sauce or maybe the waffles with pickled herring in sour cream sauce, Milk Duds, and Torta del Casar stinky cheese. Maybe it's best if I go with a lower priced option, since rare, imported European cheese is definitely out of my budget these days."

After we place our orders, we relax and chat companionably together while sipping coffee. Eventually, the server approaches our table laden with plates and a variety of flavored syrups arranged on a large tray. Our smiling server carefully sets our meals on the table and patiently explains the various types of syrups. There are the usual syrups flavored with maple, blueberry, and strawberry. However, there are syrups flavored with herbs and edible flowers. There is a syrup made from calendula flowers, one with chive blossoms, and another with thyme, and finally, a syrup made with lovage herbs.

"This looks oddly delicious. Thank you for recommending this unique eatery. It's quite an interesting experience. I'm glad we took the time to stop here for a meal and to get to know each other better." I say a silent blessing over my meal and I give thanks to God of Heaven before digging into my strange and wonderful breakfast. I bravely pour squash blossoms syrup over my waffles topped with pickled okra, Red Vines Twists, and horseradish sauce.

The conversation halts while we enjoy our meals. Miss Ginger is treated to a dish of gourmet Fatty Ratty Protein Blend wet cat food. She has lovely table manners like any true lady would, while I accidentally slop squash blossoms syrup and pickled okra into my lap. I sigh with exasperation, and use my napkin to clean up my spill. *I wish I could be a great lady like Miss Ginger but somehow the skill eludes me. I'm still socially awkward, clumsy, and accidentally messy after all these years of trying to be ladylike.* I sigh with disappointment in myself.

"Ah, what a satisfying breakfast. I'm stuffed." David smiles and takes Miss Information's dainty hand; he gallantly raises it to his lips and kisses it sweetly. "Well, ladies thank you for the delightful company and conversation this morning. A meal is always more meaningful when shared with family and friends. If you'll please excuse me, I'll go pay the bill for us." David kisses his wife's cheek and strides inside to the cash register.

After our unique breakfast, I say good bye to Miss Information, Miss Ginger, and David who are traveling in the Little Lemon Drop directly to Fragrant Bean. They are part of a large group of volunteers who help set up the festival booths and exhibits before it opens to the general public in a few days. I cheerfully wave to my new friends and climb up into the Tumbleweed to resume my leisurely trip along the Extraterrestrial Highway.

Once I'm safely belted into the driver's seat, I say a silent prayer to God of Heaven. While driving, I can't help but think about Lew. All the years we spent together from high school and onward into mature adulthood plus our plans to move to Italy after we retire. We've been working together toward this goal for decades. I've been diligently studying the Italian language on the Duolingo app. I've been faithfully depositing my wages and the inheritance from my dad into our bank accounts to fund our permanent move to Italy.

I've been learning about the culture of Italy. I even studied the regions and their various cuisines in order to choose where Lew and I would enjoy living. My heart is set on the rural hills of Tuscany. I would love to manage an olive tree grove and to someday have a small pasture with a grazing herd of sheep in order to learn how to make pecorino Toscano cheese. I researched a few family farms that allow internships where I can work for them for an agreed upon number of years and in exchange, I will learn how to care for the sheep and how to craft the traditional Tuscan sheep's milk cheese. It sounds so wonderful to me and thanks to Lew and Louanne and their betrayal, all of my cheesy dreams and my ability to relocate to Italy are dead, just like my marriage. I'm still stunned by the turn my life has taken. *What am I going to do with the rest of my life? I don't have a clue.*

What a shock it is to discover Lew chose to fall in lust with my boss. I wonder how long they have been in a stealthy, adulterous relationship with each other? Being betrayed by my husband is deeply painful but did he have to do it at the diner where I work? It's such a public place and now the whole town knows what happened. It's cruel.

My thoughts turn to other significant family memories as I navigate the Tumbleweed. I think about my creative and hardworking Italian dad Pasquale. He was skilled in working with his hands and he restored an antique truck and worked in home construction. His true talent became evident when he designed and built his own small castle to live in as a permanent home. Unfortunately, he passed away when I was still in college. It's an incredible accomplishment that he actually designed and built himself a really clever castle in Tucson, which he named Mollohan Castle. I remember back when I was still a teenager and my dad would sometimes work local construction jobs and forego monetary compensation and instead, he worked in exchange for building materials or the use of a heavy crane to lift the dome onto the top of his castle. In total, my dad spent nine years building Mollohan castle.

After his passing, we held a memorial service for him in Mollohan Castle with his many friends and a few family members in attendance. My dad's ashes were released from the castle's ramparts to blow off into the desert winds swirling away from his beloved castle and into the great beyond. Mollohan Castle still stands today in Tucson, but after my dad's passing his castle transferred into new ownership outside of our family. I'm pleased that Mollohan Castle has become a popular site for destination weddings and family gatherings. My dad would be happy that his castle is a place of joy and celebration today.

My amazing mom Joy is resilient and headstrong. She's very practical and the most organized person I know. She and I have always been close friends and we enjoy each other's company. Unfortunately, she has been missing for the last decade. Tears fill my eyes as I remember the mysterious night that she vanished. My mom was a serious UFO researcher and she volunteered with MUFON for many years. She went missing late one night in the desert surrounding Sandy Town.

Mom always investigated with another local MUFON researcher, Patti Bee. Unfortunately, at the time of the local UFO sightings, Patti Bee was away on a trip to Iceland to cool off. On the night the unusual event occurred in Sandy Town, my mom unwisely decided to proceed in the investigation on her own. It was a very rare mass sighting and there had been many reports of nocturnal lights made by a large number of townies. All of the witnesses described seeing nearly the same thing. Such an occurrence is quite rare, especially when the details in eyewitness reports are so similar. Mom didn't want to waste the opportunity to investigate and record evidence to back up the eyewitness reports. Mom never returned home from her solitary research trip into the desert wilderness.

The Sandy Town Sheriff's Mounted Posse searched for two weeks. Lew and I, with a group of mom's friends from MUFON participated in their search and then we also kept searching for another two weeks afterward. Lew was very supportive and generous with his time and resources. I appreciate his efforts to help me search for my mom. He was my rock during that scary time. My mom's friends were so caring and they were dedicated to helping us search for her. I'm grateful to everyone for their support. By that time, Patti Bee had returned from Iceland. Her cooling vacation was cut short when the island heated up from a local volcanic eruption. Patti Bee decided that if cold Iceland was going to become so hot, then she might as well head back home to the heat of the desert. The cool thing is that Patti Bee brought home her handsome import from Iceland, Bjartur, her new life partner. Naturally, they both joined us in the search team and they were a huge help during the search for my mom.

The only thing that was recovered from the desert wilderness was mom's pink Jeep which was still packed with most of her survival and research equipment. Everyone in town was deeply disappointed after the numerous searches proved fruitless. Years later, Patti Bee and I still believe that my mom was abducted by a UFO. *If only there was a way for me to search the heavens for my mom.*

It feels like I have lost everything and everyone that I love. Unfortunately, I have been living with the burden of unbearable heartache for much of my adult life. I still miss my parents so much and now my heart aches for the loss of Lew and our marriage too. I believe life is too short and too precious to stay in a relationship where I'm unloved and unwanted. God didn't create us to be mistreated or to be unloved and unwanted. God created us to worship Him and to serve Him and to thrive. I choose to trust God of Heaven and to hope that my life will work out for the better, even in this distressing time. My life goal is to serve God of Heaven, to be blessed, to thrive, and to always speak the truth about God of Heaven and Jesus Christ. This is my chance to start my life over. It's time to find my own unique and peaceful path through life.

During my drive, the day gradually turns scorching hot and very windy. The sun is a sizzling spotlight shining down on me through the windshield. The Tumbleweed is bucking and twisting like a wild horse due to the gusty winds slamming against its bulky shape. After fighting the wind, I feel fatigue in my arms from wrestling with my wildly disobedient Tumbleweed. It's time to find a roadside rest area and take a lunch break.

Chapter 10

Theme song: "Hands Up" by MercyMe from the album Always Only Jesus

Thirty minutes later, I find a remote rest stop with concrete parking and an expansive view of the remote desert wilderness. I slowly pull in and find a parking space not far from several semi trucks. I feed Rex and Patch lunch and refill their water bowl. I collect a granola bar, the leashes, and a handful of recyclable and biodegradable dog waste bags for cleaning up after my dogs.

"Sorry guys, no freedom this close to vehicles and the highway. Come on, you two need a potty break."

We step down out of the Tumbleweed and are blasted with gusts of hot wind. I unload Topaz after securing her lead rope onto her rope halter and I tie her to the trailer where I can see her while I clean up. My trailer has a solar powered roof vent with a fan that provides good ventilation and helps cool the interior. Inside it is shady and reasonably comfortable because of the rubber coating that I had applied to the metal roof. The coating helps minimize heat transfer from the roof into the stock trailer, which also features open slats in the sides that further maximize ventilation. I tie Patch and Rex inside with me and I quickly eat my granola bar before cleaning the trailer. Lunch and this job do not mix well together.

Afterward, my boys and Topaz calmly walk with me to a sandy area away from the parked vehicles. I'm thinking that boondocking here in the parking lot for the night will be a very wise decision. It feels like these gusty winds are getting progressively worse. My long hair is whipping around my face and it stings when it lashes across my eyes. I blink furiously and pull my hair away from my face, tucking it behind my ears. Despite the discomfort of the strong winds, we still manage to enjoy our stroll. Not much dampens the enthusiasm of Patch and Rex for a walk. Topaz seems to be unflappable and I think she feels safe with the Blue Heelers for company, it's kind of an unusual little herd, but it works for us. It also really helps in these windy conditions that she is an experienced traveler.

Later back in the Tumbleweed, I use my YouTube app on my smartphone to play several Christian praise and worship songs to start my Bible study. The first one I choose is "Voice of Truth" by Casting Crowns from the album Casting Crowns. While the beautiful music fills the Tumbleweed, I happily dance around with my hands raised up toward Heaven as I joyfully praise God. I stumble a little while dancing because the Tumbleweed is still being buffeted by the strong winds and it's rocking on its suspension. *I'm dancing in a dancing camper.* Sadly, I'm singing off key and I'm glad that no one, other than my God, is here to hear me. *I'm also very grateful that to God every voice is sweet when it's singing praises and prayers.*

The second song I choose is "Rain in the Rearview" by Anne Wilson from the album Rebel (The Beginning). The last song I play is "I Love Jesus" by Mac Powell from the album I Love Jesus. Out of breath, I flop onto my sofa and make myself comfortable with my Bible study guide. I open the YouVersion app on my smartphone. I choose *The Listener's Bible: NIV Edition.* I happily settle in for some well-earned relaxation for the rest of the afternoon. It's a relief to be off the road for a while. I'm learning to love RV living and carrying my little home and my adorable companions with me while traveling in my camper really appeals to me. I'm looking forward to a new view in my windshield in the morning, but for now, Bible study and rest are needed.

For dinner, I prepare a garden salad and I open a bottle of sparkling water. In addition to my leafy greens, I add sliced carrots, grape tomatoes, fresh avocados, sliced turkey breast, and then I top it with whole cashews, almonds, and dried cranberries. As a final touch, I add olive oil as a salad dressing. While I'm relaxing over my nutritious meal, the dogs enjoy their food.

Afterward, I step outside and into the stock trailer where I feed Topaz and add water to her buckets. Together, we go for another short stroll in the sandy area near the parking lot. Topaz brays loudly, enthusiastically announcing our presence to the empty pet walk area. I laugh and run my fingers along her fuzzy neck. The rest area has completely emptied of other travelers by now. It's late afternoon and the Tumbleweed looks lonely. *I think I'll bring out my telescope later for some peaceful stargazing.*

Back inside the Tumbleweed, I take my acoustic guitar out of its case and I play some of my favorite classic rock songs. I'm just a beginner rhythm guitar player but I really enjoy playing my guitar. My dogs appear completely unimpressed with my musical performance and they immediately fall asleep in their beds. *Tough audience.* Undaunted, I carry on playing in my own private rock concert.

Chapter 11

Theme song: "Eye of the Storm" by Ryan Stevenson featuring Gabe Real from the album Fresh Start

In the evening, I step down out of the Tumbleweed with my telescope packed inside my backpack. My portable camp chair is slung over my shoulder by its long carry strap. I hold tight to my travel mug filled with caffé mocha.

The wind is swirling and rushing around me and I gather up my long sweater and pull it tightly closed for warmth. Patch and Rex accompany me with their leashes clipped safely onto their collars. Two pairs of dark coffee eyes stare up at me unhappily.

"Boys, you know the safety rule, leashes on around the parking lot. It's just for a short while and then you can have your freedom. Come on."

Topaz is comfortably lying down in the clean bedding inside her trailer and she climbs to her feet as we approach.

"Would you like to join us for a hike?" I ask as I clip a rope onto her halter. She loudly squeaks out a hee haw in answer.

Together we hike out into the desert for several miles. I soak up the natural beauty as the sunset gradually transforms from apricot to blood orange and then finally to deep cherry. I remove the dogs' leashes so they can enjoy a good run. Topaz placidly plods along with me as I admire the landscape. As night gradually descends, I choose our stargazing spot and prepare to set up my equipment. I unpack my gear and set out the water bowl for my companions.

I set up my tripod and push its legs firmly into the sand. I scavenge around for a few rocks and stack them against the legs to help steady it against the gusts of wind. Finally, I secure my telescope onto the tripod and make the necessary adjustments. Despite the windy conditions, I feel peaceful and stare up into the starry sky. The brilliance of the glowing galaxy above me takes my breath away. I sigh contentedly. *This is my happy place.*

With another blissful sigh, I relax into my camp chair and I feel a sinking sensation as its legs sink deeper into the sand. I sip aromatic hot coffee from my travel mug. *My new homegrown coffee has great flavor. I'm so pleased with my coffee growing efforts.*

Before leaving the Tumbleweed, I ground some of today's freshly roasted beans to enjoy my own homegrown coffee during my stargazing. These coffee beans are from the first few crops that I've been growing in my shower and they are far stronger than any I've ever tasted. They also have a delicious aroma. *I can't believe how amazing the coffee is from these particular coffee beans. I'm feeling pretty happy right now. I guess having long conversations every morning for the last four plus years with my coffee shrubs has finally paid off. I almost feel guilty for harvesting their coffee fruits. Almost.*

As I contentedly smile and sip my delectable coffee, I'm pleasantly engulfed in a tiny cloud of steamy coffee scent rising from my mug. My smile disappears as the wind picks up and steals the delightful coffee cloud away from me. *Hot coffee is just the thing I need to stay awake and alert while stargazing.* I open Pandora and select the Anne Wilson station. I happily settle in to enjoy the mesmerizing beauty of the night sky and my favorite contemporary Christian music. Anne Wilson's song "God Thing" from the album My Jesus Anniversary Deluxe Edition is playing.

After several peaceful hours of sky watching and enjoying music, I observe dramatic flashes of lightning streaking across the sky in the distance. *Heat lightning? Yeah, probably. There's nothing to worry about.* The next song that starts playing is Zach Williams's "Rescue Story" from the album Rescue Story.

I'm startled when suddenly the night sky right above me is violently pierced by luminous white lightning bolts, flashing and sizzling over and over again. I flinch and involuntarily duck my head as deafening claps of thunder boom in the sky above me. It's so close to me that I feel the unpleasant vibrations inside my chest. Intensely brilliant otherworldly flying lights appear through the lightning storm. They are zooming across the sky at unimaginable speeds. I'm dazzled by their extreme brightness and high-speed maneuvers.

It's the same giant purple crochet needle that I saw last night and it's getting closer to me, much closer. A lightning bolt strikes the desert floor not far from me. Immediately Topaz, Rex, and Patch run away to hide in the desert scrub plants. *Oh no, they deserted me again! Cowards!* I clamp my hands over my ears and collapse to the gritty sand as the searing jolts of electricity reverberate around me, making me cower in fright. I scream into the night as tears flow from my eyes. I crinkle my nose from the distinctive odor of ozone emanating from the lightning all around me. I gasp for oxygen. Hiccup!

"Not again! How is this possible? Am I being hunted by this aggressive flying purple crochet needle, for heaven's sake?" I sit up and swipe hair out of my face and wipe my tears on my long-sleeved shirt.

Chapter 12

Theme song: "Heaven Help Me" by Zach Williams from the album Rescue Story Deluxe Edition

The UFO is glowing intensely blue and it's descending rapidly toward me. With trembling hands, I reach for my smartphone, open my camera and press record on the video button. Hopefully, I can get clear video this time. Unfortunately, the lightning intensifies around me and once again I'm forced to lie flat on the sand as the deadly bolts zing and zap all around me. I try to hold up my smartphone and continue recording video. I can feel the fine hair on my arms rise up in response to the electrifying atmosphere covering me.

"Help, Heavenly Father, please rescue me! This can't be happening again!" In fear for my safety, I cry out to God of Heaven for help. I'm gasping for breath in my state of panic. Hiccup! *Oh no, not a panic attack, I don't have time for one!*

The purple spotlights appear over me, shining down so brilliantly they're obscuring my vision. I'm panicking and my breathing is getting erratic. I look around me and I realize there is no one out here in the desert wilderness to help me. *Solo night hikes in the vast empty desert are a very dangerous habit. I can't believe I'm experiencing a case of Unidentified Aerial Phenomenon again! I'm convinced that UAP and UFO sightings are definitely not for me!*

The strange spacecraft zooms lower through the lightning storm. It hovers in the sky and then silently begins to drop lower and much closer to the desert floor. It passes over my head with a gritty rush of blowing sand.

"Ow! What on earth? Go away, freakish crochet needle!" I feel another blast of wind and sand rushing over me and I screech in terror.

I jump up from the sand knocking over my little tripod chair. I clutch my smartphone in one hand and my thumb hits the stop recording button by accident. With great determination, I hold my tumbler of hot coffee tightly in the other hand. *No matter what happens, I refuse to spill my homegrown coffee that I worked so hard to grow!* I stare in horror as the alien spacecraft touches down onto the sand. In fearful fascination, I watch as the spacecraft lands and then sinks down several inches and settles deeply into the soft cinnamon-colored sand. *Well, that level of minute detail is certainly confirmation that I'm not experiencing some strange hallucination. I believe that I'm really seeing this UFO, it's not just some weird psychological manifestation created by my grief-addled brain.*

Backing farther away, I raise my arms to shield my squinted eyes as lightning flashes around me. The otherworldly spacecraft is completely silent but it's blowing wind and sand all around me. I turn and run away from the UFO and my dogs and Topaz come thundering out from their hiding spot among the desert scrub plants. They follow me as I run away.

When I stop and look back, I notice it's brightly lit up and the smooth exterior surface of the craft is extremely glittery. It emanates a rush of blowing airflow and gritty sand is blowing all around it. The blue and purple lights are illuminating the desert.

"This is not good! Not good! This is weird, can't be possible! Not happening! Not happening?" Hiccup!

My furry companions crowd against my legs, they push and lean hard against me. I'm sure they are as scared as I am. Topaz snorts loudly and dances around me on her long lead rope, ready to bolt again. Patch whines loudly and Rex looks up at me with panic in his eyes.

Chapter 13

Theme song: "Even When You're Running" by Casting Crowns from the album Only Jesus Deluxe Edition

"Let's go, run! Come on guys, run! Run!"

I leave my telescope mounted on its tripod. My fallen camp chair resembles a turtle on its back with little legs pointing pathetically up toward the sky. I'm running with Topaz beside me and the Blue Heelers nosing me in the back of the knees and nipping at my heels. My backpack is thumping painfully against me while I hiccup and gasp for breath. I cling fiercely to my home-grown coffee which is safely enclosed inside my travel mug. *Thank goodness, there's no chance of spillage.*

I hold tight to my smartphone as I run, fervently wishing I didn't hike so far away from camp. Now that I'm not recording video, Pandora starts playing music again. Anne Wilson's song "Strong" from the album Rebel (The Beginning) is playing loudly. It's a long run and I'm drenched in sweat and desperately out of breath as we escape back to the safety of the Tumbleweed.

Topaz gladly hops into the sanctuary of her trailer. I secure the door with shaking hands. The boys and I hop inside my camper and I frantically slam and lock the door.

Frozen with fear, my dogs and I stand inside the Tumbleweed. We're breathing harshly, unable to move, and overheated from our run. We're gasping and panting for breath, trembling, and staring at each other in shock.

"Guys, we're out of here!" I'm finally released from my frozen stance or paralyzed trance of fear and I immediately take action.

I make a desperate dash and launch myself into the driver's seat. I have trouble inserting the key into the ignition because my hands are trembling so badly. I start the motor and release the parking brake. I'm grateful that I always keep Topaz's trailer hitched up to the Tumbleweed, so I'm always ready to make a quick exit.

All of a sudden, both of my dogs start growling and barking ferociously. I jump in fright at their aggressive snarling. I lay my hand over my erratic heart, willing it to calm down. Then I hear the menacing sounds behind me and my heart intensifies its rapid rebellion in my chest.

Dreading that I will expire from a heart attack right here in the driver's seat, I try to slow my breathing and control my panic. Then I hear the sinister sounds of sharp talons screeching across the floor, the slide of many shuffling footsteps coming toward me, and ominous gurgling growls right behind the driver's seat. Terrified, I squeeze my eyes tightly closed. Hiccup! *Maybe if I don't turn around and look it'll go away. It's surely a hallucination from extreme dehydration after that long sweaty run through the desert. Yup, that makes perfect sense.*

I realize with surprise that I'm still clutching my smartphone in a painful grip. My Pandora app is playing Crowder's song "Run Devil Run" from the album American Prodigal Deluxe Edition. *Oh, perfect. What a timely message. Thank you, Heavenly Father for reminding me that your protection covers me no matter where I wander.*

After a few shaky breaths, I slowly turn around in my seat, with my eyes still stubbornly and tightly closed. I*'m very much afraid of what I will see when I open them. Maybe it will go away if I don't acknowledge that it's here inside my Tumbleweed?* My heart is still hammering alarmingly in my chest. Reluctantly, I slowly open my eyes. I'm afraid that I'll never be able to stop screaming.

Chapter 14

Theme song: "Unstoppable" by Crowder from the album The Exile

I see two hideous alien creatures standing just behind the driver's seat in my kitchen area. Not surprisingly, I run out of breath pretty quickly and my screams of terror are extinguished. Holding up my left hand, I fiercely shake my olive wood bracelets with the little holy crucifixes attached. The blessed bracelets rattle as the crucifixes and beads bump into each other.

Sucking in a breath of air, I shout in my most commanding voice. "I command you to leave this place! Begone devils! Leave my Tumbleweed! Get out of here now!"

I start coughing uncontrollably. The aliens stare back at me without blinking their enormous, brightly glowing eyes. *Why aren't they leaving?*

The otherworldly intruders gurgle and screech at me. "You have Earth coffee! We smell Earth coffee! We require much coffee!"

I'm filled with dread and trembling uncontrollably. "How on earth did you two things get in here? The door's locked! What are you? Get out of here!"

There's no doubt in my mind that I would crumple to the floor if not for my driver's seat, my legs are trembling that fiercely. My alien trespassers squeal in fright and pop up into the air. Levitating above the floor, they float like grotesque children's character balloons until they are hovering near the ceiling. I stare in disbelief at the floating, glittery, purple beings. Hiccup! *Great more hiccups. They always show up with my panic attacks.*

Slowly, the bizarre aliens sink down to the floor and they land with an ear-piercing screech from their curved sharp claws. Tottering on their freakishly long feet they ominously lumber toward me. I cringe at the scraping sound caused by their knife-like talons against the floor as they move forward.

Good heavens, this can't be happening to me! This isn't possible! Alien visitation is definitely not for me! I desperately try to think of some way to escape this nightmare. Realization sinks in that the Tumbleweed is my only means of escape and somehow these creatures got inside my safe haven. *There is no escape. I must find a way to rescue myself. Maybe I can negotiate with them? Perhaps if I give them what they want they will leave?*

I start to look closely at the aliens. I try to observe everything about them. Maybe I will find something that might help me resolve this situation. I notice they're very tiny and much shorter than me. They appear hairless and are definitely not human, not even close. *What are they?*

The aliens walk upright like humans. They have impossibly tiny, bowling pin shaped purple bodies. They stand on three long hideous feet, attached to three thin, short purple legs. Their long narrow feet are gold and glittery. They have too many toes with horrific, knife-like talons. *Not that I have time to count. I'm just very observant and I have a thing about toes, they scare me.* They have two arms and hands, like me, but theirs are covered in gold skin that looks bumpy and glittery. *Hmm, that's kind of cool and disturbing. Yes, definitely disturbing.*

Their small heads are hairless and they look exactly like Italian Rosa Bianca eggplants. They even have a fringe of greenery hanging down over their foreheads, kind of like leafy bangs. Their noses are long and pointy. *Long pointy noses, just like mine. At least we have something in common.*

The skin on their faces has a pattern of mottled colors. Their gleaming facial skin is smooth. Their faces display blended colors of vibrant purple and white with bright green freckles dotted along their cheeks. I'm shocked at their uncanny resemblance to Rosa Bianca eggplants, it's so weird. I peer into their large luminescent green eyes and I see what looks like swirling galaxies spinning in their depths. *Whoa, cool eyes. Green just like mine.*

"Patch, Rex quit it now. That's enough barking."

I turn off the motor and cautiously slide out of the driver's seat. Patch and Rex climb into their pet beds. Feeling frightened, goose bumps rise all over me. I'm desperately trying to think up a solution while hot tears drip from my eyes. I'm so drenched in sweat that my clothes are damp and I feel sticky and hot. I glance at my dogs and they seem calm now as they watch me from their beds. *Okay, so no danger any longer, I guess?* I trust their instincts and I try to calm down but I feel shaky all over. We're all blinking and staring at each other awkwardly.

Chapter 15

Theme song: "Hello, my Name Is" by Matthew West from the album Into the Light

The intruders stare at me with their large green eyes that are spiraling with clusters of luminous starry light. They sidle toward me, lumbering awkwardly on their hideous and freakishly long feet. Their clumsy gait causes their curved knife-blade talons to screech along the floor. *Oh no, they're damaging my floor. How can I get rid of these devilish intruders? Maybe I should spray them with Raid Defend Ant & Roach repellent? It's probably my best defense against these things.* The screeching is painful to my ears causing goosebumps to rise all over me. Stealthily, I take a few steps toward the under-sink cabinet to grab my can of Raid Defend when the creatures start making loud gurgling sounds again.

With a harsh growl they speak at the same time. "We are Fic and Gan. We journeyed from the Wreximus Maximus galaxy. We are outlawed brothers from planet WatSoG. We need Earth coffee! We require much Earth coffee! Now!"

So, aliens come to Earth for our coffee? That's the reason? Hmm, interesting. Their eyes are shining like flashlights. They are so intensely bright that these two creatures would make excellent night lights. I realize with a start of surprise that I understand them perfectly. *English? How can they possibly speak English?*

"Oh, coffee? Uh, yeah sure. I, um. I have coffee." *If I give them coffee maybe they will leave. This sounds like a better plan than spraying them with my can of Raid Defend.*

I give them a trembling smile, trying to stay calm. *Oh wait, I better not smile. Maybe they will think I'm showing my teeth as a threat. Careful! They could still be very dangerous.* I can feel weakness in my legs as they continue shaking from my fear and adrenaline response. *I wish this was only a terrifying nightmare and that I could wake up and it would all be over.*

"Wake up. Wake up, Sedona."

Still feeling shaky and unsteady, I open the cabinet and carefully gather two ceramic coffee mugs for my alien guests. One of the mugs has a color image of Leonard Nimoy as *Star Trek's* Mr. Spock with a raised hand displaying the iconic Vulcan greeting. The other mug features William Shatner as Captain Kirk, beaming a jaunty smile. Below the color image is an excerpt from the famous *Star Trek* motto "...to boldly go where no man has gone before." I laugh with nervous hysteria when I see the two mugs gripped tightly in my hands. Still giggling uncontrollably, I retrieve a third mug with the word MUFON printed on it. Other than my flying saucer key ring, it's the only thing I have left of my mom.

I open the cloth sack of roasted coffee beans and then turn to the coffee grinder on the counter. I hiccup as I inhale the tantalizing scent of my homegrown coffee beans. I pour the beans in and press the button to start the grinder.

Watching curiously, Fic and Gan shuffle closer to me to see the coffee bean grinder in action. I cringe at the unpleasant scraping and screeching of their curved, razor-sharp talons along the floor. They stand so close to me in my small kitchen, that I feel the cold, vanilla-scented breeze emanating from their freakishly tiny bodies. I inhale curiously. *Vanilla? How can they make the room cooler just by standing here next to me? Can they be a non-pharmacological intervention for hot flashes? I would love that! I wonder if that means they don't have a warm-blooded circulatory system?*

I snort at my ridiculous wandering thoughts. *Two uninvited alien outlaws have appeared out of thin air inside my locked camper, after landing in the desert next to my stargazing spot; and I'm wondering about their circulatory system and anatomy? I really need to focus on the problem at hand. Why are they here? What else do they want? I've got to get them to leave as soon as possible.*

"Our coffee will be ready soon. Now I will brew the freshly ground beans. You see, that's the secret to great coffee flavor. I always use freshly ground beans and filtered water for my coffee."

They watch me with intense fascination as I add filtered water and the fresh ground beans to the brewer and then I press the switch. The rich soothing aroma of fresh coffee fills my nose and I sigh with contentment. *It's truly bizarre that I find myself entertaining alien guests. I never would've imagined that such a thing could be possible.*

The tantalizing smell of bubbling hot coffee wafts around my kitchen area. I stare at my guests as they sniff audibly and swivel their heads to follow the scent as it floats around the Tumbleweed. When the coffee is ready, I pour steaming coffee in each mug and slowly ferry them to the u-shaped dining booth.

"Come on, you might as well sit down and relax so you can properly enjoy your coffee." I graciously invite my alien guests to join me as I pat the soft cushions. "We haven't been properly introduced. Hello, my name is Sedona Manda Elske Dung. These are my animal companions, Rex and Patch." I gesture toward my dogs who are snoring in their pet beds and I see that my hand trembles slightly.

The alien brothers take a seat and gaze into their coffee mugs for a long moment before picking them up and taking a sip. I laugh with nervous hysteria as I stare at my two guests, sitting politely at my table clutching *Star Trek* mugs with their long claws poking my childhood heroes in the eyeballs. *Where are Captain Kirk and Mr. Spock when you really need them? I wish they would beam in here right now and help me.*

I'm enveloped in another cool breeze, sent from the mysterious aliens, this time the scent of citrus accompanies it. They look at each other, drink more coffee and then they start making strange growling noises at each other. Now the freakish creatures bounce up and down on the seat with their jaws opening and snapping shut repetitively. I shudder at the snapping sounds and goosebumps race across my skin while I'm held captive by my fear. I sit immobile with wide, frightened eyes entranced by their odd behavior. I'm watching my strange guests acting like scary, possessed dolls in a Halloween horror flick.

Their childish bouncing is making the fabric on the seat cushions squeak obnoxiously. I cover my ears with my hands to block out the unpleasant sounds. *I wonder if they are unhappy with the flavor of my coffee or what else is going on in their alien minds at this moment?*

Turning toward me again, they speak at the same time. "Your Earth coffee is pleasing. This is very acceptable to us! We approve this! It is very required to consume more coffee! It is worthy of our great effort to arrive! We traveled through many galaxies to visit you. Your weak human brain is not able to comprehend the great distances we have journeyed. Now that we are landed on Earth, we will remain here with you, living in this cumbersome land vehicle that you inhabit. We require that you will provide us with much sustenance and very much Earth coffee!" Fic and Gan stare at me with their flashlight eyeballs and then they turn back to silently gaze at each other.

Chapter 16

Theme song: "Make Room" by I AM THEY featuring Cheyenne Mitchell from the album Chapel Sessions

What did they just say? Alien outlaw roommates? No thank you! Alien room-mates are definitely not for me! The brothers have an odd way of speaking at the same time, in perfect unison. This situation is disturbing but they haven't harmed me or my dogs. *Well, at least they're friendly and they love coffee as much as I do. I don't want roommates at all, especially not alien outlaws, but what choice do I have?* I doubt that they will leave if I ask them and after all, they can just materialize in the Tumbleweed without my permission. I sigh in defeat at the impossible situation.

I guess we'll learn to live together and to get along in peace and harmony. It does state in the Holy Bible: "The alien who resides with you shall be to you as the citizen among you; you shall love the alien as yourself, for you were aliens in the land of Egypt: I am the Lord your God." Leviticus 19:34 (NRSV) Yes God of Heaven, you are my God and I will trust and obey you Heavenly Father. In Jesus' name, amen.

"So, did you visit Earth just to taste coffee or are you tourists?" I'm start-ing to get more comfortable with them as my curiosity takes over. I wipe my tears on my long sleeves. "If you're tourists, you don't want to miss Rome. It's called the Eternal City and it's one place you must visit. I've been learning about Italian history, art, and culture because I was planning on retiring to Italy. There are ancient basilicas filled with rare paintings and sculptures, ex-cellent museums, and rare, historically significant architecture and stunning public squares with huge fountains decorated with marble sculptures. Plus,

Italy also has a lovely coffee culture that you two must experience. Go and taste their famous coffee recipes. I'll give you directions to Rome. Why don't you just fly over to Italy in your crochet needle? There's nothing to see here except sand and rattlesnakes. I really think you would prefer to live in Italy."

The intergalactic, non-tourist brothers just sit silently and glare fiercely at me. They don't look too pleased with my efforts to get them to vacate my premises. So, I decide to try another tactic. I smile cheerfully to appease them.

"Why did you come to Nevada when Brazil exports the most coffee on Earth? There's so much coffee growing in Brazil that you would never run out. I really think that you would prefer to live in Brazil. I can give you directions to go there. Or why not visit Costa Rica or Ethiopia? They have amazing coffee too. You could travel there. Why did you decide to land at my stargazing spot? How did you get inside my Tumbleweed?" I boldly return the glaring eye contact from my new alien roommates as I sip my coffee.

Still glaring humorlessly at me, they finish their coffee and indicate they want a refill by clacking their long, sharp claws together while gesturing toward their empty mugs. "No more travels! No touristing! Your coffee is necessary. For certain, we were correct about the quality of your coffee. It is superior, truly out of this world! We came here because there is no coffee on WatSoG. We need to drink coffee to rejuvenate our brain powers after space travel of great distances and we choose you to provide us with assistance. We will domicile in your cumbersome land vehicle and you will brew us much coffee. You will provide us with much sustenance and very much coffee. We demand that you teach us to grow coffee! This is very acceptable to us! We approve this!"

Well, it was worth a try and I thought that my logic was pretty good. I mean, I would rather be in Italy if it were possible, so why wouldn't intergalactic tourists want to be there as well? I sigh in defeat and a pathetic tear rolls down my cheek as I grind and brew more coffee beans. I bring out the cherry filled, sugar-glazed coffee cake. I retrieve a cheery yellow bowl and fill it with fresh baby carrots. I might as well enjoy myself and I have enough snacks to share. I place a slice of cake on three red plates, gather forks, and pour more fresh coffee into our mugs. I ferry our feast to the table.

Fic and Gan inhale the strong aroma of the steaming coffee in their mugs. They open their mouths, stretching their lips wide and reveal their fangs to me. They are a sickening shade of green and they also appear very sharp. I startle in fright and then laugh nervously.

"WatSoG is our home planet located in the Wreximus Maximus galaxy. We were outlawed then forced to leave our family because we quit our jobs in the cafeteria. This is very not acceptable in our culture! We were designated as cafeteria workers at our hatching and we are required to serve for our entire lives. On our planet, there is no individual choice of career. All WatSo-Gians are assigned to work in the same careers as all of the previous generations of our ancestors. We are the first to quit our jobs and to become outlaws in the entire history of our world!"

"Why did you quit, knowing that you would be banished?" It seems unfair and I feel a pang of sympathy for these alien outcasts. I watch them, fascinated that I'm having coffee and a friendly chat with aliens.

"The cafeteria we worked in did not serve coffee. None is served anywhere on WatSoG. We used the suggestion box to request a change from the no-coffee policy. Management denied our request and we filed a formal appeal of their decision. When our appeal was denied, we were fined a monetary fee equal to fifty times our collective lifetime wages as punishment for our audacity to question the authority of the bosses. There is no way that we could ever pay the fines. Rather than become indentured servants, we decided to quit. Since our banishment, we have been traveling the universe in search of coffee."

"That sounds like an extremely harsh punishment for using the suggestion box at work. I'm sorry that you encountered trouble at your jobs. Unfortunately, it's also pretty common here for beings to have disputes at work. The sad truth is that conflict with others is practically a way of life here on Earth. Your home planet sounds very far away. How did you learn about Earth?"

The brothers share more about their travels, while I grab a handful of baby carrots and offer some to my guests. Then I toss one to each of my dogs. Both dogs raise their heads and catch the carrots and happily begin crunching. Fic and Gan bounce up and down a little on the seat cushions when they taste the carrots. Now that I'm not frightened of them, it's almost kind of cute watching their enthusiastic reaction to Earth food.

"Many years ago, WatSoGians traveled to Earth and its moon. Our grandparents, Tti and Unee, were members of both expeditions to Earth and they tasted coffee during their visits. When we were hatchlings, our grandparents told us stories of their experiences during their travels and how much they loved drinking Earth coffee. They told us that during their first Earth expedition they landed at a place called Roswell, New Mexico. While they were visiting that location, they met several friendly Earthlings who had a cattle ranch. The Earthlings hosted the WatSoGians at a barbecue party and our grandparents told us about a food called barbecue ribs and something called coffee ice cream. Do you have coffee ice cream?"

"The freezer in my camper is too small to keep ice cream. I do have lots of salad to share with you."

Chapter 17

Theme song: "Broken Things" by Matthew West from the album All In

"Oh, I watched some television documentaries about the 1947 Roswell UFO crash incident. I also watched other documentaries about rumors that the authorities detained aliens." I'm staring excitedly at my new friends now, breathless to hear more of their outlandish tale.

"Our grandparents were personally invited as special guests of honor to enjoy an exclusive vacation at an ultra-private resort in Nevada named Area 51. Tti and Unee advised us to visit Nevada because they thoroughly enjoyed their vacation at Resort 51. Unfortunately, today exclusive vacation Resort 51 is now designated as a top-secret military installation and it is under a very tightly controlled high security lock down. They do not allow otherworldly visitors anymore so we cannot go there to enjoy the comforts of the spa, the heated salt-water pool, or the ten-seat hot tubs. This is very unacceptable to us! We do not approve this! Since we cannot visit Resort 51, we decided to find coffee instead." While chatting with me, the brothers try a few more carrots.

By now, my jaw is hanging open in surprise and I quickly snap it shut. I sit up straighter with intense fascination. "Area 51? Your grandparents were detained at Area 51? I didn't really believe the wild rumors about crashed UFOs and aliens being detained at Roswell and Area 51. Incredible! The alien part, it's really true! Your grandparents, were they harmed at Area 51? I've heard lots of rumors that alien autopsies are conducted there and also that crashed spacecraft are studied, reverse-engineered, and stored at Area 51."

Fic and Gan stare at each other and then turn their luminous gazes to me. "No! No one was harmed at luxury Resort 51. There was no crash! You are badly mistaken! Our grandparents are excellent pilots with a perfect flying safety record! What is alien autopsies? It sounds delightful. Is alien autopsies a relaxing Earthling spa treatment? Can we get one too? Tti and Unee reported that everyone on the expedition had a wonderful time visiting Earth. They told us that the humans were friendly and everyone socialized together, relaxed, and enjoyed lots of Earth cuisine and drinks. That is where they first tasted coffee."

"Oh, good. I'm so glad to hear it was a pleasant visit. Never mind about the alien autopsies. They are most certainly not a relaxing spa treatment! Trust me, you don't want an autopsy, ever! Alien autopsies are definitely not for you!" I relax again and rest my back against the cushions.

"Our grandparents and the other members of the WatSoGian expedition made a second trip many years later. They returned in 1969 to spend time on Earth's moon. There is a popular lunar resort there, located deep inside a large crater on what humans refer to as the far side of the moon. It is where Tti and Unee enjoyed a vacation with their friends and all of the expedition members. While out exploring the surface of the moon, the WatSoGians witnessed the first moon landing by Earthlings traveling in a small craft called *Lunar Module Eagle*. Have you heard of it? A few weeks later, they returned to Earth for another visit. Tti and Unee said they enjoyed a visit to a very rare, colorful canyon in a place called Arizona. Have you heard of it?"

"Hmm. I've heard of the *Apollo 11* lunar mission and I've seen the Grand Canyon in Arizona. Its impressive geological beauty is very rare and spectacular. Why don't you go visit the Grand Canyon? I'm sure that they serve excellent coffee in the restaurants in Arizona. I think that you would be much happier living and touristing in Arizona. If you agree to leave, I will give you some of my coffee beans to take with you." I place another slice of coffee cake on their plates. They gobbled up the first slices very quickly. *I wonder if the WatSoGian lunar expedition is responsible for the old rumors about the Apollo 11 astronauts' possible sighting of a UFO during their lunar mission? Apparently, there were reports of them seeing a light or an object moving outside of their lunar craft window.*

"Nice try, there will be no departing and no touristing to Arizona, Sedona. We will remain here with you. The WatSoGian expedition was, according to our grandparents, an intergalactic Grand Tour."

I giggle helplessly at their use of the antiquated expression. *Wasn't a Grand Tour common among wealthy Europeans back in the 18th century?*

"After retirement, Tti and Unee always wanted to return to Earth for the delicious cuisine and to consume much more coffee. Once we were banished, Tti and Unee provided us with the navigational coordinates. They suggested that we travel to Earth and experience coffee for ourselves. Our intergalactic travels have diminished our brain powers. Now we require rest and much coffee to help us recuperate. We first decided to come to Nevada to vacation at Resort 51. Since it is now off limits to aliens, we tracked you down instead because your highly aromatic coffee drew us to your location."

Fic and Gan eat more coffee cake while chatting with me. After their first few enormous bites of coffee cake, the alien brothers levitate up into the air above the dining booth. While the brothers are floating near the ceiling and noisily chewing their mouthfuls of cake, they accidentally unleash a rainstorm of cake crumbs down onto my hair. They send a chocolate scented breeze in my direction. *Does that mean they like the flavor of the coffee cake or is it an apology for raining crumbs down on my head?* I decide they are very weird but pleasant guests even though they literally popped into my home uninvited.

"Fic and Gan, I desperately need your help. Something terrible happened to my mother and I want to share her story with you. Because you and your family have unique space travel experiences, I think you're my best chance for assistance. I hope you can help me. My mom disappeared more than a decade ago. Her name is Joy and she was a researcher of UFO sightings. One night many years ago, there were many eyewitness reports of nocturnal lights appearing in the empty desert surrounding Sandy Town. My mom went out into the desert alone to search for any evidence. She wanted to witness the nocturnal lights phenomena for herself. She never returned from her investigation that night. Do you think it's possible that my mom was abducted by aliens?" Tears flood my eyes as I share my concerns about my missing mom. While awaiting their response, I inhale the soothing chocolate aroma therapy breeze sent by the brothers. I smile at them while brushing crumbs out of my hair.

"We have been informed that abductions of innocent citizens are occurring throughout many galaxies! Our home is a peaceful and very civilized society that strives for a high quality of life for its citizens. The major deficiency is that WatSoG does not cultivate coffee, nor does it import any. This is very unacceptable to us! We do not approve this! WatSoG also maintains very good diplomacy and peaceful relations with its allies and other neighboring planets. Unfortunately, this is not the case in every galaxy. There are many uncivilized planets where war mongering is the accepted way of life. They pillage and plunder other planets. There are vicious creatures whose actions are not peaceful. It is probable that your parent was taken hostage by one of these marauding species. We will send a message home to inform Tti and Unee. They will report it to the WatSoGian Intergalactic Peace and Citizen Safety Council. Perhaps with their assistance, it will be possible to investigate this encounter." As the alien brothers speak at the same time, they slowly float back down to the seat cushions in the dining booth.

"I still can't believe that there's no coffee served on WatSoG. It's no wonder that you were willing to travel such a vast distance to visit Earth. Now I understand your insatiable desire for consuming coffee. I'm grateful for any help you can give me. I'm curious, though, if you're here on Earth with me, how can you report my mom's suspicious disappearance all the way back to your grandparents on WatSoG?"

"We maintain communication with WatSoG through a network of transmissions of our interconnected brain waves. The limitless capabilities of WatSoGian brains are superior and much more complex compared with the pathetic limitations of the barely advanced abilities of the puny human brain. We have the ability to transmit our thoughts vast distances through space. WatSoG is not so far away that we cannot send a message home. We agree to provide you with assistance in this matter and we will make it so."

Chapter 18

Theme song: "Wishful Thinking" by MercyMe from the album Welcome to the New

The next morning before sunrise, I step out of the Tumbleweed which is still parked at the deserted rest stop. I get busy setting up the small corral and hanging the tarp for Topaz to have a shelter. I fill water buckets and hay bags. I lead Topaz into her corral and brush her fuzzy coat. I also clean out her hooves with the hoof pick. I pull a carrot from my pocket and hand it over. Back inside her trailer, I get a good workout by shoveling out manure and soiled bedding then I add fresh wood shavings. I refill the trailer water buckets and hay bags. I hop out of the trailer to visit with Topaz. I make a fuss over her and coo silly words while I scratch her on the neck and withers. She raises her head, stretches her neck forward, and rotates her upper lip with delight, expressing her appreciation. I gaze at the cool beauty of the dark sky. After she is content, I gently hug her warm neck. I feed her another carrot and go back inside.

When I climb up into my camper, Fic and Gan appear instantaneously, materializing right out of thin air before my eyes. "Mercy me! Gentlemen, please knock on the door first before you appear inside. My heart can't withstand the shock of your unannounced entrances. Here let me show you how to knock on the door before entering."

I step outside and they dutifully follow me. I stand before the closed door and knock on it as hard as I can. Both brothers jump scare at the loud sounds and levitate up into the air. At their unexpected movements, my heart lurches in surprise and I'm startled all over again. My roommates are floating just above me and their knife-like toenails are dangling near my face. They are quite repulsive. The nails are pumpkin and squash colored and are quite disturbing. Ew! I laugh aloud at our mutual social blunders because now they feel exactly how I felt a few moments earlier. I really hope I get used to their sudden movements and frequent springing up and levitating into the air.

"So, is today moving in day for you? Do you need help bringing your personal belongings over from your crochet needle? I'm happy to help you." I smile pleasantly at the intergalactic brothers and after my last night alone in the Tumbleweed, I feel ready to welcome my outlawed alien roommates.

"What is moving in day? What is personal belongings? Coffee! We require much coffee now!" Fic and Gan speak at the same time as they float through the door into the Tumbleweed and make themselves at home in the dining booth.

"Never mind, don't stress yourselves. I've already made coffee for us and I want to take a hike this morning with my animal companions. I need to retrieve my stargazing equipment. Come on, here is your coffee. Follow me, gentlemen."

As the landscape is bathed in a peachy glow from the approaching daylight, we hike out to my stargazing spot. Patch and Rex enjoy their morning run and they are already accustomed to the presence of Fic and Gan. The brothers are floating above the sand and are effortlessly moving along with me as I walk beside them. They each clutch a travel mug of caffé mocha in one hand. They are sipping and grinning as they glide along with me. I notice the brothers seem to be amused by Topaz and they reach out long claws to gently scratch her shaggy neck as she walks along with me.

As we cover the miles together, I realize I'm beginning to feel more comfortable with my new roommates. When we reach my stargazing equipment, I'm glad to see it's undamaged. I pick up my fallen camp chair and set it upright. I quickly break down my telescope and tripod and stow them inside my backpack. I set out the large water bowl and fill it with cold water. Topaz stands next to my camp chair and I leave her a large pile of baby carrots on the galaxy fabric seat. I drop her rope on the sand, taking advantage of her ground-tying training, so I don't have to worry about her wandering too far away.

"Sedona, now you must come with us to investigate our spacecraft."

The crochet needle sits dark and silent in the desert. When the brothers approach, it illuminates and begins vibrating and humming loudly. A ramp extends and settles onto the sand, then an entrance door glides open.

"Stay here Rex and Patch. I'll be right back, I hope. Fic and Gan, I'll be allowed to stay on Earth and you will let me leave your spaceship after our tour, right? You're not going to abduct me, right?" Suddenly I feel very concerned and I have doubts about my safety.

"Touristing, Sedona! As you would say, it is just a tourist visit. We are not ready to fly again so soon. We require more quantities of rest and touristing on Earth before we can navigate our craft. Someday we will bring you on a spaceflight. Be patient!"

"You misunderstood me, I'm not asking to go for a ride in your…oh never mind. Let's move on, please."

I notice that my dogs happily continue exploring in the nearby desert scrub plants. I feel confident they'll enjoy their outdoor romp more than looking inside a spaceship. I trust them to keep Topaz company. The brothers motion for me to enter their crochet needle and I tentatively precede Fic and Gan inside.

"Even though I'm standing right here, I still have trouble accepting that this is real! Wow, it's so cold in here that I'm getting goosebumps. I like your interior decor it's sleek and very minimalist. Do you have a cafeteria or any food service on board?"

"Negative. Now you comprehend why we need sufficient time to rest and to consume sustenance and much coffee. We have the need for more sustenance very soon." They pause to sip caffé mocha from the travel mugs imprisoned between their long claws.

When I walk, I feel an unusual springing sensation coming from the flooring almost like it has shock absorption properties built into it. It's a strange sensation just like trying to walk inside a bouncy house. All of the smooth surfaces feature an endless purple and silver geometric design which illuminates with pulsing green light with every step I take.

"This is an incredible experience. It's beautiful the way that the geometric designs on the walls and floors are shifting and changing shape as they illuminate. I've never seen anything like it."

I feel dizzy after watching the fluctuating green lighting and the rhythmic movements of the shape shifting geometric patterns. Feeling disoriented, I stop walking and rapidly blink my eyes to clear my vision. I feel better and we continue exploring the crochet needle. As we walk, I spy soft purple lights glowing along the ceilings. I notice the walls have alcoves set into them at regular intervals. Inside the alcoves are curved benches with thickly padded cushions. *Oh my, those benches look inviting and perfect for reclining and reading a good book.*

Fic and Gan show me their unique smile. For a moment, I startle at the ferocity of their pointed green fangs. Immediately, a lovely coconut scented breeze floats serenely around me. I feel relaxed and content enveloped in the deliciously scented cloud.

"Fic and Gan, how do you do that? I always experience a soothing scented breeze in your presence."

"It is helpful to reduce your stress levels. We want to help you feel comfortable with the new experiences. Keep calm and carry on! Just do what the famous Earthling expression advises."

"It's good advice. I'm pretty fond of that old expression. I really like your crochet needle. How long have you had it?"

"We started flying when we exceeded our hatchling age. On WatSoG, it is referred to as being ascendant. On Earth, you would call it being a teenager. We studied the star systems and the physics of space flight. We had craft navigation and flight lessons. After completing our exams and test flights, we were officially permitted to fly within the boundaries of WatSoG space. We did not venture out into new galaxies until our banishment."

"So, how exactly do you fly this thing? Can you explain it to me?" I gaze at my surroundings in wonder. *This entire experience feels so surreal. I'm actually walking around inside an authentic alien spaceship.*

"This spacecraft is specifically tuned to our individual brain wave patterns and also linked to our WatSoGian DNA. We use the immense power contained within our brains and our DNA to navigate it. This natural process contained within us also powers and propels our spacecraft. WatSoGian brain cells and DNA are uniquely evolved for this purpose. Our brains are vastly more powerful and contain exponentially greater abilities than those of humans. We simply envision the coordinates of where we want to travel and our spacecraft responds and flies to that location. Our ability to travel vast distances is without limits but there is a physical cost. Our brain cells are weakened and some are burned out and this results in our abilities being diminished after long travels. We only just learned while visiting you here on Earth, that drinking your specific blend of coffee can assist our brain cells to regenerate and to help increase our abilities after our long spaceflight. We believe that the various combinations of chemical compounds that are released when your ground coffee is brewed with very hot water is responsible for these phenomena within our brain cells."

Ah, okay then. That explains why they can't ever get enough coffee. They constantly drink it and I'm having trouble supplying their endless demand for the brewed beverage.

"You must save a lot on fuel costs." I grin at them. I'm not sure they understand my sense of humor yet. "I really like the design of your spaceship it's uniquely beautiful. The shape of it reminds me of an Earth instrument called a crochet needle, except that your spaceship is much larger, of course." I gaze with amusement at the brothers. I pull my smartphone from my back pocket and find an image of a purple crochet needle and hold it out for them to see.

"There is an uncanny resemblance to our spacecraft. What is the purpose of this Earthling crochet needle? Does it also fly? It seems entirely too tiny to carry passengers and cargo!" The curious brothers tap their long claws on the image displayed on my smartphone as they speak.

"Oh, a crochet needle doesn't fly or carry passengers and cargo. It's used in the fiber arts. Essentially, it's a hand-held tool for creating stitches in fibers such as yarn or thread. With a specific pattern of stitches and enough hours of crocheting, it transforms the fibers into clothing or household items such as beautiful sweaters and cozy blankets. I would like to learn to crochet, but at the moment, I don't have any experience with the fiber arts. Does everyone on WatSoG have a spaceship like this one?"

"This model is the most common transport on our planet. Every family has similar spacecraft. Although, most of the government officials are assigned a luxury spacecraft that is shaped very much like the yellow Earth banana that we saw lying on your kitchen counter. Our parents gave us this Spin-Class starship upon graduation from our education. This is the customary time to become independent on our world and for us to take our places in the cafeteria to work. We use the Spin-Class to travel both on and off Wat-SoG and to visit neighboring planets. There are many wonderful worlds near WatSoG that are friendly and they are great family vacation destinations."

"Well, that sounds perfectly ordinary. We Earthlings enjoy vacations with our families too."

Fic and Gan continue chatting with me while they glide a few inches above the floor. "We once took a trip with our parents and Tti and Unee to a planet where it rains colored diamonds. The planet is called IdskeOBlue and we wanted to go swimming in the Acidic Rainbow Sea. It is a top-tier planet also located in the Wreximus Maximus galaxy. It is well loved for its blue diamond pebble beaches and multicolored mineral waters. The beaches are aglow with colorful radiant light. There is also gourmet food in their cafeterias! This is very acceptable to us! We approve this! It is one of the few planets near WatSoG that offers gourmet food. Unfortunately, they do not serve coffee! This is very unacceptable to us! We do not approve this!"

"Fic and Gan, I'm trying to imagine walking on beaches covered in glittering diamonds. It sounds painful and beautiful at the same time. I would love to see it. I can just imagine it. I would walk along the beaches wearing shoes to protect my feet and I would carry a cloth shopping bag and fill it with diamonds. On Earth, some people like to collect sea shells and driftwood from our beaches. Are visitors allowed to collect the stones on IdskeOBlue? It's nice to daydream about visiting another galaxy but I don't think I could ever travel so far from Earth." I look at Fic and Gan as I speak. The thought of Fic and Gan walking on beaches with their parents and grandparents makes me think of my lost mother. I sincerely hope they can help me search for her.

"It is not permitted to remove the diamonds from the beaches. If visitors took away the beautiful stones, then the beauty of the beaches would also be removed. However, it is permissible to capture digital photographic images while visiting the beaches and post the digitized images to SpaceTravelChats and StarryPictograms. That is what most visitors do."

"Oh, well it's good to know that the rare blue diamond beaches are protected places. Are Spacechats and Starrygrams or whatever they're called, are they WatSoGian social media?"

"What is socials medias? There is no such thing on WatSoG. SpaceTravelChats and StarryPictograms are online platforms where family and friends can follow each other. It allows them to share digital media such as digital photographs and video footage of their pets, their vacation travels, and their favorite cuisine. There is no socials medias on WatSoG, rather it is digital media shared online between friends and family. Many of the premier citizens of

WatSoG have millions of followers on their online platforms and they wield great influence over society. In fact, they are often referred to as influencers and they are adored and trusted by their many followers to dispense good advice. Sedona, you ask odd questions sometimes."

"Oh, okay. I think we're actually talking about the same thing. I understand."

We walk farther inside the crochet needle. Eventually, the shape of the spacecraft shifts into a long and very narrow hallway, instead of the much wider and rounded shape of the crochet handle section that we first walked through. Finally, the narrow corridor opens into a narrow and sharply curved room that terminates in a pointed end, the hooked end of the crochet needle. It's the flight deck and it is dominated by an enormous space shield window. It resembles an oversize semi truck windshield but its size is scaled up and it's clearly engineered to withstand the stress of space travel.

The centrally located space shield window is flanked on both sides by panoramic space windows. I notice numerous purple benches designed for reclining. They are topped with thickly padded green cushions. The benches are strategically placed below the space shield. Several benches are placed beneath all of the panoramic windows. They provide incredible views of the outdoors while the spacecraft is parked here in the desert.

I'm very surprised at the lack of instrument panels and flight crew stations. In my mind, I foolishly imagined the bridge of *Star Trek's USS Enterprise* NCC-1701 and this bridge looks nothing like it. I'm kind of disappointed at the emptiness of the room. It's very odd that no machinery or technical instruments are on the bridge. I can't believe the only things to see in here are a bunch of benches and panoramic windows. Outside, I see Rex and Patch lying in the shade of a big sagebrush shrub near Topaz. I smile at the trio; they look quite comfortable while they await our return.

"Can you explain to me about this room? Why is it so empty of machinery or flight instruments? Do you have a flight crew on board?"

"No flight crew or staff of any kind are needed. There is also no need for instruments or machinery. Do you remember that we explained to you that this spacecraft is tuned into our brain waves and linked with our unique WatSoGian DNA? That is the only requirement for this spacecraft to travel. We simply lie comfortably on the benches and take extremely long naps. This frees up our brains to power and to guide the ship while we rest."

"Oh." I want to laugh or cry because it's such a letdown. I'm standing inside an authentic alien spaceship and it's actually pretty boring here on the bridge. Although to be fair, the rest of the interior decor is pretty amazing. "Thank you for the tour of your crochet needle-ish spaceship, gentlemen. My stomach is rumbling. It's time we get back to my Tumbleweed and make breakfast." I wisely decide to feed my voracious alien roommates before they can become cranky from hunger.

Fic and Gan look at me with a puzzled expression on their faces. "Breakfast? What is breakfast?"

I smile at my otherworldly friends. "Come on, please escort me back through your spaceship and when we return to my cumbersome land vehicle, I'll show you what breakfast is. I'm sure you'll like it. Breakfast is always served with coffee. I promise."

We walk back through the seemingly endless corridors and finally exit the crochet needle. The ramp retracts and the door closes up behind us. The spaceship powers down and becomes totally dark and silent. I pick up Topaz's rope, collect the empty water bowl and stow it in my backpack. I collapse my tripod camp chair and sling its long strap over my shoulder.

Together we hike the miles through the warming desert back to the rest area parking lot where the Tumbleweed awaits, still all alone. I'm glad the rest area is deserted. It would be hard to explain the presence of my alien roommates to other people and naturally it would start a disastrous nationwide panic. *Secretly, I'm also very relieved their spaceship was empty. I don't think that I could handle more than two WatSoGians. The general public just isn't ready for alien visitation. Honestly, I'm not either.*

Back in my kitchen, I ponder my biggest problem. I need to find a way to disguise their alienness and to help them blend in with the general public. I think of my friend Sam and her unique skill set and I smile with hopefulness. Perhaps there is a way.

For Fic and Gan's first Earth breakfast, I make chocolate chip Belgian waffles and top them with homemade whipped cream and fresh sliced strawberries. I fry up a pound of cherry wood smoked bacon. I cook them just slightly crispy so they are not too crunchy. To impress my new roommates, I add orange wedges to our plates as a fancy garnish. Naturally, I serve copious amounts of hot coffee.

Fic and Gan are thrilled to try more Earth cuisine and I get the feeling they will be happy here even though they are far away from their family. They devour all of the bacon slices and four waffles each. I'm left with just one waffle for myself but it's enough to satisfy my hunger. *I wonder how such tiny beings can consume such large quantities of food? I'm definitely going to need more groceries soon, now that I have voracious roommates living in the Tumbleweed.*

Chapter 19

Theme song: "Better than Sunshine" by Crowder from the album Milk & Honey Deluxe Edition

After breakfast, I show my intergalactic roommates the coffee plants living in my shower. I go over the basic parts of the plants and explain that they require soil and a specific amount of daily water and light to thrive. I show them my grow lights hanging from the ceiling.

"Ah, these lights perform the function of the sun to nourish the plants, yes? This hose hanging up on the wall, what is the function of it?"

"Here, I will show you how to use the hand-held shower head to water the coffee plants. Take hold of it like this. Be careful with your claws so you don't puncture the hose. Now hold this end, then turn this knob and spray a little water. See? You did it."

"SilyEeeeeeGrrrrrWrtrs! UooTypeitNowwwHerEeee!"

"Is that WatSoGian? What are you saying?"

"The rough translation into American English is something like: Caring for the coffee is very acceptable to us! We approve this! Can we drink them now? Much coffee!" Both brothers grin their horrific smile at me.

"Not yet. First the plants need time to grow more coffee cherries. Be patient, life takes the time it needs to grow, to nourish, and to prosper."

Fic and Gan are very excited when they see the garden soil in the pots briefly fill with water. I laugh as they eagerly place their long claws gently into the wet mix and suddenly, they pop up into the air and begin floating above the floor.

I feel their cool lemon-scented breeze flowing around me in the small bathroom area. I explain the process of waiting for the coffee fruits to mature on the plants before they can be harvested.

"After I pick the ripe coffee cherries, I set them outside in the sunshine for a few days. Once they become very dry and wrinkled, I use a hand tool to remove the seeds from the cherry husk. Later the dried seeds can be roasted in the coffee roaster and then they are called coffee beans. Do you understand?"

"This is very acceptable to us! We will help you take care of the coffee lifeforms and you will teach us to make coffee beans. We require much coffee!"

We step into the kitchen area and the brothers watch me closely as I use the bean grinder and then pull shots of espresso for iced lattes. Once our glasses are filled, I ferry them to the dining booth.

"Fic and Gan, I think you are attentive students and that you genuinely want to learn about coffee. I'm on my way to Fragrant Bean for the annual coffee festival and I think you would enjoy the activities at the festival. Maybe I can get you into the coffee growing and coffee bean roasting classes with my friend Sam and I. Sam is a fan of sci-fi and alien lore, so I think she will enjoy meeting the two of you. This could be a fun trip."

"Sedona, this is very acceptable to us! Let's go touristing with your friend Sam and get much coffee. We approve this!"

"You must understand that other humans shouldn't see you or learn where you come from. You will have to impersonate human beings in order to go to the coffee festival. I think my friend Sam can help us. She can change your appearance and help you to blend in with all the humans. We need her expertise to create convincing disguises. For your safety, we need to keep your true identity a secret. I don't think other humans can handle aliens living among us. My friend Sam has a unique skill set that will surely help us with this problem. What do you say, are you interested in my plan?"

Fic and Gan stare into each other's eyes and then they agree to come with me. "As you wish, Sedona. We will comply. We want to go to Earth coffee festival!"

"Okay, so here's the deal. Until Sam can change your appearance, you two can't be seen by other humans. You will ride with me in the Tumbleweed and stay out of sight. I believe it's safe enough to leave your crochet needle where it's parked, since this area seems to be mostly uninhabited. This area is very remote and far from tourist attractions so it's unlikely that anyone will find it."

"We agree this is acceptable to us. Our spacecraft will become invisible in our absence and it will remain locked down until we return. It will only activate upon tuning into our brain waves and DNA. We will travel inside your cumbersome land vehicle with you. We are in need of sustenance and much coffee now. Do you have any games for us to pass the time while you navigate your land vehicle?"

Fic and Gan stare at me with their vibrant green eyes and I see the miniature galaxies swirling in their luminous depths. It's eerily mesmerizing. I force myself to look away.

"I have an entertaining card game that you might enjoy. I can teach you how to play it. I also have Star Trek Monopoly, which is a fun board game. I need a few minutes to get us ready to travel." I smile at the thought of the intergalactic brothers playing a *Star Trek* game.

I step outside and spend a few minutes preparing the Tumbleweed for the drive. I load Topaz in her stock trailer and stow the portable corral panels. She has plenty of hay and water and the bedding is fresh. I check the hitch, the tire pressure on both vehicles, and the charge on the battery banks. Finally, I'm satisfied that everything is ready to travel.

I'm grateful to have the array of solar panels on the roof of the Tumbleweed and I'm impressed at my dad's DIY skills. He reconfigured and set up the Tumbleweed to operate only on a solar power system complete with battery banks that store the solar power for all operations. I love the freedom of being able to camp anywhere without the necessity of having to plug into shore power. I appreciate that traveling on solar power instead of fossil fuels makes it much more economical for me to travel and live in my camper.

Once I'm back inside, I prepare snacks for my roommates. I place a bowl filled with baby carrots, sliced celery, and apples on the table. Their glasses of iced coffee are nestled securely in the cup holders. I retrieve my Star Trek Galactic Enterprises card game from the cabinet. I'm certain this entertaining game will keep my mischievous roommates busy while I drive. I explain the rules of the game and play a practice hand with them.

"Well gentlemen, these snacks and iced coffees should keep you happy while I drive. Enjoy your card game. If you get bored with this game, you can play Star Trek Monopoly. Since you speak English so well, I think you should be able to read the directions and figure out how to play the game. It's in that cabinet over there. Remember to keep the window shades down, no one else is supposed to see you two."

Rex and Patch curl up in their pet beds, familiar with my travel routine by now. I put on my pink sun glasses and cap, gather my long hair into a ponytail and slide into the driver's seat. I buckle up my seat belt and start the motor. I raise my foot from the brake and allow the Tumbleweed to slowly roll forward. I carefully pull out of the parking lot and onto the deserted highway. It's a relatively short drive from here along the Extraterrestrial Highway to Fragrant Bean. I feel butterflies in my stomach as I think about introducing Fic and Gan to my friend Sam.

Chapter 20

Theme song: "City on the Hill" by Casting Crowns from the album Come to the Well

Today our trip is gradual uphill driving and we're gaining quite a bit of elevation. After a while, I'm starting to feel slightly fatigued. I'm enjoying the beauty of the high desert landscape but I'm very happy when I finally pull into Fragrant Bean. It's an old western settlement from the 19th century situated on a high plateau. I drive with caution through town and head toward the parking lot reserved for campers.

The town is very quaint and thanks to its unique location it is blessed with incredible panoramic views of the region. It features several historic adobe buildings with exposed wooden beams that date to the town's early settlement. Not surprisingly, Fragrant Bean has modernized over the centuries and the town's architectural style has changed over the years as a result. Some of the adobe buildings have been altered over the years and now include brightly painted shutters and wooden covered porches charmingly decorated with rocking chairs, potted flowers, and blooming cacti.

The town design is pedestrian friendly and encourages walking. It has gravel trails that are wide and level to accommodate large crowds of festival visitors. The walking paths have human and pet water fountains. Numerous benches with shade coverings are stationed along the entire length of the trail.

There are several diners in town with covered outdoor patios paved with flagstones. They are decorated with colorful potted plants and they have brightly painted tables with comfortable seating. Cooling fan misters are stationed in the outdoor dining areas. There is also an old adobe building with exposed wood beams that houses the town's only authentic old-fashioned general store. A covered front porch constructed with wood planks was added to the store front. Green and pink rocking chairs invite visitors to sit and enjoy the shade. Colorful flower boxes adorn the front windows. There are also countless gift shops in town that are popular with visitors.

My favorite attraction in town is the Fragrant Bean Museum of UFOs. It's housed in a massive shiny silver metal warehouse. The museum has a replica of a classic flying saucer with blinking red lights perched vertically on the apex of its roof. The building is bathed in red and blue flashing lights. It is filled with exhibits that contain artifacts, eyewitness accounts, documents, photos, and videos plus other memorabilia of UFO sightings and close encounters. It also has an extensive collection of exhibits covering the evolution of spaceflight and the U.S. space program.

Ha! I wonder if the UFO museum would like to add my close encounter of the third kind to their case files? What a bizarre and exciting thought. I could become part of a museum exhibit in my favorite museum. Of course, I realize this is not possible because it would endanger Fic and Gan. Sam and I will definitely keep this situation top secret. Maybe we can just enjoy a visit to the museum with our new friends. I can imagine how fun it will be to tour the exhibits with Fic and Gan. How extraordinary to be able to take two intergalactic aliens into a UFO museum and no one else there will know who and what they really are.

The Tumbleweed passes under a bright pink banner illustrated with piles of coffee beans and cheerful green and blue coffee mugs with little plumes of steam rising up from them. The town banner proclaims: "Welcome to the Fragrant Bean Coffee Festival. Go ahead and inhale! Roasted coffee beans are tasty beans with a naturally fragrant aroma." *Who on earth writes this nonsense?*

The festival is held in the large town square and park area at the center of town. The town square is paved with huge square-shaped paving stones in lovely shades of terracotta, yellow, blue, and green. At the park's center, there is a three-tier concrete fountain splashing and bubbling melodiously. It releases a cool mist into the surrounding area which makes the nearby benches popular with visitors.

Across from the fountain and benches are four irrigated greenhouses filled with several varieties of coffee shrubs. The greenhouses will hold the coffee seminars and demonstrations. The biggest draw of the festival are the coffee bar tents. They are a popular gathering place for friends and family to enjoy the fruits of the festival.

Inside, each of the three spacious tents are shady and cool. They have large ventilation fans to keep guests comfortable. Bright green tables and chairs fill the crowded space. At the back of each tent is the main attraction, a long coffee bar where baristas serve an expansive menu of coffee drinks from around the world. Finally, at the far end of town is the huge gravel parking lot filled with happy campers.

Once the Tumbleweed is parked and level in our reserved space, I give instructions to my roommates. "Fic and Gan, for your safety you must stay inside. Please wait here for me. I have another fun card game for you to play and here are more snacks and coffee. This is my Yes, Yes Yeti Risk-Taking Card Game! These are the instructions for the game. Do you think you can figure out how to play it while I'm out searching for Sam?"

"We flew to Earth using our brain powers! Do not underestimate us. Our brains are far superior to yours. We understand that you mean well but your species is very much inferior. Human games are entertaining and we approve this! Sedona, we will stay here in your domicile land vehicle. We will study the instructions and master this new game while you are retrieving your friend." Fic and Gan nod at me and send a delicious peppermint breeze toward me.

I smile while inhaling the refreshing aroma therapy. My roommates seem to enjoy learning to play new games and they look comfortable seated in the dining booth. I caution them to keep the window shades closed. I place a plate filled with baby carrots, sliced apples, and Havarti cheese on the table. Next to it I place a bowl of chocolate covered almonds and another bowl filled with trail mix. I refill their glasses of iced coffee. *I'm worried it's a mistake to leave them alone but I need to go find Sam. What could possibly go wrong?*

I step outside and get to work setting up my campsite. I extend the patio awning and place several camp chairs in its shade. I hang up my galaxy-shaped wind chimes and then set out a large water bowl for my dogs.

I spend a few more minutes setting up Topaz's small corral securing her shade tarp across one side. I spread a comfortable layer of clean wood shavings over the gravel surface. I hang water buckets and hay bags along the corral fence. When I bring Topaz out of the trailer and into her corral, she looks around curiously and squeaks out a loud bray to announce her presence to the other campers. I spend a few minutes grooming her fuzzy coat and I use the hoof pick to clean out her hooves. I give her hooves a pedicure with my hoof rasp to keep them neatly trimmed. I'm satisfied that she is comfortable and I leave her a few carrots.

One of the things I love about Fragrant Bean is that it's pet friendly. Well behaved pets on their leashes are welcome throughout town as long as you clean up after them. They are even welcomed in special areas including the outdoor dining areas, some of the gift shops, the outdoor market, and even in the greenhouses and coffee bar tents. I climb up into the Tumbleweed and call Patch and Rex, then clip their leashes to their collars. I tie several recyclable biodegradable pet waste bags to the cotton leashes.

"Fic and Gan, I hope you enjoy your card game. You can also get the Star Trek Monopoly out of the cabinet if you get bored with the Yes, Yes Yeti Risk-Taking Card Game! I'll be back. Come on Rex and Patch, let's go find Sam."

Chapter 21

Theme song: "Even in Exile" by Crowder from the album The Exile

I can't wait to see Sam. She travels with her Red Heelers, CJ and Rocky. They inhabit an old pink-painted Airstream Bambi that she tows with her vintage wood-paneled station wagon. This makes it easier to spot her in a crowded campground. I smile and wave as I pass people at their campsites. I find my friend after only about ten minutes of walking through the parking lot camping area. As I get closer, I start running when I see Sam sitting outside in a camp chair under a wide floppy hat. We have been friends since childhood and we try to go camping together a few times a year, especially at the coffee festival.

Sam is a sweet and compassionate person. She's also very creative and a talented artist. Best of all, she is a loyal friend and fun to spend time with. She has a steadfast and optimistic outlook on life and she never complains about any problems; she just fixes them instead of complaining. That's a very handy skill; she's a real overcomer. I want to be more like Sam. I'm blessed to have her in my life and I never take that for granted. She is my chosen family. Sam loves baking and decorating Yule log cakes and not just at Christmas time, but all year long. *Sam is always so joyful that she reminds me of a jolly Christmas elf.*

Sam has Mediterranean blue eyes. She has a groovy short layered shag hairstyle, which I love. She always wears long dangle earrings that she designs and makes herself. She is usually dressed in one of her own creations and she is almost never without her trademark pink flip flops. Today, her outfit is a pink peasant blouse embroidered with red hearts paired with bell-bottom jeans.

I wave enthusiastically as I jog up to her. "Hey girl! How are you? It's great to see you." We hug and smile joyfully at one another, feeling like reunited sisters after a long absence. "Sam, I have an important breaking news story to share with you. Can we sit inside and talk for a while?"

"Sedona you look different. You have a new and unsettled aura around you. Is everything all right? Come inside please. It's fabulous to finally see you again. How are you really? Do we need a healing energy intervention?" Sam leans down to pet Rex and Patch and they smile up at her. "It's good to see you boys. You're both looking very fit. CJ and Rocky will be thrilled to see you guys."

She holds the door open and I climb up the steps into the Bambi with Patch and Rex following close on my heels. Rocky and CJ greet us happily and I step inside to make room for Sam to enter the small confines of her adorable Bambi. We settle on the sofa while the four Australian Cattle Dogs sniff each other and wag their tails enthusiastically. Their tails thump the cabinetry with a rhythmic tattoo as they continue to circle and sniff one another. I look around the cozy space and I spy strings of butterfly-shaped LED mini lights hanging all around the trailer. They are taped up to the walls and some are wrapped around light fixtures and others are entwined in the handles of the cabinetry. They blink on and off casting a festive glow around the cool and shady interior. There are also handmade fabric flowers in every shade imaginable adorning every available surface. The overall effect is quite charming and it feels like I've stepped into an enchanting fairy garden.

Sam is also a prolific watercolor artist. There are sheets of paper featuring stunning landscapes and figures dressed in chic clothing designs taped to every available inch of wall space, including all the cabinets, refrigerator, and microwave oven door.

"Aw, hey Rocky. I'm so happy to see you again." I smile at the handsome dog as I run my fingers gently through his soft strawberry blonde and white speckled fur.

We sip iced water with lemon slices and Rocky lies down across Sam's feet. CJ stays with Rex and Patch and they all try to pile into a single pet bed, ignoring the other bed for some reason. It's comical watching them spin in circles and scrape at the bed with their claws and then try to lie down together in the same bed. Patch loses his balance and steps out of the bed in defeat. Rex finally gives up trying to claim a space and settles for the floor at my feet. CJ is beaming with pride as he triumphantly lies in the comfort of his own dog bed.

"Well Sedona, what's your news?"

"Brace yourself, it's heartbreaking. I caught Lew and Louanne in a stealth love affair. Unfortunately, I caught them in the act, literally. I was incredibly furious and I quit my job and left town right away. I finally left Lew and his crappy attitude and his bad behavior behind me. I'm done." The finality of the words breaks my heart all over again and tears slide down my face.

"Oh, Sedona. I'm so sorry for your pain and heartbreak. I'm so sad for you, you deserve better treatment from your husband. How could Lew dare to treat you so badly? I'm shocked that Lew would break your marriage vows. What is wrong with that man? He should have respected you and appreciated you. He should have cherished every moment that he spent with you. Wait a minute! Isn't Louanne your cousin?"

Sam leans in and gives me a fierce hug. She understands my emotional pain and heartbreak very well. She and her husband Whim separated last year. They were college sweethearts and they were happily married. Until Whim up and left her, because of a dream he had on Christmas morning. He left their home so early, that he didn't even eat a slice of Sam's delicious homemade Yule log cake or even stop to open any of his gifts. He ran out of their house while it was still dark, wearing only his SpongeBob SquarePants slippers and sailor-themed pajamas.

Whim left Sam to pursue his childhood dream of sailing around the world solo using his third-grade science project. It was a homemade bamboo raft held together with chewing gum, Silly Putty, and Silly String. The only means of propulsion that he installed on his science project was a hand stitched, open weave, light weight burlap cloth sail. The frail sail was secured to the raft's bamboo mast with more chewing gum and Silly String. *I wonder how that solo sailing trip worked out for him? It's no surprise that Sam hasn't heard from him since he left her. Bless his silly, whimsical heart!*

Afterward, Sam left their home when the lease expired and moved into her Bambi full time to pursue her theatrical clothing design and seamstress dreams. I'm happy to see that Sam is thriving on her own and it gives me a feeling of hope and encouragement to know that I can do the same thing.

"You're right, Sam. Louanne Pooey is my cousin on my mom's side of the family. She's the daughter of my mom's older sister. I've learned a devastating and very painful lesson that Lew is not the person that I thought he was. He's no longer the kind man that I married. Lew is unwilling or is unable to maintain a healthy relationship and his behavior is shocking. I'm sad and disappointed that Louanne would participate in this disaster. I hold them both equally accountable for their sinful behavior. I'm working through the process of forgiving them. I want to forgive them but it's going to take some time."

"Sedona why would Lew and Louanne behave this way? I just don't understand it."

"Me either Sam. Unfortunately, I think their sinful behavior fits the pattern of toxic people. In my experience, Lew only recently adopted this bad behavior. In the case of Louanne, this type of unhealthy behavior has been going on for several decades."

"Sedona, I had no idea. How sad. It sounds like you tried to have a healthy relationship with both Lew and Louanne. Perhaps they don't deserve to be in your life if they are purposefully causing you harm. Especially if you have given them years of second chances and they do not treat you better. Do you think that they deserve forgiveness?"

"You're right Sam. Maybe I love them too much for my own good. I sincerely believe in unconditional love and unconditional forgiveness and I try to practice them every day, but I also believe in self-preservation too. It's past time for me to make changes. For my own well-being, I'm avoiding close contact with Lew and Louanne. It's sad because I still love them even after what they put me through. The only thing that I'm really qualified to do is to pray constantly for their healing and for them to change. I won't stop praying for them. I'm still in shock that Lew and Louanne are having an affair. It never occurred to me that Lew would ever break our marriage vows. He knows that marriage is a sacred covenant between God of Heaven and a wife and her husband. It's a very serious promise and commitment. Breaking vows that are promised in the name of God of Heaven truly have serious and eternal consequences when we break them." I sigh with disappointment at how my life has turned out.

Sam nods her head. "I truly understand how sad it is to love someone who can't get their life together. I will start praying for both of them as well. Unfortunately, marriages frequently fall apart for various reasons and then our vows are irrevocably broken. It makes me sad."

"Me too, Sam. I'm trying to move forward with my life and I will try to stop focusing on Lew and Louanne, because it's too painful and unhealthy. Even so, I have to tell you the complete truth of what really happened. Full disclosure, I'm guilty of bad behavior as well. You won't believe this mess girl, but I totally lost my Christian dignity when I caught them in the act. In a fierce rage, I hurled rotten diner trash at them. They were covered in smelly, rotting goo, and burned kitchen waste and it was disgusting. I bet they stank for a week no matter how much they showered afterward. I'm so ashamed of myself and my bad behavior. In that moment of hurt and anger, I failed to love my neighbors and to forgive their sins and I did not behave as Jesus would want me to behave. I'm sure God is disappointed in me. After the trashing of the trashy couple, I had a terrible panic attack. The whole town saw me have an emotional break down at the diner. The townies were eating their meals and watching my performance with intense fascination as if it were dinner theater. The gossipy townies witnessed the very public demise of my marriage. It was humiliating. I immediately quit my job and ran away. I'm so mortified at my bad behavior. I'm willing to change and I will work on being a better person." I sniffle and try to hold back my tears.

"Sedona, we all lose our tempers sometimes. Just don't be too hard on yourself. It sounds like it was a pretty awful and stressful situation. Sometimes you just can't hold it together. I know that is not the person you are normally, it's very out of character for you, so maybe you're allowed one huge freak out. Just don't repeat the performance, leave it in the past. Don't dwell on it any longer, just let it go and try to focus on moving forward with your life. I believe this situation calls for a slice of Yule log cake. I baked one last night just for us, since we're camping here at the coffee festival. It's a coffee flavored cake with whipped cream filling and espresso frosting. I added a topping of chocolate covered roasted coffee beans. I decorated it with tiny fondant coffee mugs and just for you, I added cinnamon sticks arranged into crosses, since I hope the flavor is heavenly. I also added whipped cream frosting piped along the edges. Coffee and cream are the theme. It's very cute and coffee festival appropriate. I think you'll like it." Sam hops up off the sofa and steps into the kitchen area to fetch our slices of cake from her tiny refrigerator.

"Thank you, Sam. A slice of your wonderful Yule log cake makes everything better. On a much happier note, I have more exciting news to share with you. It's major news. Truly top-secret news. Promise me that you will not tell anyone what I'm about to tell you. This is life changing on a whole other level and you'll be thrilled, I promise." I dry my wet eyes on my long sleeves and take a sip of water.

Rex and Patch watch me closely as they lie on the floor nearby. It's a bit crowded in Sam's small trailer, with four dogs and two people, but it's the first time that I've felt at home in a very long time. I inhale a deep, cleansing breath and I begin to feel relaxed and peaceful.

In a few minutes, Sam comes back with two slices of cake for us. She hands me a fork and a napkin and I balance the plate on my lap. The Yule log cake is beautiful and it smells just like a delicious cup of good coffee. The cake appears traditional in its form and it's shaped perfectly like a log or a branch, except that Sam always makes hers in unexpected flavors. My slice of cake is elliptical and has spirals of cream filling. I notice that Sam used food coloring for the tiny sculpted fondant coffee mugs. Cute pink, blue, and green mugs are pressed into the espresso frosting along with the cinnamon crosses. Delicious chocolate covered coffee beans are pressed into every available bit of left over space in the frosting. I smile with genuine joy at her baking skills. In between tasty forkfuls of coffee cake I share my otherworldly news with Sam.

"Okay Sam, try to stay calm while I explain what happened to me. A few days ago, I was boondocking out in the desert for dark skies and stargazing with my telescope. Topaz, the boys, and I were out very late and we were completely alone in the remote desert not too far from the Extraterrestrial Highway. I had a very disturbing and weird experience. I saw a UFO!"

"No way! Sedona, are you kidding me? You're teasing me, right? Why are you inventing science fiction, woman? Are you planning on becoming a novelist?" Sam laughs with genuine amusement and shakes her head at me in disbelief. She takes a huge bite of Yule log cake and smiles with satisfaction at the sweet results of her baking.

"Sam, I actually saw it two different nights, in two different places. The second night it flew in and landed next to me. It was terrifying. Topaz, the boys, and I ran several miles all the way back to the Tumbleweed. I left my stargazing equipment out in the desert, that's how scared I was. Then, next thing I know, there are two alien creatures inside my camper. The creatures just materialized out of thin air, suddenly standing there."

"Mercy me! I don't want to doubt you Sedona. I know you're an honest and reasonable person, but this kind of thing seems implausible. Did you drink too many lattes? Maybe you had too much caffeine and you thought you experienced something out of the ordinary? What if there was some kind of toxic mold festering in the coffee beans that caused you to have hallucinations, could that explain what happened to you?"

Sam's Mediterranean blue eyes are huge in her small pixie face as she wrangles with my unexpected news. I giggle at her valiant attempts to use logic and to try to rationalize what happened to me. I know she is kind and that she means well. She won't be able to believe it until she sees it for herself.

"Sam, it really happened. It's true. They are here with me and seeing is believing. You can meet them for yourself. They're my new roommates in the Tumbleweed and I brought them here to the coffee festival to meet you. They are very gentle and friendly. I promise they're harmless."

I continue eating my Yule log cake and watch Sam for any signs that she finally believes my outlandish tale. Sam's face blanches at my words. It takes her a few moments to gather her thoughts and finally she recovers her voice.

"You're not kidding me. Goodness gracious. I thought maybe you were playing an elaborate prank just for fun. Now I see that you are entirely serious. Whoa." Sam tilts her head and squints at me.

"Their names are Fic and Gan. They're brothers from planet WatSoG and they are banished from their home and so they traveled here."

Suddenly, Sam squeals with excitement and all four dogs jump up from their naps, startled awake by the high-pitched sounds she is making.

"They were banished because they quit their jobs in the cafeteria where they worked. They told me coffee is not served there and they used the suggestion box in the cafeteria to ask the management to start serving coffee. Apparently, that was a serious problem for the cafeteria management, because WatSoG does not grow or import any coffee. When the management denied their request, both brothers quit their jobs. Apparently, it is forbidden and they are the first WatSoGians to ever quit their jobs. I feel sorry for them because they didn't really do anything wrong. Poor things just wanted to drink coffee."

"Aw, I feel sorry for them too. Are they sad being away from home and family?"

"It's possible, they do talk about their family fondly, so they seem to have strong bonds with them. I noticed they want to eat all the time. I wonder if that could be a response to feeling homesick or sad? They are extremely tiny beings but it seems to me that they eat as much as an elephant. I can hardly keep up with the demands of feeding them. They are also serious coffee drinkers. They can't get enough coffee. I wouldn't want to be around them if they were denied access to coffee. So naturally, I brought them here to the coffee festival."

"Sedona, what else do you know about them? Tell me more please."

"Well, they told me that it was their grandparents that introduced them to coffee. Apparently, their grandparents were members of two WatSoGian expeditions to Earth. Like other tourists, they visited a few famous places and then tried lots of local cuisine and drinks. So, their grandparents really loved coffee and smuggled some back home and shared it with Fic and Gan. Imagine that, aliens and coffee! Fic and Gan said that's why they traveled to Earth after their banishment. They simply can't get coffee anywhere else." I finish my outlandish tale, breathless with nervous energy. *Maybe there's too much caffeine in my slice of coffee and cream themed Yule log cake? Nah, that's simply not possible.*

"What a story. Aliens and coffee, indeed. Do you think other WatSockerians will come here to Earth to try our coffee? What if we get overrun with intergalactic tourists who want to drink up all our coffee? What will we do?" Sam's Mediterranean blue eyes sparkle with mischievous delight at the possibility of more alien tourists arriving on Earth.

"It's WatSoGian not WatSockerian, Sam. Pronounce it like WatSawgIan. Got it?"

By now, Sam is frantically jumping up and down on her sofa with excitement at my news. She is a major sci-fi fan, after all. I'm relieved at her positive reaction. She has no idea how much I need her help. I'm glad the news about my new roommates is way more interesting to Sam than the disaster of my love life. I want my disastrous marriage left in the rear-view mirror and I'm focused on moving forward. I really need her support to safely manage the outlawed alien brothers.

"Sedona. Introduce me to your roommates. Can we go see them now? Please! I'm so excited to meet them!"

"Of course. We desperately need your help, Sam. We need to disguise Fic and Gan as humans. Nobody else can know they are here. Do you understand what's at stake? If anyone else sees them, Fic and Gan will be in danger. Sadly, if they are ever discovered by the authorities, they would become laboratory specimens and their lives would be over. This is serious, Sam. There will be no alien autopsies. Not on my watch. Their very lives depend on us." I give her a stern look.

"Okay, Sedona. I completely understand. Of course, I will help you. Anything you need. Have you told them about your mom's mysterious disappearance yet? Maybe they can help you find her."

"As a matter of fact, they are aware of alien abductions occurring in many galaxies. They agree with me that my mom was likely abducted by lawless, uncivilized aliens. They are going to help me. First, they will send a message home to WatSoG to alert a committee called the WatSoGian Intergalactic Peace and Citizen Safety Council. We'll wait and see what they recommend we do next. It has been a big adjustment since leaving Lew and then suddenly acquiring alien roommates. But you're right, I think they will help me search for my mom. You know I still believe she is alive. The only logical explanation for her disappearance is that she is a victim of alien abduction. It's the only thing that makes sense, since she went missing while out hunting for evidence of UFOs right after a mass sighting occurred. She knew how to stay safe while researching and gathering evidence for MUFON. My mom was well trained and more than capable of handling herself in the wilderness."

We hug each other again to offer comfort during this trying time. I'm so grateful to God for my dear friend Sam. *Everyone needs a brave and loyal friend like Sam.*

"We need to get back to the Tumbleweed. I've already left my roommates alone too long. I'm worried they might cause trouble if I leave them alone any longer. I think it's going to take time for them to get better adjusted to living here among humans. We need to train them and to properly socialize them." I sigh and grab Sam's hand. "Let's go."

Sam hops off the sofa and takes our plates and utensils to the kitchen. She quickly washes and dries them and returns them to the cabinet. "Okay, I'm ready."

Chapter 22

Theme song: "Live with Abandon" by Newsboys from the album Restart Deluxe Edition

We climb up the steps into the Tumbleweed, close the door, and remove the dogs' leashes. They immediately scamper to the water bowl for a refreshing drink. Displayed on my walls, I see a Christian dating website. Photographs of women and their profiles are glowing on my living room wall. Fic and Gan are serenely floating above the cushions of my sofa, bobbing gently in the air. It appears that they are using their enormous eyes to project the dating website onto my wall. How on earth is this possible? While I do have satellite dish internet service and a laptop computer in my RV, I didn't share my network password with my new roommates. This clearly has otherworldly origins. *I wonder how many other amazing things they can do, and I hope I don't find out.* I glare at Fic and Gan with disbelief at their shenanigans.

"Turn it off, please."

In apology, they send a cool banana-scented breeze to me as they float back down to the sofa cushions. The twin beams of light emanating from their eyeballs extinguish and the dating website blinks out of existence.

Sam looks around and audibly sniffs the air. "Sedona? Do you smell ripe bananas?" Sam, feeling suddenly shy, stands behind me when I approach the aliens.

"Fic and Gan, this is my friend, Sam Dori Image. She will help us. Sam, meet Fic and Gan."

"Hello, Fic and Gan. Welcome to meet you, um, welcome. It's nice to meet you." Sam fidgets with her dangle earrings as she smiles shyly and giggles.

Fic and Gan float up into the air with excitement and suddenly the room fills with the delicious aroma of chocolate covered strawberries and fragrant blooming roses. *Oh my, it's love at first sight.* I smile as Sam slowly approaches the levitating brothers. Meanwhile, all four dogs pile into the pet beds and settle down for a short nap, happy to be together.

Fic and Gan, still levitating, and appearing completely mesmerized, stare into Sam's eyes. *If they were cartoon characters, they would all have red hearts circling around their heads. Well, this is awkward.* The three of them silently stare at each other unwilling to break eye contact for several long minutes.

I clear my throat to break the spell. "Okay, snap out of it, folks. We need a plan if we're going to pull off the transformation of Fic and Gan in time for the coffee seminars."

"You're right, Sedona. We need to get started immediately." Sam finally breaks eye contact with the enchanted, levitating brothers and quickly starts planning. "I will need my costumes and sewing supplies from my trailer. My roller suitcases have dress patterns, fabric, thread, scissors, sewing needles, and left over costumes from my work with the theater companies. Also, we need my best sewing machine, no make that two sewing machines, I'm putting you to work, Sedona. Plus, we need my cosmetics case and my cases with wigs and hats." Sam taps her foot while pondering her plan of action.

Sam places her index finger on her chin and tilts her head to one side while she muses. "Oh, and my jewelry case too. That reminds me, Sedona I made you a new pair of earrings. Fic and Gan, please stay here with our dogs." Sam smiles at them. "Sedona and I will run back to my Bambi and fetch my supplies. Ready?"

I smile and nod affirmatively at her excellent plan. I admire her quick thinking and her organizational skills. "Gentlemen, no more internet surfing please. Don't forget you must stay inside. There are plenty of snacks on the dining table. Why don't you play another card game while we're out?"

"Sedona, they won't eat our dogs or harm them, right?" Sam loudly whispers as we climb down the stairs.

"No, don't worry Sam. Our dogs are perfectly safe. Fic and Gan are very gentle. I serve them meals, plus lots of coffee and snacks. I've watched them share tidbits of their meals with my dogs. They like them, don't worry. Everyone will be fine while we are gone."

Together we jog back to Sam's Bambi. By now, several neighbors are taking an interest in our coming and going. A few people watch us go by and they smile and wave at us. A young guy whistles as we pass his RV. We ignore the whistler, but we wave hello and smile at several kids riding their bikes and say hello to other kids walking their dogs.

We step into Sam's Bambi, laughing and happy to be together. We're excited about our new adventure. We begin to gather all the supplies that we need in order to transform Fic and Gan into human beings.

First, we locate her bubblegum-pink roller case that is filled with supplies including thimbles, measuring tapes, scissors, sewing needles, dress patterns, sketch pads, and colored pencils. Next, we pull out from under Sam's bed the seashell-pink case that is packed with fabric, thread, and accessories like rhinestones, sequins, beads, and lace. We wrestle from the closet two sewing machines stored in their flamingo-pink roller cases.

Finally, we gather the blush pink and magenta cases filled with jewelry and cosmetics. Sam finds her baby pink bedazzled purse and sunglasses. We take a moment to gulp a drink of water. Afterward, we ferry the various cases outside and then lock her trailer door. We stroll back to the Tumbleweed, chatting together while pulling the large assortment of wheeled cases.

Chapter 23

Theme song: "Getting Started (Radio Version)" by Jeremy Camp from the album When you Speak Deluxe Edition

A few minutes later we are back in the Tumbleweed, and our dogs greet us enthusiastically as we step inside, dragging the roller cases with us. I help Sam arrange the small roller cases on my sofa and we open them and get organized for the night's work. Sam takes Fic and Gan's measurements. She mumbles quietly while she's taking the measurements. As she jots down the numbers on her sketch pad, I sneak a peek at my roommate's measurements. I laugh aloud.

"Oh, my goodness. Height 39 1/2 inches, inseam 18 inches, waist 10 inches, hips 13 inches, neck 7 1/2 inches, chest 10 inches, arm length 17 inches, and head 6 inches. This won't be too hard to pull off in one night. Right, Sam? What do you think?"

"It's entirely possible. These outfits will be so small that we should be able to make several of them pretty quickly. It's more like making clothes for life-size dolls than for people. Together we can get it done in time for tomorrow's classes."

I refill the dogs' water bowl and feed them, setting out extra bowls of food for CJ and Rocky. I step outside to check on Topaz and bring her several carrots. There are a few kids standing near her corral watching her curiously. I spend a few minutes chatting with them. I let them know that it's okay to pet her gently on the neck, but that it's not safe to climb the corral fence or to go inside it.

I step back inside and Sam is sketching outfits for Fic and Gan using colored pencils. She works efficiently due to many years of practice. She draws a dapper pin striped navy suit jacket with a matching vest. A light blue dress shirt paired with wide leg navy trousers and a wide silver tie. She also sketches a dressy golfing style outfit with a long-sleeved pink shirt and a sweater vest in green and yellow plaid, paired with tan trousers and white golf shoes. Next, Sam draws a classy pair of black slacks and a yellow button-down shirt with a skinny green tie. The slacks are paired with silver dress shoes. Her sketches are beautiful.

"Sam, I think you're forgetting that Fic and Gan have three legs and three feet. How are you going to conceal that fact from the public?"

She laughs good-naturedly. "Aw, I wasn't thinking very clearly. You're right. I'm so used to working for humans that I didn't think about their unusual anatomy, other than their tiny measurements, of course. Okay, let's explore other options."

Sam starts creating a new plan and while pondering, she rhythmically taps her chin lightly with her pencil. "Designing outfits to hide three legs and three feet, it's a first for me. Let me rethink my entire plan. To start, we know cosmetics and wigs will be necessary. Hats will be a good option. We will use tinted eyeglasses to hide their flashlight eyes. Also, Fic and Gan are unusually tiny and so much shorter than most human women, hmm. So, what to do? I've got it! We're going to turn them into adorable little old ladies in lovely long dresses. Grannies! It's our best option."

I'm so surprised and delighted with Sam's creativity, that I laugh aloud with joy. Fic and Gan stare at us with bewilderment. "What a brilliant plan, Sam. It's truly inspired and I think it will work wonderfully. You're a genius. Thank you so much."

Fic and Gan, still looking confused, speak up. "Explain the meaning of grannies. What is adorable little old ladies? What is grannies?"

"Fic and Gan, on the Christian dating website you probably noticed the difference between men and women. When men and women partner up together in holy matrimony, they often produce offspring, called children. Children are young humans who develop and grow up over many years into men and women. Old men and adorable, little old ladies are men and women with many years of living completed. This time in a person's life is actually an advantage because humans gain experience and a lot of wisdom as they mature and grow older."

"You can use the internet to look up information about the human life cycle for further clarity if you need to. Please avoid all online shopping websites, dating websites, and anything immoral, illegal, and unsavory. We have a respectable reputation to uphold. Well, it's probably best if I supervise your time on the internet to keep you out of trouble."

Sam continues working during our chat. She removes the sketches of the men's suits and golfing outfit from her sketch pad and tapes them to the wall. She begins new sketches of outfits that will conceal the alien anatomy of my roommates. After she is satisfied with her work, she reveals her new designs. Her new sketches consist of a collection of modest maxi dresses in various prints and fabrics styled with high necklines. The accessories include belts, long formal gloves in many colors, plus various styles of feminine hats with colorful hat bands.

There are also sketches of different wigs in numerous hair styles, scarves, and eyeglasses. For eyeglass keepers, they have long, thin strings decorated with colorful beads. To complete the fancy granny ensembles, she also illustrates various styles of hand bags and diminutive walking canes.

"Fic and Gan, will you wear these outfits if I make them for you? These long dresses are perfect for concealing your additional legs and feet. The opera gloves will hide the unique gold and purple skin on your hands and arms. The various scarves, wigs, hats, and tinted eyeglasses will also help you to blend in and look human. You'll have to wear heavy cosmetics on your faces and necks to disguise your beautiful Rosa Bianca eggplant skin tone. I haven't figured out how to disguise your feet and lethal-looking toenails." Sam shudders with involuntary disgust at their hideous feet. "I'll search in my suitcases to see if there are any men's shoes left over from previous theater performances."

"Sam, it will be as you wish. We will cooperate. This is very acceptable to us! We approve this! We require to consume much Earth coffee at the festival!" Fic and Gan stare at Sam while speaking at the same time. They reveal their gruesome smile. Sam looks shocked for a moment and then laughs nervously.

"Sam, that's their version of a smile. I think." She hands me a lovely pair of handmade sterling silver and turquoise earrings. "Oh, wow these are beautiful. You're a talented jewelry designer. Thank you so much, Sam. I love them." I give her a quick hug of gratitude for her kindness.

Sam always travels with at least two sewing machines in case one of them needs repair. She travels year-round, throughout the country to work for various theater companies in need of her expertise. Her skills are in high demand and it has turned into very steady work for her. She keeps all of her supplies in the Bambi so that she is always ready to design and create or repurpose costumes at a moment's notice. Sam gives me helpful instructions before we begin working on the tiny dress designs. She is an expert and I'm happy to improve my sewing under her guidance.

We spend the rest of the day and much of the night working on the diminutive outfits for Fic and Gan. I help Sam measure and cut fabric using the dress patterns that she created for us. The humming, whirring, and clattering of the sewing machines becomes the musical soundtrack for our evening together.

"I'm glad that Fic and Gan are so tiny. We don't need a lot of fabric to create their outfits and I can easily repurpose fabric from old costumes from my work. This is going to be a successful project, if we put in enough effort."

"Sam, I appreciate your costume design expertise and your sewing skills. Sewing is not something that I'm great at. Thank you so much for your generosity and your willingness to help us. Fic and Gan will be able to finally mingle among the general public with their new disguises. There's no way I could do this without you. I'm grateful for your help."

"You're welcome. I'm happy to help and I'm more than thrilled that you trust me enough to invite me into your adventure. This is truly a once in a lifetime opportunity."

After a few hours of work, we take a break for dinner. We enjoy a brief rest while dining. We start with mocktails made with sparkling water, cranberry, and lime juice with a sprig of mint. For our entree, we enjoy hard shell tacos filled with spicy shredded chicken, black beans, and topped with shredded cheese, chopped jalapenos, sliced avocados, diced tomatoes, onions, and sprinkled with fresh chopped cilantro, parsley, oregano, and lime juice. For dessert, we treat ourselves to a slice of Sam's incredible coffee and cream themed Yule log cake. I think it's the first time that Fic and Gan have tasted such an amazing dessert and naturally it's a big hit with the voracious aliens. By bedtime, we have finished four adorable granny disguises.

Chapter 24

Theme song: "Better Days Coming" by MercyMe from the album Always Only Jesus

For breakfast, I serve my guests western omelets with a side of fresh fruit and cinnamon dolce lattes. After enjoying our meals, we search through Sam's suitcases for the accessories that best compliment the granny disguises. By 11 a.m., Fic and Gan are transformed into adorable old ladies. Sam and I share a high five as we take a good look at our new grannies.

"Mercy me, they really do look like very tiny grannies. I'm amazed that we managed to pull this together in just one night." I say to Sam as I stare in disbelief at my new grannies.

"They really do look like human grannies. I don't think anyone will figure out their true identities. I'm so relieved that there were a few extremely tall men playing parts in the last production that I worked for. Otherwise, I don't know how I would have found shoes large enough for their long skinny feet. Size fourteen narrow is hard to find on short notice and who would think that we would need shoes that big for beings that are only 39 1/2 inches tall. I'm relieved it worked out so well. Now, the challenging part is to teach them how to act like grandmothers. Let's think about our own grandmothers' behavior and try to use them as a guideline for training Fic and Gan." Sam advises.

"Oh, good idea. We definitely need to teach them the art of the grandmotherly lifestyle." I can't take my eyes away from the incredible transformation of the WatSoGian brothers.

Granny Fic appears genteel in a navy with white polka dots maxi dress. His tiny waist is cinched with a wide white belt. He is wearing Yates Oxfords fancy men's dress shoes in saddle tan. The rather enormous shoes effectively disguise his scary alien feet and knife-like toenails. Sam cleverly placed riser platforms inside both brothers' borrowed shoes, raising their extra feet up off the ground. This trick solves the problem of their extra legs and feet being visible. Now they are safely hidden inside the skirts, thus concealing their otherworldly origins.

To disguise his glittery purple neck, Granny Fic wears a wide white scarf. His Rosa Bianca eggplant head is adorned with a silver shoulder-length wig, charmingly curled at the ends. A jaunty straw hat is perched on his wig. It is accented with a navy and polka dots hat band and a pink fabric flower. He wears dark blue eyeglasses perched on his long pointy nose. The glasses have oversize plastic frames with tinted lenses to help conceal his glowing eyes. They have a fancy eyeglass keeper chain attached to them and it is decorated with pink and white beads.

His hands and long claws are disguised with opera length velvet gloves in navy and he wears a collection of pink and white bangle bracelets on each arm. Granny Fic carries a white wicker hand bag with pink scarves entwined around both wooden handles. In his other hand, he grips a tiny white wicker cane.

Sam has artfully applied a heavy layer of cosmetics to conceal his unique and beautiful Rosa Bianca eggplant skin tone. Fic is completely transformed from a three-legged, knife toed, glittery purple and gold alien creature into an adorable, tiny old lady. I grin when I notice his pretty coral lipstick. Sam snaps a photograph for her portfolio.

Gan looks refined in his clever grandmother disguise. He wears a lemon-yellow maxi dress. The fabric print is festooned with large orange and pink flowers with green leaves entwined with trailing vines. His wide basketweave belt is tan. He is wearing enormous Bordeaux wine colored Yates Oxfords fancy men's dress shoes in size fourteen narrow.

Granny Gan also wears a wide pink scarf around his neck to hide his alien skin tone. His gray wig is shoulder length and is artfully cascading with a series of light waves. He wears a wide brim straw hat with a yellow hat band encircled with orange and pink fabric flowers. His oversize tinted eyeglasses have thick pink frames with a dangling eyeglass keeper decorated with tiny green, orange, and pink beads.

To effectively disguise his glittery gold hands and long claws, Granny Gan wears opera length green velvet gloves. He wears a collection of pink and orange bangle bracelets on each arm. He carries a yellow wicker hand bag with green scarves entwined along both wooden handles and a tiny tan wicker cane. Sam has also applied heavy cosmetics to all of Gan's exposed skin and as a result, he looks quite human. Granny Gan smiles a bright pink lipstick and pointy green-fang grin as Sam snaps another photograph for her portfolio.

Before heading to the coffee festival, we give the brothers a crash course in proper ladylike manners. We spend a lot of time explaining the art of the genteel grandmotherly lifestyle. The alien brothers also practice walking in their new shoes. They learn to properly sit in a dress. We teach them to sit with their knees and ankles pressed tightly together and how to use the classy Duchess Slant to preserve their modesty and to demonstrate that they are high-class grannies. We also review correct and polite human behavior. We explain the concept of waiting in line patiently. We teach them about purchasing items in stores and restaurants. As a precaution, we advise them to stay close to us at all times while we are in public. Most importantly, we ask them to never smile an open-mouthed grin.

Sam and I look at each other and cross our fingers. It feels like we are mature matrons who are launching young debutantes into polite society. *What could possibly go wrong?* At this point, I feel quite nervous about my roommates' public debut. I hope Sam and I can successfully pull this off and keep their true identities a secret.

I nervously dispense last minute advice to my roommates. "Please remember to keep your legs covered by your long dresses. Don't forget that three legs and feet are not human traits. Also, no levitating, don't show your fangs, and no projecting the internet from your eyeballs. Oh yeah, please don't touch anyone or talk with anyone. You would definitely scare people. Do you understand?"

I smile at Fic and Gan. "We will have fun, I promise. Just stay very close to Sam and I. Please try to act like us and only do what we do. The good news is that you can drink as much free coffee as you want. You will get to try every type of coffee drink from around the world. It will be worth the effort of blending in with humans. There will also be coffee made from different coffee bean varieties, so you can experience the wide variations in flavor. Plus, there are lots of gift shops to visit. Oh, this is very important, Sam and I will call you Granny. Remember, you are now Granny Fic and Granny Gan. It will allow other humans to accept your disguises and it will also make us a family. We want you to blend in with the community and to behave like ordinary humans."

Granny Fic and Gan agree to be on their best human-ish behavior. Sam and I take a few minutes to get ready. I wear my new turquoise earrings. I pair them with a turquoise maxi dress with embroidered sunflowers. I slide into my black cowgirl boots also embroidered with pretty sunflowers. I wear my pink cap with the baby blue embroidered cross. I drape a wide, white and blue prayer shawl around my shoulders and tie the ends in front.

Sam changes her outfit in the bathroom while I'm getting dressed in my bedroom. She changes into one of her own creations. It's a flowy white maxi dress with a high neckline and it's beautifully decorated with a profusion of deep pink and purplish blue mophead hydrangea blooms. All of the flowers and leaves are sequined and they sparkle bright pink, purple-blue, and green in the sunshine once we're outdoors. Naturally, Sam still wears her trademark pink flip flops. She accessorizes with a purple floral pattern scarf and a straw cowgirl hat with a cheery pink hat band.

"You look great. I love your outfit." Sam and I compliment each other at the same time. We laugh and collect the leashes and pet waste clean-up bags for our dogs.

"Alright, let's go for a walk around the festival. We're going to have a great time today." I grin as I take in the sight of Granny Fic and Gan in their adorable granny disguises. "Hold on one moment, please. I need to take a photograph of everyone dressed in their Sunday best." I use my smartphone to snap a quick photo of Sam standing with our dogs beside our new diminutive grannies. I quickly post the photo to my IG account, making our new family Instagram official. I make sure to tag Sam in my post.

Chapter 25

Theme song: "On our Way" by MercyMe featuring Sam Wesley from the album inhale (exhale)

One by one we climb carefully down the steps and exit the Tumbleweed. It's so comforting to be with Sam, especially now that we are introducing Granny Fic and Gan to the general public for the first time. I'm hoping she and I can safely manage them and keep their behaviors under control and prevent them from accidentally revealing their true identities.

I can't help but marvel at the odd turn my life has taken recently and it's still hard to believe that so much has changed in such a short time. *Even in my wildest dreams, I never imagined that I would leave my husband, meet two outlawed alien brothers, who then become my grannies and my roommates in the Tumbleweed, and then reunite with Sam all in just a few weeks.* My life has gotten so weird lately, but I have to admit it's also filled with adventure and that's always intriguing.

Together we walk very slowly and cautiously through town. We're traveling at a snail's pace to allow Granny Fic and Gan to get accustomed to walking in long dresses and enormous shoes. They toddle slowly along while clutching their hand bags in one hand and using their walking canes for support in the other one.

Our dogs are happy with the slower pace and they stop and sniff the ground along the path. As we're ambling along, we smile and say hello to several people. The gravel trails in town are filling quickly with large crowds of festival visitors. I sincerely hope we are blending in. So far, it appears that no one has noticed anything unusual about our freakishly tiny grannies. I slowly begin to relax and enjoy the day.

Our first stop this morning is the festival information booth to say hello to Miss Information. She is stationed inside an enormous blue coffee mug. It has a wide counter along the front side. Miss Information leans out of the large opening with her forearms resting on the counter, where she manages stacks of flyers, brochures, maps, and of course the ubiquitous newsletter: *The Fragrant Bean Coffee Scoop.*

"Well, hello there Sedona and friends. I was hoping that you would stop by my coffee mug. How are you enjoying the festival so far?"

"Hi, Miss Information. We're happy to be here and it's delightful to see you again. I brought my family to meet you. This is Sam, she's a costume designer for several theater companies and a baker of the most delicious Yule log cakes, and not just at Christmas time but all year long. Here you go, we brought you a slice of Sam's coffee and cream themed cake to try. I hope you like it. These are my two grannies, Granny Fic and Granny Gan." I smile with delight at the sight of Miss Information thriving in her natural habitat among the leaflets and print newsletters.

"Hello, Miss Information. It's nice to meet you." Sam steps forward and shakes hands with Miss Information and takes the proffered map from her hand. "Oh, thank you. This festival map will come in handy."

"You're welcome, Sam. I designed and printed it myself. Thank you for sharing your coffee and cream themed Yule log cake. It's perfectly appropriate for the coffee festival. How thoughtful of you and it looks very tasty. It's a pleasure to meet all of you as well. Sedona, your grannies are fashionistas. Hello Granny Fic and Gan. Ladies you are very stylish."

"They're so stylish thanks to Sam's creative talent. She designs and makes all of their outfits. Isn't that great? Miss Information, we're on our way to the coffee bar tents. Would you like us to bring back a coffee for you?"

"Thank you, but I have a nice cup of peppermint tea on the counter behind me. Don't tell anyone else, but the baristas always make a pot of tea and bring it over here for me. Isn't that sweet? We've all worked here together for a number of years and so they kindly remember me over here all alone inside my coffee mug." Miss Information winks conspiratorially at us and waves fondly as we depart.

After our stop at the information coffee mug, we visit one of the coffee bar tents. We all take a deep breath inhaling the tantalizing coffee aroma swirling through the crowded space. My ears perk up at the familiar hissing and grinding sounds coming from the steamy coffee machines. We patiently wait in the long line leading up to the coffee bar. When we finally reach the bar, each one of us chooses a different coffee drink. Granny Fic gets a foamy Italian cappuccino sprinkled with cocoa powder. Sam orders a Swedish drink called kaffeost. Granny Gan tries a Norwegian egg coffee. I decide to be absolutely adventurous, by skipping my usual caffé mocha and instead I try my first Italian bicerin.

I place a ten-dollar bill inside the tip jar for our barista and then I retrieve four complimentary dog treats from one of the jars arranged along the counter. We walk around and search for an available table in the crowded tent. Luckily, we find one near the entrance/exit tent flap and we happily settle into our chairs to enjoy our fancy coffee drinks.

"We are very pleased with new flavors of Earth coffee drinks. This is very acceptable to us! We approve this!" Fic and Gan say at the same time.

Sam and I are suddenly engulfed in a sweet-scented breeze sent by our happy grannies. We both inhale deeply. We're so lucky to have access to free aroma therapy.

Sam smiles widely and identifies the scented breeze. "Mm, delicious. This is my favorite scent from my childhood, fresh baked chocolate chip cookies and hot cocoa with marshmallows."

Sam and I hand out the dog treats. I smile at the loud crunching sounds coming from under the table.

"What an enjoyable way to spend our vacation. There are lots of different coffee drinks to try and we have two weeks to indulge our coffee habit. Don't forget, we need to walk over to the greenhouses soon." I comment.

A few minutes later we exit the tent and slowly follow the crowds toward the center of town and over to the greenhouses surrounding the public square. It's a pleasant morning for a leisurely stroll. The day is beginning to heat up. I feel a hot breeze caressing my face and lifting my long hair off my back. We stop to water the dogs at one of the pet fountains placed along the walking trail. After the dogs drink their fill, we continue strolling along the walkway. Abruptly, Granny Gan trips on his long yellow dress and falls down onto the gravel path. Granny Fic is so startled that he suddenly levitates several feet off the ground. He is gently bobbing up and down, floating above the crowd looking exactly like a child's character balloon.

Chapter 26

Theme song: "Good God Almighty" by Crowder from the album Milk & Honey

In what feels like slow motion, I watch the hem of Gan's long dress slide down his legs toward his granny underpants as he lands flat on his back. Like an upside-down beetle, all three of his purple legs are sticking up and waving frantically in the air. His dress shoes gleam brightly in the sunlight. His third foot is bare and his knife-like claws gleam menacingly in the light. His straw hat falls off and his wig is tilting precariously, hanging halfway off his glittery purple head. *Calamity!*

There are several large groups of people walking along with us to the greenhouses. The crowd of festival visitors stops suddenly and are now curiously watching the commotion my otherworldly grannies are causing on the gravel walkway.

I hear a little girl shout. "Mommy, look! Why is that little old lady suddenly much taller than Daddy? Look over there, at that one, Mommy! That other old lady fell down on the gravel. She has purple legs! Why does she have three legs, Mommy?"

Oh no she didn't! Granny Gan has been publicly outed by a kindergartner! More curious people come over to get a closer look at what is happening. A sizable crowd is gathering around us now. Heads are turning our way to watch the antics of our intergalactic grannies. Quickly, Sam jumps up and grabs Fic by the shoes and pulls him back down to earth.

"Please keep your feet on the walkway."

I'm already on the ground with Granny Gan, helping him sit up and then Sam and Fic immediately close ranks around Gan, shielding him from the curious crowd. Sam and I quickly help him regain his feet. We work together to restore his outfit and to smooth down the hem of his dress. Sam straightens his wig and replaces his hat. I hand him his cane and hand bag, which went flying during his fall.

"Oh, Granny Gan. Are you alright? Did you get hurt?" I inquire sympathetically.

"Dearest Granny Gan, are you okay?" Sam asks and gently rubs his back reassuringly.

"I remain intact and all systems are go. My modesty has been tarnished but no permanent damage has been sustained. Keep calm and carry on, ladies." Granny Gan wisely advises us.

The man and woman with the children step closer and kindly ask if we need help. Their little girl is curiously watching every move we make.

"Thank you, but Granny Gan is unharmed. Thank goodness it was only a minor fall and she is feeling better already. We appreciate your concern for our granny. Thank you everyone, but please don't be late to your next activity on account of us. Thank you and please enjoy your day at the festival." I respond pleasantly and smile reassuringly at all of the curious people gathered around us in a large crowd. I hope my words will get the crowd moving again, as we stand quietly at the center of the crowd and wait to see if there will be a public outcry and further trouble over our grannies' otherworldly origins.

The father of the little girl who publicly outed Granny Gan smiles benevolently at us. Then he leans in close to us and wisely remarks. "All beings are welcome along the Extraterrestrial Highway." He nods his head sagely and then winks conspiratorially at Sam and I.

His partner is standing close to their children with both arms wrapped protectively around them. She gives us a wobbly smile and watches us warily. She appears very afraid of what she has just witnessed. Looking flustered, she quickly takes the children's hands in a firm clasp, unwilling to let go of them. We hear their persistent little girl protesting vehemently as they begin to walk away.

"Mommy! Daddy! That old lady had purple legs! I saw it! I saw that she has three legs! What kind of granny is that?"

"Shush now. Don't say another word, ever again, about what you think you saw here. Forget it and never speak about it. Never mind, my darling. Everything is fine. Nothing happened. You saw nothing. Let's keep walking over to the museum. You will enjoy the museum, it's very fun." The couple finally walks away with their children.

The curious crowd gathered around us slowly disperses as they lose interest. People begin walking away and resuming their conversations. No one else comes over to confront us. *Good heavens. That was a very close call. That could have become a very serious problem.*

"Alrighty, that was an experience that I hope we don't repeat. Let's try to avoid attracting any more attention. I think everything is fine now, thank goodness. Granny Gan, are you feeling well enough to continue walking?" Sam asks while giving Gan a close visual inspection to reassure herself that his granny disguise is properly restored.

We all lean in to make sure he's truly unharmed. The brothers send us a gentle breeze infused with the soothing scent of lavender flowers in bloom. I sniff appreciatively.

"Affirmative. All systems are go." Granny Gan replies with a toothy grin.

"Very funny, Granny Gan. I'm truly glad that you're alright." I respond with an amused smile. "Just be more careful from now on. Your secret was nearly revealed and we're lucky that everyone was willing to let it go."

Chapter 27

Theme song: "Love Broke Thru" by TobyMac from the album This is not a Test

Outside greenhouse number one, we wait politely in line with a large crowd of people for our first seminar to begin. Our leashed dogs sit patiently at our feet. Eventually, the long line of people (plus two aliens and four dogs) moves slowly inside. Curious attendees wander in small groups around the greenhouse to get a closer look at the different varieties of coffee shrubs.

It is surprisingly sticky and humid inside the greenhouse. The air feels like a heavy wet blanket clinging to me. It's a weird sensation, but the dampness feels soothing after our long walk in the dry desert air. I take a deep breath and inhale the earthy aroma of plants and soil. I see countless water droplets covering the inside of the glass walls and ceiling. The damp heavy air pulses with a calming soft green-tinged light. It feels like I've entered another world. The greenhouse is very large and it's filled with potted coffee shrubs of various sizes. Overhead is a network of irrigation pipes dotted with moisture and a series of sprinkler heads. Every now and then I hear water dripping off the pipes and landing with soft splatters on the sandy floor, which quickly absorbs the moisture.

Our facilitator, Missi from Mississippi, is nearly, almost-a-professor of botany. She wears purple eyeglasses. She is dressed in a purple top decorated with an artsy flowering coffee shrub. Over her purple top, she wears an unbuttoned white long-sleeved shirt. Her black skinny jeans are paired with a white belt decorated with metal conchos. Missi manages to look both intellectual and fun. She also wears a headset with a microphone so she can be heard throughout the large greenhouse.

Her left hand showcases a very beautiful diamond bridal set in white gold. Her rings are so sparkly, that I can see their radiant brilliance from where I stand in the back of the crowd. She wears white Doc Martens ankle boots with chunky lug soles. They are adorned with roasted coffee beans and tied with purple laces. *Greenhouse chic fashion style, I love it. I need to ask her where she shops. Her boots are so unusual. It looks like she has glued real roasted coffee beans all over them as a unique decoration.*

"Welcome coffee lovers. I'm Missi from Mississippi. I'm almost-a-botanist, and my special area of study is *Coffea*. This is my ninth-year teaching at the festival here in Fragrant Bean. Thanks for attending my seminar. I'm nearly a professor at the unknown, underfunded, and sadly unaccredited University of Delightful and Delicious Coffee in Washington state, as is my wonderful husband, Murphy. We facilitate the botany program together. Murphy has a lecture later this afternoon in greenhouse four that still has some openings, so please feel free to drop in if you're interested. Please feel free to email me later with any questions. My email address is printed on the class hand-outs. I'm excited to announce I have arranged a special treat for you today. As you know, the Fragrant Bean Coffee Festival is all about coffee education and sampling delicious international coffee drinks. I invite you to step up to the coffee bar and order a complimentary coffee from my friend Corree. Corree is an amazing barista and we're very lucky that she is here with us today. She has many years of experience crafting international coffee drink recipes. Corree is an award-winning barista and she is a world-renowned expert in the barista arts. She has lived all around the world and during her extensive travels, she has spent years training with some of the top baristas. If you don't know what type of drink you want to try, be adventurous and ask her for a recommendation. While you're waiting in line for Corree to craft your coffee orders, our fantastic baker KittyKelly will circulate around the greenhouse and hand out complimentary pastries, still warm from the ovens. KittyKelly is also a close friend of mine and she has generously donated her time to bake for you. Today, we have Italian prosciutto e pecorino Romano formaggio cornetto, cornetto con cioccolato, and beautiful Scottish scones. We have plain scones and also scones with blueberries and raspberries. Please enjoy yourselves."

The crowd buzzes loudly with enthusiastic conversation at Missi's unexpected announcement of free gourmet food and coffee. There's a rush to be first as everyone hurries over to the coffee bar at once. Since we have our little grannies and our dogs with us, Sam and I hang back. We wait patiently for the crowd to organize a line and settle down before taking our places at the back of the long line. Granny Fic and Gan are thrilled to get another chance to drink more coffee and to try all of the different pastries.

Chapter 28

Theme song: "This I Know" by Crowder from the album *Neon Steeple Deluxe Edition*

"We only have two hours in the greenhouse today, so I'll try to move through the information quickly, while demonstrating at the same time. Full disclosure here, I read information on the internet to help me prepare for today's seminar. My online sources are the website of the National Coffee Association of U.S.A., Inc. plus several informative Wikipedia articles about coffee beans, coffee plants, and coffee drinks. In my class hand-outs: I attest and I certify that every word you read is from my own authentic creative process, that I dredged up from my own memory, and that I created it from my own biological brain, and that I physically typed every single word with my own hands. I'm a practitioner of authentic human-powered creativity and genuine human-powered creative writing. However, I give credit to general knowledge contained within books and widely distributed on the internet. I also give credit to, and I thank the National Coffee Association of U.S.A., Inc. and also Wikipedia for teaching me what I needed to learn. They are a wonderful source of information that is generously made available to the general public. I enjoyed reading all of the information and I'm happy to share it with you in this lecture."

Missi pauses her monologue to enjoy a fruit scone and an Italian caffé latte. Unfortunately, she spills coffee on her white work shirt and it leaves a large brown stain on the front. I can't take my eyes off the giant brown blemish on her shirt. *Look away, Sedona! Look away.*

Missi bravely continues speaking while wiping crumbs from her hands. "As you probably already know, because it's widely common knowledge, Ethiopia is the birth place of coffee. Today however, it is grown around the world. The beverage coffee has a long history of being a favorite among many different cultures and nations around the world. The shrubs that produce it are properly called *Coffea*, but coffee is the common term that we all use. There are a wide variety of plants that grow coffee cherries, whose seeds, called coffee beans, give our lives a delightful, delicious, and healthy boost."

Missi smiles indulgently at her enchanted listeners. How clever, she really knows how to captivate her audience. Just feed us scrumptious fresh pastries and delicious coffee while feeding us information at the same time. She's brilliant. It's no wonder that her lectures are always well attended. The happy crowd nods and blinks contentedly at Missi while munching on pastries and serenely sipping coffee. Everyone pays close attention as Missi begins her demonstration.

She brings out several potted shrubs in various sizes and stages of growth and places them on the table in front of her. One of the potted plants has huge dark green leaves and is covered in numerous fragrant white flowers. Another plant is covered in plump green and red coffee fruits. Missi explains that the coffee fruits contain the seeds that once dried, are removed from the dried fruit and are then roasted. Once they are roasted, they are called coffee beans. There are also several bags of roasted coffee beans on the table. The warm lush plants and aromatic coffee beans emit a pleasantly strong aroma. Together they smell delicious and the scent wafts through the greenhouse.

"Botanists and coffee growers have worked diligently and have experimented in the development of hybrid plants. Research is still ongoing in the field of hybrid coffee plants. As a result of years of hard work, coffee experts believe coffee flavor has improved. Further research will ensure the continued production of coffee on a global scale."

Missi steps over to the coffee bar again and orders an Italian caffé lungo from Corree. KittyKelly promptly appears at her side and hands her an oven-warmed cornetto con cioccolato. Missi takes a few minutes to enjoy her snack, then she absently wipes her hands on her white work shirt. Now the huge dried coffee stain on her shirt is festively decorated with streaks of melted chocolate. I studiously avert my reflexive stare and I cover my mouth to hide my unintentional giggles. I'm thoroughly enjoying this lecture. After finishing my delicious fruit scone, I surreptitiously wipe berry juice from my hands onto my forearms and rub the juice in like moisturizer. *Why doesn't KittyKelly hand out napkins with the pastries?*

"Currently the most common type of hybrid is *Coffea arabica*. Ongoing research into developing hybrids may change this at some point in the future. Previously cited sources believe that *arabica* originally began in Yemen. It was discovered at some point by clever researchers that *Coffea arabica* was written about in ancient historical documents dating to the twelfth century. According to what I read on the internet, apparently it was developed from two plants, *Coffea canephora* and *Coffea eugenoides*. Today, *arabica* is widely available and is currently a top seller for coffee growers. *Arabica* is cited by the expert sources that I previously mentioned, as currently being the most consumed coffee around the world and making up the largest portion of the global coffee produced at this time. Valid concerns about the long-term effects of climate change and *arabica's* susceptibility to leaf rust has led to an effort by researchers all over the world to continue studying and developing new hybrid varieties of coffee. Having much needed genetic diversity in the world's coffee supply can only be a benefit to coffee drinkers. I'm curious to know how many of you festival visitors are gardeners?"

In response to Missi's question, a large portion of the crowd raises their hands, including me.

"How many of you gardeners have tried to grow coffee plants?"

A few people raise their hands along with me. Granny Fic and Granny Gan suddenly raise their hands too. Sam and I smile indulgently at our grannies, amused at their enthusiasm.

"How wonderful, keep on growing ladies and gentlemen. According to the articles that I read on the internet; coffee shrubs can sometimes also be grown successfully in manageable pots for individual use at home. The articles on the internet indicate that it is important to keep your coffee shrubs in a greenhouse or an indoor heated space like a sun room. While many coffee varieties grow at high altitudes, and are very hardy, they should always be protected from frost. For indoor growing without a greenhouse, you must remember to provide the necessary amount of light. You can really learn a lot of useful information from trustworthy and reputable internet websites. Thank you to all of the experts who contribute their knowledge to helpful internet articles. I learned a lot, and I found it very interesting to learn about coffee plants. I hope you did too."

Missi smiles as she saunters around the greenhouse handing out ripe coffee fruits for everyone to inspect. She continues teaching and delivers a fact-filled lecture about plant structures, growth rates, and soil requirements. She indicates with a long pointer the structures of the plants as she is speaking.

Afterward, Missi asks the class to line up and we are invited to the table in small groups to inspect the coffee shrubs up close. This gives everyone a chance to ask questions before the seminar is over. I notice that Granny Fic and Gan are paying close attention to the lecture. I hope they are learning enough to be able to grow their own coffee plants in their crochet needle. I'm relieved that the granny disguises are working.

"Take a hand-out from the table. Thanks everyone for attending my seminar. Please enjoy more coffee and pastries before you exit the greenhouse."

We follow the long line of people and step outside. After hours inside the moist air and the soothing green-tinged lighting, it's a bit of a shock to be out in the intense dry heat and bright sunlight again. It takes me several minutes to adjust to the drastic change.

Chapter 29

Theme song: "Big Tent Revival" by Zach Williams from the album A Hundred Highways

"I think we should head back to the Tumbleweed for lunch." I suggest to my friends. As I say the word lunch, I notice Rex and Patch flick their ears toward me and comically tilt their heads when they hear the familiar word.

Granny Fic and Gan frantically wave their arms at me and adamantly exclaim. "No, no, no! First, we need lots more coffee. We must try more types of Earth coffee drinks. Humans are creative with the coffee. This is very acceptable to us! We approve this! We require more paste to eat. It is good with the coffee drinks." Fic and Gan refuse to take no for an answer. We immediately walk back to the coffee bar tents.

"Grannies, it's pronounced paystree. You're right, pastries go great with coffee. We'll have to stop by a bakery in town to get more pastries. They only serve coffee in the big tents." I explain while trying to hold back amused laughter.

The coffee tasting tent is still very crowded and we wait in line patiently to order our drinks. Once we all have our complimentary coffees, we walk around in the hopes of finding a table. After a few minutes, we're lucky enough to stumble across a family that is just leaving and we thank them as we settle into the last available table. Our dogs lie down under the table in the soft sand and I hand them a dog treat.

"This is a great way to spend the afternoon. What a good idea, grannies. Coffee always revives me and my energy level will be restored too." Sam sighs contentedly as she relaxes back into her chair and sips her Spanish cortado coffee.

"Agreed. We love to drink lots of Earth coffee! It is pleasant to have Earth friends and to spend time at a coffee shop. This is very acceptable to us! We approve this!" Granny Fic and Gan reply at the same time.

Granny Fic is sipping a caffè Americano and Granny Gan is drinking a red eye coffee. I shake my head with amusement at my over-caffeinated friends, as I happily drink my decaf almond milk caffè mocha. I'm enjoying their company and I'm grateful we are growing closer like a family.

While relaxing at our table, I see Missi stroll inside and line up to get a coffee. Several minutes later, she is walking around the crowded tent with her coffee looking for a place to sit. Smiling enthusiastically, I stand up and energetically wave my arm to get her attention, then I beckon her over to our table. She nods at me, raises her coffee in acknowledgment, and with a big grin on her face she strides confidently over to our table.

"Hello again everyone. I recognize all of you from my lecture. Can I join you?"

"Have a seat, professor. I enjoyed your seminar today. I'm Sedona. This is Sam, and this is my Granny Gan and here is my Granny Fic." I say while gesturing to my friend and my intergalactic grannies seated around the table.

"Hello ladies. It's a pleasure to meet you all." Missi smiles kindly at them while settling comfortably in the empty chair.

Granny Fic and Gan incline their heads politely and smile closed-lip smiles at Missi in a genteel and ladylike manner. They continue to politely sip their coffees, with their pinkie fingers extended, all the while trying to keep their eyes lowered. Missi startles visibly as she notices their unusual star-lit and brightly glowing green eyes.

"Complications from cataract surgery." I say mildly to Missi.

She sardonically raises her eyebrows at me. We introduce Missi to our dogs as well. They've been standing politely and wagging their tails in the hopes that Missi brought more dog treats from the bar. They politely sniff her hands and then they lie down again under the table when there is no chance for more treats.

"Is this your first time visiting the coffee festival?" Missi inquires, then takes a sip of her Italian caffè al ginseng.

"I've been a regular for several years. This festival marks my fifth year coming to Fragrant Bean. Sedona and I like to meet up and camp here for the festival." Sam replies and takes a sip of her Spanish cortado coffee.

"We are parking lot dwellers every summer. All of the information I learned from your seminars really prepared me to start my own coffee plants several years ago. This is the first year they have produced fruits. I'm finally able to roast my own beans this year. Drinking coffee from my own home-grown beans is very rewarding." I smile at Missi and I hope that this is the start of a new friendship.

"Which variety of coffee are you growing?"

"I'm growing *Coffea canephora robusta.* Unfortunately, I have a very small home, my camper to be precise, and I have very limited space for my plants. Sadly, I'm separated from my husband and my lifestyle has become nomadic lately. So right now, I'm living in my RV with my two dogs, a miniature donkey, both of my grannies, and my coffee plants. The plants are living in my shower stall with grow lights hanging from the ceiling. Luckily, they are thriving in their unusual home. My life has definitely gotten a little weird lately."

"Oh, I see. Well, God bless you Sedona. You really are living an adventure. You're growing *Robusta* coffee; that's a solid choice. According to the internet articles I read, *Robusta* coffee is widely available, it can thrive in lower elevations, and it is well loved by coffee drinkers. Did you know that donkey manure is a good source of fertilizer, if you properly compost it first? Have you tried using your donkey's manure as fertilizer yet?" Missi seems very enthusiastic about manure, composting, and fertilizer.

"Mm, I leave the manure out in the desert where it won't cause offense to other people. While it's a good idea in theory, I've been traveling from town to town lately and not staying in one place for very long. There's just no way to carry a pile of compost in my camper and my livestock trailer is too small to accommodate composting, since I use it as a home for Topaz when she's not in her corral."

Missi smiles kindly and nods her head in understanding. "A lack of space does pose a stumbling block to proper composting, I suppose. Murphy and I are currently on sabbatical from university to work on research into new types of fertilizer and new hybrids of coffee plants. Murphy and I have a five-acre homestead in eastern Washington state. We have two greenhouses set up with automatic irrigation systems. Say, I have an idea Sedona. I'm currently looking for a volunteer to work with me and with your experience, you're a good candidate. If you would like to work in the greenhouses with me, you can live in your camper with your companion animals, and stay as long as you like. There is a gravel parking area that has utilities hook ups right next to my greenhouses and it has plenty of space for large vehicles. I really could use a volunteer at this time. Contributions from your donkey would be very helpful to my fertilizer research."

Chapter 30

Theme song: "Me on Your Mind" by Matthew West from the album My Story Your Glory

"Missi, you're an answer to my prayers. I would love to work with you. It's a great opportunity for me to learn more about growing coffee and I appreciate your offer. Would it be helpful to have several assistants? My grannies want to learn more about growing coffee and I've been teaching them what I know so far. After all, many hands make for lighter workloads."

Granny Fic and Granny Gan begin to rise up from their chairs and levitate in their excitement at the possibility of working in the coffee greenhouses with me. Sam and I gently reach over and place our hands on their arms to remind them not to levitate in front of other people. They sink back down onto their chairs.

Sam smiles and looks at Missi. "What about me? I would love to volunteer as well. Would you like several assistants? I also live in my camper. I have a small Airstream Bambi; it doesn't take up much space. I could easily park my station wagon and camper next to Sedona, if you're interested?"

"It's an almost-a-botanist's dream come true. I would love to have all of you helping me with my research project. It really is too big for me to tackle without assistants. The group of students that worked with me last year are now studying abroad. I'm worried about your grandmothers; they seem extraordinarily tiny and frail. Working in the greenhouses is very physical and hard labor. I'm confident you and Sedona can handle the work, but what about your grannies?"

"Oh, don't worry about my grannies. I promise you they are much stronger than they appear. In fact, they are freakishly capable for their tiny size and they are deceptively youthful. Looks can be very deceiving. They are full of youthful vigor and they're really very physically fit. They've been wishing for a chance to work with coffee plants and they are very determined to learn how to grow coffee. It won't be a problem, truly." I raise my eyebrows sardonically at Missi.

"Complications from cataract surgery?" Missi inquires mildly.

I grin broadly at Missi. "Something like that."

Sam laughs aloud at our weird conversation and our little grannies appear slightly perplexed as they continue to sip their coffees.

"Thank you, Missi. This is just what I needed. I was hoping for an opportunity to learn more about coffee growing and this gives me the chance to further develop useful skills that could lead to new career options. Well, that was a delicious caffè mocha. It's my favorite coffee drink, but sadly it's empty now. I hope everyone enjoyed their coffee too. I have an idea. Would you all like to spend some time together wandering around the festival and visiting the market and the vendor's tents to see what else the festival has to offer? We can stop by the bakery too. I promised my grannies I would get them more pastries."

"I'm in." Sam says.

"Me too. I'm done working for the day and I haven't had the chance to wander the festival yet." Missi replies.

After my friends finish their coffee, we all stand up, stretch, and head out of the tasting tent. We spend several companionable hours at the festival together, chatting and browsing the booths in the market and the vendor's tents full of coffee related products until the evening.

Granny Fic and Gan are particularly excited about the selection of pastries in the bakery. I let them choose a baker's dozen to take back to the Tumbleweed. We also browse the coffee machines. I purchase a multi-purpose coffee maker that is similar in function to the one I keep in my Tumbleweed. It's designed to make espresso as well as brewed coffee. I hope they will be able to re-engineer it to work inside their crochet needle, once they finally return to their spaceship.

Sam loves to collect t-shirts and she finds a bright pink one artistically designed with a pretty flowering *Coffea arabica* plant on the front of it. The text on her new t-shirt cleverly states: "Coffee helps you bloom with natural energy."

For myself, I buy a small spiral bound recipe book of popular coffee drinks. This will come in handy while teaching Fic and Gan how to make coffee. I'm looking forward to trying out new recipes with my grannies.

Chapter 31

Theme song: "Thrive" by Casting Crowns from the album Thrive

I invite everyone back to the Tumbleweed for dinner. Missi's tall bearded husband Murphy joins us after his lecture. He takes long purposeful strides to his wife and enthusiastically wraps her in a big bear hug lifting her feet off the ground. Missi laughs as she clings to her husband and then slides back down until her coffee bean Doc Martens are on the ground again, then she kisses him affectionately.

"Welcome Murphy. I'm Sedona. It's nice to meet you. We had the best time today with Missi. Her lecture was great and I learned a lot of useful information that will help me with my own coffee plants."

"We also had coffee together. It's the first time I've encountered anyone who likes ginseng in their coffee. I really enjoyed Missi's lecture today as well. I'm Sam by the way. It's nice to meet you, Murphy."

"It's nice to meet you ladies as well. Missi's lectures are the best. She always spends extra time with anyone who has a genuine interest in botany. We're both happy to meet other coffee plant nerds. By the way Sam, do your friends call you Sam or should I use your full title? Kidding, I'm jesting. When you get the chance, try the caffé al ginseng, it's delicious. Thanks for the dinner invitation for Missi and I. We were planning on spending the evening in our room at the B&B, going over our research notes and doing some work on our papers. It's great to have a night out with my lovely wife and to meet her new friends." Murphy smiles playfully. He stands with his arms wrapped around Missi and leans his bearded chin on top of her head for a moment. She leans comfortably against him, secure in his embrace.

"Missi, do you want to meet my donkey Topaz before dinner?"

"Oh, absolutely. She looks very content in her little corral. I like the set up that you arranged for her. I declare you definitely do have your donkey domicile down to a decent design during your days drifting in the desert." Missi alliterates as she gently pulls away from her husband and walks toward Topaz's corral.

"Ha, nicely done. I enjoy alliteration too."

We all snicker with amusement at Missi's clever quip. We're standing together around the corral and Topaz comes over to say hello. She is thrilled to be the center of attention. Missi has many questions and while we discuss Topaz's diet, she enjoys feeding her carrots. Missi asks to inspect the hay and she collects a handful and pulls it apart to identify the various grasses it contains. I smile with amusement as she pulls out another handful of hay from Topaz's hay bag and places it inside small plastic baggies for further analysis. Topaz is watching every move we make and then she brays loudly demanding her dinner. We all laugh at the obnoxious sound of her squeaky bray. Then Missi helps me feed Topaz while I refill the water buckets.

For our meal, I prepare a large garden salad and my specialty, *panini con prosciutto e pomodori con formaggio*. For our mocktails, I prepare delicious prickly pear agua fresca. After dinner, I serve dessert coffees with crispy cannoli from the bakery in town. We happily settle into camp chairs outside under the stars to enjoy the brilliant light show displayed above our heads. We relax and chat about our day. Later, I bring out my acoustic guitar and begin strumming a variety of classic rock songs. I can hear Topaz in her corral nearby, singing along in her loud squeaky bray.

After a while, several groups of neighborly campers visit us bringing their camp chairs and our little circle of friends grows. Sam switches on my flameless candles set on a little table nearby, to add enough light so that nobody trips in the darkness. We end up laughing and singing together as the crowd of happy campers multiplies. Pretty soon, we have most of the town's parking lot dwellers visiting with us. Several people bring party snacks, baked goods, and cold drinks to share. This is one of my favorite parts of the RV lifestyle: Friendly neighbors love to stop by to swap travel stories, recipes, travel advice, and to simply share food and fellowship. *La dolce vita. Che bello.*

Chapter 32

Theme song: "Happy Dance" by MercyMe from the album Lifer

A few guitarists also stop by and join us. We end up playing and singing until very late. People start dancing and I watch as Granny Fic and Gan join them. I smile and nod my head to catch Sam's attention; I gesture with my head toward our grannies as I continue to rhythmically strum my guitar. Sam smiles and nods at me in understanding. She jumps up and moves over to the group of happy dancers. She joins in and begins dancing with and supervising our intergalactic grannies.

Pretty soon my grannies, still holding onto their canes, are happily dancing with a large group of smiling young ladies. Children are playing together and they start up a game of tag. Loud laughter and childish squeals of delight add a chorus of voices to our musical performance. I spy Murphy and Missi dancing together and I smile at the couple. At one point, my grannies start to float up off the ground and Sam gently takes their hands to help them stay grounded.

Gradually, sleepy campers disperse with their families back to their RVs and the parking lot quiets down for the night. Sam and I take a few moments to pick up trash and tidy up my campsite.

"Missi and Murphy, I'm so glad you joined us tonight. I hope you had a fun time. If you're too tired to drive back to your B&B, you're more than welcome to stay with my grannies and I in the Tumbleweed. There's a comfortable guest bed if you want to stay over."

"No need, it's a short drive to our B&B. Will I see you all tomorrow at my next seminar?" Missi inquires while taking her husband's hand. They lean into each other for a sweet kiss.

"I can't wait to see what you have in store for us in your lecture. I'm looking forward to it. Murphy, it was very nice to meet you. Good night you two." I wave to the sweet couple as they depart.

Granny Fic and Gan join me as I walk Sam back to her Airstream Bambi. Naturally, our leashed dogs accompany us. Topaz is snoozing in her corral with stalks of hay hanging out of her mouth, so I leave her to enjoy her rest. The starry sky above us illuminates our path through the camping parking lot and back to Sam's trailer. We say good night to Sam and my little family and I head back to the Tumbleweed for a long rest.

"Sedona, the gathering of the humans was pleasant. This is very acceptable to us! We approve this! We need more sustenance after our boogie-woogie dancing. We require more cannoli or paste to eat." Granny Fic and Gan say at the same time.

"Good, I'm glad you enjoyed dancing and socializing with all the campers. It was fun. You can have pastries or cannoli when we are back in the Tumbleweed. I might join you in a midnight snack, I love cannoli."

Sam comes over to my Tumbleweed early in the morning for breakfast. We chat in the kitchen, while I teach Fic and Gan to make a new coffee drink. I choose a Northern Italian recipe from my new recipe book to help my grannies learn the barista arts. We're making caffè marocchino. First, Granny Fic and Gan learn to pull shots of espresso. Then they learn how to steam milk. Next, they learn how to make hot cocoa using just cocoa powder and heated whole milk. I patiently help them attempt to layer each individual ingredient one level at a time in our mugs. Since it's our first try at creating this complicated drink recipe, we make a terrible mess of it.

My grannies especially enjoy adding the cocoa powder to the bottoms of the mugs before layering in the steamed milk, espresso, and then hot cocoa. As a finishing touch, I help them top the drinks with a little milk foam. Then my grannies sprinkle cocoa powder onto the surface of the foamy clouds floating in our mugs. By the time our drinks are ready, my kitchen counter is splashed with spilled espresso, milk, and cocoa powder is smeared all over.

Once our fancy drinks are ready, we get to work on our breakfast. My grannies and I dice vegetables and add them to the eggs in the frying pan, while Sam sets the table. She feeds the dogs and then joins us at the table. I say a blessing over our meal. We enjoy a hearty breakfast of eggs scrambled with diced jalapenos, bell peppers, onions, tomatoes, and pepper jack cheese. After breakfast, we make another round of caffé marocchinos for our travel mugs, then we clean up the kitchen. Afterward we all step outside with our dogs for a morning walk.

My grannies ask to walk Rex and Patch so I relinquish the leashes to them. Sam hands me CJ's leash and she walks with Rocky. We walk the dogs through the campground area for a short stroll, while enjoying our fancy caffé marocchinos. When we return to the Tumbleweed, I check on Topaz in her corral. She still has plenty of water and hay. I spend a few minutes grooming her and then I give her a carrot.

"See you later, Topaz." I say as I head back inside.

"Okay, Fic and Gan, check this out. I made these new outfits for you. I hope you like them." Sam smiles and shows us her latest creations.

"Granny Fic and Gan, I want to see how they fit you. I can make alterations if needed." Sam hands our grannies the new dresses.

"Sam, what adorable clothes. They still remind me of those life-size doll dresses. Except your designs are more mature in their styling and clearly the quality of your work is much finer. You are very talented. Our grannies will look enchanting in these lovely dresses."

Sam and I help Fic and Gan get changed. The new outfits are matching blue and white floral print maxi dresses. The brothers are already wearing their cosmetics to disguise their Rosa Bianca eggplant faces. They wear shoulder length blonde wigs with vintage 1940s victory rolls. They are carrying the same canes and hand bags from yesterday. Once again, the intergalactic brothers are transformed into tiny, sweet grannies.

"It's time to walk over to our coffee seminar. Granny Fic and Gan would you like to walk Patch and Rex again?"

"Affirmative. We will walk your canine companions. We require more Earth coffee. This is very acceptable to us!"

Chapter 33

Theme song: "All of Creation" by MercyMe from the album The Generous Mr. Lovewell

By 10 a.m., we are back inside the humid greenhouse for the coffee roasting seminar hosted by Missi and her friends Corree and KittyKelly. Like yesterday's lecture, there is a very large crowd of coffee lovers spread throughout the greenhouse and many people are strolling among the fragrant coffee plants.

Missi is dressed in a lemon-yellow peasant blouse embroidered with green, pink, and blue coffee mugs with little plumes of steam rising from them. She wears a long blue denim skirt embellished with embroidered flowering coffee shrubs. Her outfit is paired with her signature coffee bean Doc Martens tied with yellow laces today. She is carrying a clipboard with her notes and she is wearing her headset microphone. *Her greenhouse chic fashion really suits the coffee nerd lifestyle.*

She stands next to a long table set up at the front of the class. The table surface is crowded with several large boxes filled with small cloth pouches of dried coffee beans. The table is also laden with stacks of stapled hand-outs for the participants. A large commercial coffee bean roaster stands on the ground nearby. As I pass the table, I inhale deeply and savor the coffee bean aroma.

"Welcome everyone. It's nice to see so many of you here again for today's coffee roasting seminar. Please take a few minutes to visit Corree at the coffee bar for your complimentary coffee. We have a special experience for you today. My friend Sedona shared her Grandma Bruno's authentic Italian cream puffs recipe passed down in their family for generations. There are also fruit-filled and cheese-filled Danishes. For our savory option, KittyKelly made

Mediterranean puff pastries. They are topped with feta and pecorino cheeses, spring mix lettuces with baby spinach, sliced Rosa Bianca eggplants, grape tomatoes, olives, Tropea red onions, fresh herbs, and drizzled with olive oil. Please enjoy."

While everyone is lining up to get their gourmet food and coffee, Missi conducts a safety inspection of the exhaust ducts connected to the commercial coffee bean roaster. The ventilation system is crucial to vent potentially harmful emissions to the outdoors. Missi turns on the exhaust fans to circulate plenty of fresh air before starting the enormous roaster machine.

"If I can get everyone to listen up, I'll explain what we are doing today. Last night I read a bunch of information on the internet about the process of roasting coffee beans. I also read the coffee bean roaster instruction manual thoroughly. Please follow my instructions carefully so we can avoid accidental injury and death. Don't worry, I'm pretty sure it will be safe and we'll most likely be fine. Just don't touch anything and it should go well. I kind of guarantee it, almost! Remember, before you can participate in today's activity you must sign the release forms that are right over there on the table." Missi suddenly has the undivided attention of everyone in the greenhouse.

Sam and I exchange a worried glance with one another. "Sam, yesterday did Missi say that she is a professor, or that she is nearly, almost-a-professor? I really like her, but is she qualified to teach us?"

"I was wondering the same thing. I'm not sure about her credentials and now I'm feeling a bit concerned too. Let's just trust her. She's been hosting these seminars for nine years. I like her too. Let's have faith that everything will work out just fine."

During the seminar, the pastry nibbling, coffee klatsch crowd listens attentively to Missi's lecture. She gives detailed instructions about the coffee bean roaster. Missi invites attendees to join her at the potentially hazardous machinery to finally learn how to roast dried coffee beans. She asks the class to come up to the table in small groups of four people. Once the roasting process commences, the commercial coffee roaster shimmies and shakes alarmingly and rumbles loudly. It releases an overwhelming and cloying aromatic heat into the greenhouse for the next several hours. *I really hope the ventilation system is drawing out the exhaust fumes because it doesn't smell nice in here anymore and it's getting hard to breathe because of the strong fumes.* I share a look of concern with Sam.

When it's finally our turn to use the coffee bean roaster, Sam and I hold hands with our grannies as we assist them during the lesson. Granny Fic and Gan are giddy with excitement, or possibly due to the noxious fumes, and we don't want them levitating off the ground in front of the class. By the end of the demonstration, each person (and alien) is miraculously unharmed and has retained all of their original parts, still in working order.

"Every participant gets to keep the coffee beans they roasted. I hope that each of you leave here today with a layperson's understanding of the coffee bean roasting process. Let me remind you this is my last class until next year's festival. I encourage you to visit my website and sign up early to reserve your spot in next year's seminars hosted by myself, Corree, and KittyKelly. Please enjoy more pastries and coffee while they're still available."

At the conclusion of her lecture, Missi spends time answering questions. She asks for volunteers to distribute the class hand-outs. Granny Fic and Gan step forward. They stuff their pouches of roasted coffee beans into their hand bags, while shoving their canes and bags into our hands. Sam and I share a look of concern. Our grannies walk around the greenhouse giving the stapled sheets to each person, smiling the whole time. Their pointy green fangs startle a few people. Soon after, the crowd of coffee lovers are leaving the greenhouse satisfied with the day's seminar.

"Missi, are you driving over to the coffee bar tents in your truck, or would you like to walk with us?"

"Sedona, I'll walk with you. Murphy is picking up the truck when he finishes his lecture in greenhouse four. Now that my work is finished, I'm ready to hang out and enjoy the rest of the festival."

The coffee bar tent is crowded as usual and we wait patiently for our drinks. There are no available tables, so we take our coffees to go. Sam orders a French cafe au lait and I get a decaf iced caramel macchiato. Granny Fic orders an Italian espressino and Granny Gan an Italian caffé con latte. Missi chooses an American caffé breve. Once we all have our drinks in hand, we simultaneously grin at each other.

"Is anyone hungry yet? We could visit one of the diners for lunch. If not, how about we browse through the market?" Sam asks.

"I'm still pleasantly full from the Mediterranean puff pastries. They were delicious. How about you Missi? Did you get a chance to try KittyKelly's pastries today?"

"I wouldn't miss them. We ate together while we were waiting for the seminar to start. We always have to be there several hours before class to set up, and of course it takes quite some time for KittyKelly to bake those pastries. After we worked together getting the greenhouse ready, Corree joined us and we sat down for a nice meal. I won't be hungry again until dinner time. I would love to walk through the market."

I look over at Granny Fic and Gan surprised that they haven't spoken up in favor of going immediately to find more food. "Granny Fic and Gan what about you? Do you want to stop and get more food?"

"Sedona, peek inside our hand bags."

Sam and I open them and they are stuffed full with pastries. Cream puffs and fruit Danishes are crammed together causing the fillings to squish out and smear onto the fabric.

"Sedona, hand me a fruit Danish." Granny Fic says.

Granny Gan's flashlight eyes light up at the thought of snacks. "Sam, be a dear and pass me a cream puff."

Chapter 34

Theme song: "My Victory" by Crowder from the album *American Prodigal Deluxe Edition*

Back in the Tumbleweed, Sam, my grannies, and I settle onto the sofas and chairs sighing with relief in the cool air conditioning. Granny Fic and Gan access the internet, projecting it onto the wall through their glowing eyeballs. They look just like flashlights and I'm certain I'll never get used to it. They show us the website of the Fragrant Bean Museum of UFOs. We enjoy planning our visit and debating the merits of each exhibit. We study the descriptions and photos of the exhibits on the website and vote on which ones to see first.

"I vote for the exhibit about famous historical UFO investigations. To me, it's the most intriguing exhibit. It covers all the former investigations from the 1940s through the 1960s including Projects Grudge, Sign, and Blue Book. It includes information about eyewitness accounts of UFO sightings and close encounters. The museum recently installed an exciting new addition to the exhibit. They added an exhibit about the AATIP program and its related Unidentified Aerial Phenomena Task Force. It focuses on detailed reports that document eyewitness accounts of the most recent UAP sightings. I can't wait to see it."

"Sedona, we cast our votes to view the spaceflight exhibits!" Granny Fic and Gan reply. "First, we explore spaceflight. Later we will visit your paper records of visitations and sightings."

"Sorry, Sedona. I also vote to see spaceflight first."

"Okay, I yield. I know that I can't have a victory every time we take a vote on something."

The exhibits covering spaceflight of the 20th and 21st centuries are informative. They teach about spaceflight history in general. However, there is a particular focus on Project Apollo and specifically the 1969 *Apollo 11* moon landing mission. All of the various Space Shuttle program missions are also covered in detail.

Natural objects from space are included in the spaceflight section. There is a collection of moon dust, dirt, and rocks on display. The meteorite collection of the Southwest contains the best specimens found in the region. We spend a few more minutes reviewing the museum information before getting ready for tonight's dinner.

"Can I have your help, please?" I ask my friends. "I need to finish getting ready for tonight's campground dinner. Last night, I started both of my crock pots with fresh ingredients. Simmering in the crockpots are Anaheim, Poblano, and Jalapeno chili peppers. I used my favorite beans including pinto, black, and kidney beans. I added sea salt, ground black pepper, minced garlic, chopped yellow onions, beef bouillon, crushed tomatoes, tomato paste, and ground beef. It smells delicious already."

I jump up from the sofa and step into my kitchen area. I peer through the glass lids and admire my spicy chili. It's ready for a few additions. Everyone joins me in my small kitchen. All four dogs come to supervise us.

"We need to add a few more fresh ingredients to the crock pots. We still have a few hours until dinner. Granny Fic and Gan, will you please open the jars of sweet corn salsa and the cans of stewed chilies with tomatoes? Also, will you chop up these bell peppers and sweet onions for me? Don't forget to wash your claws before you use them to chop the vegetables. Go ahead and add all of those ingredients to the two crock pots when you're done. Sam, will you please slice the corn kernels off the cobs and add those as well? I will brew coffee for our guests and set up our picnic table outside."

With my arms full of supplies, I climb carefully down the steps. I set my supplies on the table and then I pour ice into the ice chests that are already full with cans of fruit juice. I spread out my tablecloth. I set out multicolored bowls and I place spoons on napkins. I set my iced tea dispenser jug on the table and add ice to my sun tea, which has been steeping all day.

I'm excited about tonight's campground dinner. It's a fun tradition at the festival, where each parking lot dweller sets up a meal on their picnic table. We all make the rounds visiting our neighbors, chatting, and tasting the various dishes.

I check on my solar lights and reposition some of them around my campsite. I want to have enough light especially around Topaz's corral so that no one trips and falls in the darkness later tonight. I also set my flameless candles onto a little pile of rocks to add a glowing ambience to our evening. I hang multicolored LED lights all along the Tumbleweed's awning to add a festive mood.

In the early evening, Missi and Murphy arrive. They're holding hands, strolling, and smiling sweetly at one another. They are so completely in love, that it makes me smile wistfully and I feel a little sadness at my lost love. Pretty soon, more campers arrive to taste our homemade meal.

I hand out steaming bowls of chili with beans. The chili is garnished with sliced green onions, chives, sour cream, and shredded cheddar cheese. Granny Fic and Gan pass around cold drinks from the ice chest. Missi and Sam hand out glasses of iced coffee and iced tea. Murphy arranges extra camp chairs for our guests, placing them in a wide circle around the glowing candles.

We enjoy chatting with our neighbors about our various RV trips across the United States as we enjoy our meals. We sit basking in the flickering glow of the chunky candles. Several campers brought their RV dogs along and there is a flurry of furry activity as the excited canines play and chase one another. Topaz watches curiously while chewing hay and swishing her tail. She has a good view of the activity in camp and brays loudly, welcoming every visitor.

Later, I fetch my acoustic guitar from its case and I begin softly strumming John Newton's famous song "Amazing Grace." Missi and Sam start singing along and soon more people lend their voices to the beautiful song. More guests join us for dinner and we continue serving hot meals, cold drinks, fellowship, and melodious guitar music.

Around 10 p.m., our neighbors thank us for the meals and wish us a good night. Slowly, our guests depart and walk back to their campers. Gradually, silence descends upon the parking lot campground. Sam and I clean our picnic table and carry glasses, bowls, and utensils into the Tumbleweed. Murphy collects trash and Missi offers to wash dishes. Granny Fic and Gan volunteer to dry them.

"What a fun evening." I say to my friends. "I enjoyed the companionship and the conversation. Thanks for helping with everything. I think our guests enjoyed themselves."

Missi, standing at the kitchen sink, looks over her shoulder at me. "The chili was good. Also, it's not very often Murphy and I get to enjoy live music."

Sam grins and nods in agreement. "People watching is good for my work. I got some inspiration for new designs." She helps Granny Fic and Gan dry the dishes and I put them away.

As I'm putting away utensils, my smartphone rings and I get it out of my purse. *Who on earth is calling me at this late hour?*

"Hello?"

"Sedona, don't hang up! It's Louanne, sugar. Listen, this afternoon there was a dreadful accident in Sandy Town!" Her voice sounds strange, kind of hollow, and I hear her sniffling loudly.

Chapter 35

Theme song: "Oh Death" by Mercy Me featuring Walker Hayes from the album Wonder & Awe

I nearly drop my phone as I cringe in dismay. *I can't believe that my husband-stealing, ex-boss, ex-cousin would dare to call me after the trauma she and Lew put me through!* A vivid flashback from the last time I saw Louanne floods my mind like a raging river. I clearly see Louanne wrapped passionately in my husband's arms. I get a faint whiff of the rotten diner trash that I used as ammunition against them. I feel my chest expand with rage as my eyes flood with tears. I crumple onto the sofa.

Through blurry eyes, I look down at my wedding ring perched on the wrong hand. The bright blue turquoise stone reminds me of the life that I left behind, and the selfish husband that I'm still legally married to. Things have been going so well here with my friends, that I was trying to put Lew and Louanne and their awful betrayal out of my mind.

I wonder why he had Louanne call me instead? Surely, he's smart enough to know that it will cause more trouble. I don't understand why Lew is doing this to me. I think it's Lew's responsibility to call first and apologize for his affair, since his adulterous actions are the cause of our separation. So far, it has been dead silence between us.

"What do you want, Louanne? You have thirty seconds before I hang up my phone." I utter through tightly clenched teeth.

"Sedona, the sheriff's department just called me. They asked me to call you. Lew had a freak accident in his work truck. He was hauling a load of full portable toilets back to Dung's Doody Thrones when his truck blew out a tire on the highway. He was driving at a high rate of speed and he lost control and his flatbed truck rolled over. He crashed down into Brown Spill Ravine. I'm sorry, but he's dead, sugar! There's no one else to call you. The sheriff is still out working at the scene. They said there's a pool of raw sewage inside the truck's cab and, he, uh. I'm sorry, honey. I'm sorry to say he couldn't escape the cab, and, and. Uh, he drowned in the pool of sewage." Louanne is sobbing uncontrollably and her words become unintelligible.

I hear deep despair in her grief. *What am I supposed to say to her? I don't trust my cousin. I can't believe it's true. I don't want to believe her.* Abruptly, I press end call, silencing my faithless cousin. I burst into gut wrenching sobs.

Granny Fic and Gan are startled at the sound of my loud crying. Sam gives them a warning look reminding them not to levitate in front of our guests. She turns to me and wraps her arms around me. Missi pats my back consolingly. Murphy pops his head in the door, checking in with Missi and she assures him that she is okay. He goes back to campsite cleaning duty.

"Lew is dead! That was my cousin Louanne." I wail. Hiccup! I'm starting to feel panicky and anxious, and now I'm having trouble catching my breath.

"Oh no. I'm so sorry Sedona. That's very sad news. I'm here for you, whatever you need, just say the word. Do you want to tell us what happened?" Sam offers compassionate sympathy while gently patting my back.

Missi hands me a cloth napkin from the kitchen and I dry my face. I share the shocking news with my friends in between sobs and hiccups. I explain to Missi why I'm separated from Lew and I reveal the grisly details of his untimely and tragic demise.

"After learning about Lew and Louanne, I needed some distance between us. I already had plans to come to the coffee festival and to be away from home for several weeks. Now, it makes me wonder if it was a coincidence or just a convenient time for Lew to reveal his adulterous affair right before my annual camping and coffee trip. Now, I'll never know for sure. I wanted to forgive him but I needed some time to process it and to pray over it. I wanted to forget that he is in love with my cousin. But I didn't want anything bad to happen to him. I, I thought he would call me. I was waiting for him to call me and to apologize to me. Now, I'll never get the chance to tell him that I choose to forgive him and that I'm sorry that I threw trash at him." I hiccup and sniffle. I try to slow my breathing back to normal. My teary eyes implore my friends to help me make sense of this terrible tragedy. *Lew didn't deserve this horrible accident. This can't be happening.*

"I'm so sorry Sedona. You've had a terrible shock. Here, you need a drink. Try this." Missi hands me a glass of iced coffee.

She hands a glass to Sam as well, and we all take a restorative sip of delicious coffee. Granny Fic and Gan toddle over to us and Missi gets them glasses of iced coffee as well. My dogs jump up from their beds to come over and investigate the proceedings. Patch lays his head on my leg and Rex licks the water condensation off the outside of my glass. Then they both lie at my feet. My chosen family surrounds me with support and I'm grateful for their presence.

"Thanks for being here. I don't know what to expect now. Do you think I need to go back to Sandy Town and plan Lew's funeral? I know Lew's lawyer, John. They are good buddies. We all went to high school together. Maybe he can help me?" I hiccup again and cover my mouth.

"Why don't you call John in the morning? As a lawyer and a friend of your husband's, I'm sure he will be happy to help you." Missi advises.

"That sounds like a good idea, Sedona." Sam agrees.

"Thank you, that's good advice. I'll call him in the morning. Will you stay here with me for a bit longer? Let's pray for Lew." I say while blinking the tears from my eyes. "That's all I can do at this moment; I trust in God's mercy and grace." Together we bow our heads and I pray aloud for Lew. "Heavenly Father, please welcome Lew into Heaven and please offer him your mercy and grace. I ask that you please bring Lew to your stream of forgiveness, and allow him to drink from the living waters, and please forgive him for his sins. I ask for this in the name of my Savior, Jesus Christ. Amen."

Chapter 36

Theme song: "You Changed my Name" by Matthew West from the album My Story Your Glory

In the morning, I place a call to Lew's lawyer. "Hello, it's Sedona Dung. John, is it true about Lew?"

"I'm afraid so. I'm sorry for your loss Ms. Dung."

"Thank you, John. My condolences to you as well, I know you were good friends. I need some advice, please. What should I do now? I'm in Fragrant Bean. Should I return to Sandy Town to begin making arrangements for Lew's funeral?" I speak softly, still having trouble accepting this unbelievable tragedy.

"Don't do that, Sedona. Stay where you are. I'm already working on the arrangements for Lew's funeral and burial. There's no need for you to return to Sandy Town. Listen, I am obligated to inform you of recent developments that have taken place since you departed town. This may be difficult for you to hear. I'm sorry if it comes as a further shock to you during this tragic time."

"What could be more shocking than Lew's tragic end?"

"Sedona, Lew and Louanne came to my office. Lew filed divorce papers the morning after you left town. The judge signed the divorce papers a few days before Lew's accident occurred. I'm sorry Sedona, but you're divorced. The laws in Sandy Town allow for a rapid divorce in a case of spousal abandonment, when there are no living children born of the marriage. The laws are very strict and crystal clear in cases where one of the spouses moves out of Sandy Town, without providing an official physical mailing address, where mail can be delivered to, and in particular, when that spouse does not return to Sandy Town within two consecutive weeks. You are judged as being culpable of unlawful abandonment of your spouse Lew, whom you left alone in Sandy Town."

"John, I don't understand this. I only went on vacation and I told Lew where I was going. I take a girls' trip every summer to the coffee festival. That's not abandonment!"

"It's entirely legal here in Sandy Town, Sedona. It is an antiquated law from the 19th century, but it is still legal. It was written into the Sandy Town legal codes at the founding of the town by Old Judge Sandy himself. As you already know, the town is named after him because he donated most of the land that the town occupies today. This act made him one of the most respected and powerful founders of the town. Being a judge cemented his complete control of the town. Rumor has it, that Old Judge Sandy was a bitter and angry man after he was abandoned by his wife Pious Purity. It happened back in 1886, when she moved back East due to his philandering lifestyle. As the sole lawyer and judge in town, and as one of the founders of the town, he wielded great power here. He wrote this law specifically as revenge against Pious Purity. These are laws from the era of the Wild West when the land and the people living here were wild and untamed. Sandy Town was just a dangerous nest of rattlesnakes at its founding, I'm afraid. Unfortunately, the legal codes here have never been updated or amended since the year that Old Judge Sandy wrote them, so it is a lawful divorce."

"Well John, I would love to know who explained this obscure and antiquated law to my husband. Hmm, John, do you wish to tell me? It's entirely out of character for Lew to go read the legal codes at the courthouse when he won't ever read a newspaper or even read the directions on his box of frosted blueberry Pop Tarts. Did you help my husband trick me and perpetrate this travesty of justice? After all, you have been very close friends since high school. Perhaps I should report this to the District Attorney who oversees our local area."

"Sedona, I only performed the duties that your husband hired me to perform as his legal counsel. My work is by the book, precisely following the laws of Sandy Town. Feel free to contact the District Attorney's office. As I said, it's an entirely legal divorce."

"Also, how is it possible for Lew to divorce me without my signature on the divorce papers? Why didn't he contact me by phone or email? Isn't my email technically a forwarding address since it's an electronic mailbox where I receive mail?"

"Sedona, an email is not a real mail box. Email didn't exist at the founding of this town. The Sandy Town laws require a physical mailing address because at its founding, mail was delivered by either train, stagecoach, or Pony Express. Today we have to use the United States Post Office system and emails are not acceptable as official notice. In Sandy Town, in the case of spousal abandonment your signature is not required on the divorce papers. Like I said, the judge already signed the divorce papers and filed them on record. It can't be undone."

"John, as the attorney on this case, shouldn't you have at least called me to notify me? Did my last name get changed in the divorce? I can't believe this is happening! What's my legal name now?" I'm completely shocked and utterly blindsided by this unforeseen turn of events.

"Sedona. Lew is my client, not you. I only represent his legal interests, so I don't have any obligation to call you or to track you down wherever you're wandering in the desert with your camper and your pets. How would Lew or I have mailed you a copy of the divorce paperwork without a forwarding address and when you live in a camper and you wander all over the desert living like a nomad?"

"John, I know I left home, but Lew knew that I was leaving for a vacation to the coffee festival with camping reservations in Fragrant Bean to visit with my friend. That's not abandonment! Going on vacation is not a crime! I only left a day or two early for my trip because I caught him sinning with Louanne! This entire situation is shady, it feels like an elaborate deception is being perpetrated against me. I'm the victim here! It's almost like Lew planned the whole thing, orchestrating events so that they coincided with my annual camping trip to Fragrant Bean! Did you knowingly help him commit this crime?" I shout loudly into my smartphone, enraged and feeling completely betrayed and defeated.

"Sedona, I acted responsibly as Lew's legal representative and everything was handled entirely in accordance with the laws here in Sandy Town. Lew acted within his legal rights. It's not a crime to file for divorce! Now, quit shouting in my ear! Calm down, Sedona. Look, I'm telling you all of this as a favor to you. The fact of the matter is that from a legal standpoint there is nothing that can be done. Whatever personal relations transpired between you, Lew, and Louanne is not my business. The divorce papers stipulated that your last name change from Dung back to your maiden name of Bruno. As a courtesy to you, I'll email you a copy of the signed divorce papers since you don't have a physical mailing address. You'll need them as proof of your legal name change. You should probably get your last name changed on your driver's license soon."

Chapter 37

Theme song: "Take it All" by Third Day from the album Revelation

"Listen up, Sedona. There's more you need to know. Lew had me complete several legal contracts for him in my office. As a favor to you, I will inform you that Lew sold the house and the fifty acres to a mining company the day that his divorce was final. In legal terms, after the divorce all marital property still remaining in Sandy Town was solely owned by Lew. However, anything that you took with you when you left town is now solely your legal property. Naturally, this would be your camper, your personal belongings onboard the camper, and your pets. Lew moved into Louanne's home the same day. He made Louanne co-owner of his bank accounts and he appointed her co-owner of his portable toilets business Dung's Doody Thrones. Lew also appointed her the co-owner of his physical business and personal property items and he made her the executrix of his will and his estate. In other words, every financial and physical item that Lew owned here in Sandy Town is now the lawful property of your cousin Louanne Pooey."

"Lew sold our home and land? To a mining company? This is criminal, I paid for half of our house and he made me homeless! How much money did he get?" I'm crying now, sobbing loudly into my smartphone.

"I can't divulge the legal specifics of the contracts to protect the privacy of the buyers and other parties with a vested interest in the property, but I am more than certain that Louanne is now a multimillionaire." John ruthlessly informs me without even a hint of compassion in his voice.

I press end call. I have nothing more to say to the vicious lawyer that helped Lew and Louanne orchestrate this travesty of justice. *Wild West era law codes indeed. Sandy Town is still a nest of deadly rattlesnakes today! I'm devastated at this turn of events; this is not how I expected my life to turn out. Stupid Old Judge Sandy, with his unethical Wild West era laws, he sounds more like an outlaw than a judge to me. I'm glad poor old Pious Purity got away from him. I hope she lived a very happy life back East. Lew, what have you done to us?* Louanne Pooey can stew in her ill-gotten riches. I truly feel a little sorry for her because no amount of worldly wealth can fix such atrocious character flaws. The only good thing that comes from this situation, is that at least I'm legally me again. I'm back to my original, independent self with my original name. I'm glad to officially be a Bruno again. I never liked the idea of giving up my own family name just to marry the person I love.

Chapter 38

Theme song: "Help is on the Way (Maybe Midnight)" by TobyMac from the album Life After Death

Thirty minutes later, Sam and Missi knock on my door with CJ and Rocky and a huge box of warm doughnuts fresh from Desert Doughnuts Delightful Dough-Nuttery Desserts. I usher them inside with a waterfall of tears sliding down my face.

My compassionate friends wrap me in a consoling hug and hand me a cloth napkin to dry my tears. After I get control of my emotions, I make chocolate chip lattes for us. My version is just a caffé latte made with my special homegrown coffee and topped generously with whipped cream and overflowing with chocolate chips. We all squish companionably into the dining booth. Sitting elbow to elbow with four dogs lying at our feet, we carefully sip our steaming hot lattes. *I love lattes, not lousy Lew.* I silently repeat this consoling advice to myself.

"Good morning, ladies. Thank you so much for coming over. Ooh, it has been a tough morning. I'm so glad that you stopped in at the Dough-Nuttery. It feels like nothing will make me feel better, but a Dough-Nuttery doughnut will certainly make a dent in my sadness."

"How was your phone conversation with John this morning? I can see by your sad and teary face that you're very distressed. I'm sorry." Missi says.

Sam nods her head in agreement, and smiling kindly, she opens the huge box of doughnuts and offers me a dry napkin and a triple chocolate doughnut topped with double fudge frosting sprinkled with copious amounts of crushed hazelnuts. *Ah, I truly enjoy a good chocolaty nutty doughnut with my latte.*

"Thank you. I think it's safe to say that I've had better mornings and more enjoyable conversations than the one I just had with John. Bless his legalistic heart."

I hand two doughnuts and napkins to Granny Fic and Gan. They smile with their pointy green fangs dripping with saliva in anticipation of the sweet treat. Their *Star Trek* coffee mugs are filled to the brim with lattes that have turned into a violent cataclysm overflowing with a volcano of whipped cream pouring down the sides of the mugs. Chocolate chips topple down the whipped cream lava flow and onto the table creating a miniature lahar slide. It's a mess and I just want to hand them a straw so they can use it to slurp up the disaster zone that has erupted onto my table.

"We love to eat paste. It is so wonderful with the Earth coffee. This is very acceptable to us! We approve this!" My intergalactic grannies exclaim gleefully.

"These pastries are called doughnuts, grannies. I thought that you might like to try this flavor first. These are caramel doughnuts with chocolate frosting and crushed macadamia nuts. I hope you enjoy them." I smile at my grannies while cleaning up my table with our napkins. I'm feeling amused at their obvious enjoyment of our morning meal. Although, so far, I've noticed that they like to eat anything and everything that I give them.

"Well, it was a terrible conversation. Lew divorced me after I left town. Lew was granted a divorce by the judge a few days before his accident. So basically, my husband divorced me for going on a vacation that he knew about and quite frankly he didn't mind me taking. It's unbelievable."

"Sedona, I can't believe it. It seems so unjust." Sam remarks.

"I have developed a working theory based on my conversation with John this morning. I believe that Lew purposefully orchestrated the shocking events at the diner. He must have meticulously planned it, so I would discover he and Louanne having public relations together up against the dumpster at the diner. How sad is that? I'm sure it was no accident that they were conducting their sinful love affair at my place of employment during my normal work shift. That way he could be sure that I would leave town a few days early. Essentially with this maneuver, Lew bought himself enough time to file for divorce and to claim that I abandoned him just by coming here for vacation." I tell my wretched tale of woe to my friends.

Sam and Missi look incredulous at my news. Sam drops her chocolate doughnut on the table, missing her napkin entirely in her shock. The almond butter frosting and crushed pecans smear on the table. Sam swipes her finger through the mess and licks it. Missi carefully sets her cherries and crushed almonds filled chocolate fudge doughnut onto her napkin.

"How could Lew betray you like that? Lew was clearly a heartless man. How could your cousin do this to you? You've always been such a faithful woman and a patient, kind, and compassionate wife. Sedona, how is this type of divorce still legal in the 21st century?" Sam utters fiercely.

"That's basically what I said to John. Unfortunately, this situation gets worse. John told me that Lew sold our home and the fifty acres to a minerals mining company. Now I have no home to return to. The sale of our land to a mining company clearly indicates that Lew knew there were valuable mineral deposits contained within it. He certainly never mentioned this fact to me.

He went to great lengths to conceal it from me and to cut me out of the proceeds. When we bought our land two decades ago, we didn't test for the presence of minerals. I actually thought that he would call me to apologize and I was planning on apologizing for trashing him. Now slinging trash seems a pretty minor offense after everything that I learned about Lew today."

"Sedona, this is shocking. I'm so sorry. It's hard to imagine Lew treating you so ruthlessly. It seems out of character." Sam comments.

"Clearly, he is not the same person that I married decades ago; he has become wicked. What's even worse is that Lew removed my name from our bank accounts and in my place, he added Louanne. The very same accounts that I have been depositing my wages and my dad's inheritance into for all these years of our marriage so we could retire in Italy. I get none of my own money back, now it belongs to my cousin. What's even worse is that when Lew sold our home and land, he became a multimillionaire. He cut me out completely and now Louanne gets to keep all of our money. She's filthy rich and I'm as poor as a church mouse. The only good news is that I'm me again. Legally, my last name was changed back to my maiden name of Bruno. I'm happy to have my original family name but sadly I'm also technically homeless. What a mess Lew has left behind."

I smile sadly as tears of shock continue to seep slowly down my cheeks. I reach for a devil's food cake doughnut topped with peanut butter frosting and crushed peanuts. I dab at my tears with my napkin.

"Oh, what a delicious doughnut but I truly despise the name. Why did some baker think it was a good idea to name a dessert devil's food? It's such a terrible name for such a tasty treat."

Sam replies. "Yup, that's why I never eat devil's food cake." She smiles and winks comically at me.

"Sedona, can't you hire an attorney to contest your divorce?" Missi asks.

"That's what I thought too, but John told me the divorce was already final because it was signed by a judge several days before Lew's accident."

"Sedona, I'm truly sorry for everything you have been through. It's cruel and unconscionable that your husband would do this to you. No words can really express it. Just know that we're here for you and we're on your side." Missi smiles at me with sympathy and compassion.

"Thank you for your support. It means a lot to me. I appreciate you and I'm grateful for good people in my life."

"Amen to that, sister." Sam replies.

"I'm glad I opened a new checking account after I left Sandy Town and all future payments of my inheritance will be deposited there. I'm devastated that my cousin has my money and I can't get back anything that was previously deposited in my joint accounts with Lew. It's a harsh situation. I'm grateful to have my camper to live in. I will still receive a monthly income from my dad's estate, so I can buy groceries. The harm Lew and Louanne inflicted on me is out of my control. The only thing I can control is my attitude and my personal actions related to the chaos they unleashed on me. My response to their bad behavior and the actions that I take now are my own choices. I choose to walk the path of peace like Jesus Christ. I choose to forgive them. I choose to accept my current situation as a blessing and a character-building opportunity. I choose to believe that God has a plan and a purpose for my life. I choose to make serving God my purpose in life. I choose unconditional love and forgiveness instead of anger and resentment. I choose God, Jesus Christ, and the Holy Spirit as my first priority above all earthly wealth and possessions. The only thing that truly matters to me is the gift of salvation from the Holy Trinity."

"Good heavens, that's inspirational wisdom. I like it." Sam comments.

"Indeed, that's a healthy and positive attitude. Good for you Sedona." Missi responds.

Naturally, I burst into tears. I can choose to heal from this pain but it will take time and effort to get there. My positive attitude and my Christian faith are a good start on the path to recovery. It's a path that I will walk on, one little step at a time, following God and Jesus, and I'll let them direct my journey from now on. Trusting God above all else will bring me peace and I need peace and healing now more than ever.

We sit quietly together for several minutes until my grief subsides and I get myself under control. When I'm feeling better, I open the box of doughnuts and pass my grannies more doughnuts. They are voracious eaters and they never seem to get full. This time, I give them raspberry cake doughnuts topped with orange frosting and crushed almonds. They bounce up and down on the seat cushions and open their jaws wide and clack them loudly together. They finally cease their antics and begin eating.

"Murphy and I are heading home to Eastern Washington state tomorrow afternoon. Why don't you and Sam caravan with us?"

"Epic idea." Sam smiles at Missi. "I would love to travel with you guys. Traveling together in a caravan through the desert? It's positively Biblical."

"Sedona, how about you?" Missi inquires. "Are you ready to get rolling?"

"I have a favor to ask first. Will you attend Lew's funeral with me? John texted me the details this morning. After our contentious conversation, he was probably afraid to talk on the phone with me again. Anyway, the funeral is in a few days in Sandy Town. It's in the direction that you are heading, so that works out."

"I'm sure we can arrange that, Sedona. I'll go talk with Murphy and let him know everything that's happened, if that's okay with you?"

"Sure, it's fine with me. He might as well find out directly from you, so that I don't have to keep talking about it."

"Why don't you call me later with the details about the funeral, okay?" Missi replies.

I nod my head and finally I can smile with genuine joy at my friends. After Missi leaves, Sam and I stay seated in the dining booth relaxing and chatting. Granny Fic and Gan are perched between us, enjoying blueberry cake doughnuts with lemon frosting sprinkled with crushed pistachios. All of a sudden, their eyes begin glowing like flashlights and they project the internet onto the wall. I look up startled by the bright light and I see a large map glowing there.

"Sedona, we must visit our friends in Washington state! They live here!" Granny Fic and Gan announce.

"What friends? What are you talking about?" I ask my grannies, stunned at this revelation. "This is the first time that you've mentioned that you have other friends here on Earth."

"Our friends are SasQueen and her family, the SasTribe from WatSoG. Earthlings would call them a sasquatch or a bigfoot creature. Humans expect them to be big dumb apes hiding in a forest or living wild in a remote mountain range. How ridiculous! They are in fact, a very civilized and advanced society. SasTribe are more intelligent and sophisticated than your ancient myths and legends give them credit for. For countless generations, they were sequestered in a very old city. They domiciled near a region of WatSoG known as the honeybees, butterflies, and flower meadows. When they eventually outgrew their ancient city, they enlisted the help of our grandparents,

Tti and Unee. Our grandparents agreed to transport the entire community during the first WatSoGian expedition to Earth. SasQueen and the SasTribe started a new colony on Earth in the remote wilderness of the Channeled Scablands in Washington state. At the time of our banishment, before leaving our family and our home, we promised an oath of honor to Tti and Unee that we would visit SasQueen and SasTribe to check on them and to bring them greetings and well wishes from home. We must keep our promise! This is very acceptable to us!"

"Sasquatch are real? The what tribe? The what lands? I've never heard of this before. Are you sure your information is correct?" I ask.

I'm feeling skeptical and yet excited at the same time. Perhaps a new adventure is what I need to help me move on with my life. "Are you sure it will be safe for Sam and I to go with you? What about our dogs and Topaz? What about Missi and Murphy? We need to consider our safety. Will your sasquatch friends welcome humans and keep us safe during our visit?"

Sam and I exchange a genuine look of concern. *This adventure could get very hairy indeed.*

"We are certain of it. It is safe for you and Sam to visit our fellow WatSo-Gians." Granny Fic and Gan assure us confidently. "We communicated with SasQueen about you, Sedona. We explained everything about you. That you helped us and how you take good care of us. Feeding us endless sustenance and much Earth coffee! This is very acceptable to SasQueen and her family the SasTribe! They value compassion and good stewardship. SasQueen and SasTribe believe it is very honorable to help others in a time of need, which is exactly what you did for us, Sedona. You and your human and animal tribe will be welcomed as honored guests. In fact, SasQueen has specifically requested to meet you and she has granted permission for all of you to visit the SasTribe commune."

"Sam, what do you think about this invitation?"

"Well, it's pretty far out of the ordinary and I'm inclined to believe that it would be an amazing experience. Most people would never get this kind of opportunity. Why don't we discuss it with Missi and Murphy before making a final decision?"

I smile and nod my head at Sam while I think over the situation. Absently, I run my fingers through my hair. "Sam, I think you make a good point. It's certainly an extraordinary invitation. Let's discuss it with Missi and Murphy in the morning over breakfast." I place a quick call to Missi and invite them to have breakfast with Sam and I in the Tumbleweed tomorrow morning.

Sam slides out of the dining booth and begins washing our coffee mugs. "Sedona, let's take Granny Fic and Gan over to the UFO museum. There's no point in wasting the rest of this beautiful day moping around here. I think a visit to your favorite museum will cheer you up."

Granny Fic and Gan levitate out of the booth. The brilliant light that was streaming out of their eyeballs extinguishes. They float in the air with their dresses dangling below them. They grab onto each other happily. Suddenly, my intergalactic grannies perform graceful pirouettes in the air. Their joyful twirling causes their dresses to flare out and swirl around them.

"We go now! This is very acceptable to us! We approve this! Sedona, we will cheer you up at the museum!" Granny Fic and Gan yell loudly as they are floating and twirling above me.

I giggle helplessly. "Good idea. Just stop your silly antics, you're making me dizzy. I always enjoy a trip to the Fragrant Bean Museum of UFOs." I fetch my smartphone and zip it into the large front pocket on my hiking shirt.

Chapter 39

Theme song: "Open Skies (iTunes Session)" by Crowder

The heat is intense as we walk along the gravel walkway to the museum. We arrive a little breathless and sweaty. Sam and I both sigh with relief at the cool air-conditioned interior. We pay the entrance fees and I make sure to get the senior discount on Granny Fic and Gan's tickets. They are holding the museum brochure open to the floor plan. They are pointing excitedly as they speed walk toward the spaceflight section.

"Slow down." I laugh with amusement at their enthusiasm. I'm glad we took the time to bring them to the museum. *I wonder how often intergalactic tourists have the chance to visit a UFO museum on Earth?*

Today, my speed-walking grannies are wearing pink cross trainers and matching pink maxi dresses. They are wearing their usual cosmetics to disguise their skin. They have on gray shoulder- length wigs styled into charming 1940s victory rolls. Perched atop their wigs are tiny blue fascinator hats with pink fabric flowers on the hat band.

They have pink eyeglasses resting on their long pointy noses. The fancy eyeglass keeper chains with blue beads dangle from the frames. Their opera length velvet gloves are also blue and they both wear blue belts around their tiny waists. For some reason, they were adamant about leaving their walking canes and hand bags back in the Tumbleweed today. I'm quite surprised by this turn of events since they normally stuff their hand bags with food and carry them everywhere they wander. My cross-dressing, granny impersonating, alien outlaw roommates are so accustomed to dressing in human fashions by now, that walking in shoes and long dresses does not slow them down anymore.

"Here it is!" Our grannies shout with pleasure at finding the exhibit they wanted to see.

They are bouncing up and down and peering closely at a small bell-shaped spacecraft. Sam and I trot over to see what they are so excited about. According to the exhibit sign, it's a realistic replica of the *Apollo 11* command module *Columbia*. The sign says that the replica is constructed with the exact same materials and specifications as the original spaceship.

Before Sam and I have a chance to get a good look at the exhibit, we are pulled inside it by Granny Fic and Gan. One of the first things I see inside are the astronaut flight suits draped across the three flight seats. Granny Fic and Gan each take hold of a flight suit and bring them over to us.

"You humans must wear these astronaut flight suits. Try them on so that you can get a realistic experience for visiting this very acceptable spacecraft museum exhibit. This is very acceptable to us! We approve this!" Our grannies grin mischievously at us as they place the flight suits into our hands.

"Why would we want to change into these smelly old suits? Absolutely not. We're not allowed to touch anything in a museum exhibit. Please put those flight suits back where you found them right now. This exhibit is only for visual inspection, touristing, and to educate museum guests. We're not allowed inside the exhibit. Let's all follow the rules. Come on, we need to leave the spaceship now." I instruct.

Chapter 40

Theme song: "Rattle!" by Zach Williams and Essential Worship featuring Pastor Steven Furtick from the album Rescue Story Deluxe Edition

In the blink of an eye, Sam and I are wearing the astronauts' flight suits and we're strapped into the flight seats. I'm experiencing nauseating vertigo at my rapid change in circumstance.

Smiling gleefully next to us, our grannies share the third flight seat with the large harness secured around both of their tiny bodies. The long skirts of their pink dresses are draped elegantly down over their legs and they manage to look both comfortable and fashionable, while I feel awkward and nauseated. Still staring at my troublesome, yet elegant grannies, I notice that their enormous cross trainers are dangling in the air high above the floor, forming a shoe-shaped protrusion in the fabric of their dresses.

Suddenly, command module *Columbia* starts to make weird rumbling sounds and now it's vibrating alarmingly beneath us. We are jostled fiercely in our seats while the module shakes and rattles violently. *I'm so scared right now and I hope I don't chip a tooth.*

"What's happening in here?" Sam shrieks in fright.

I'm fighting a feeling of rising panic as I try to turn my head to look around the interior. I notice some of the instrument panels are illuminated with blinking lights. My breathing is getting faster as my anxiety ramps up. *How did we get inside these old flight suits? This can't be good. What alarming shenanigans are our naughty grannies up to?*

"Grannies, we are absolutely not allowed inside the module. Take us back into the museum right now!" I shout at my alien roommates with panic painfully gripping my lungs and trying to steal away my breath.

I'm overcome by the sharp metallic odor permeating the interior of the spaceship. *It's quite stinky in here.* There's no fresh air circulating into the module and I'm feeling dizzy. Just when it feels unbearable, Sam and I are enveloped in a sweet lemon cake-scented breeze that floats around the module, eliminating the unpleasant metallic odor. Sam and I gratefully breathe in the dessert scented air.

Suddenly we hear a loud grating metallic screech and we feel the module begin to move alarmingly and then it careens awkwardly up into the air. *Command module Columbia is taking flight once again.* It's shimmying and rattling as it's slowly rising toward the high peaked roof of the UFO museum.

"Stop it right now! Granny Fic and Gan take us back down to the ground!"

"Don't worry Sam. We will cheer up Sedona! This is very acceptable to us! We approve this!" Our grannies cackle loudly, fully committed to their misguided mission.

Our intergalactic grannies are clearly excited by their rebellious mission. Just then, my Pandora app starts playing music. Anne Wilson's song "Rebel" from the album Rebel (The Beginning) is blaring loudly from my shirt pocket.

"Oh, I love this song! How is your smartphone playing music all by itself?" Sam shouts her question so she can be heard above our laughing grannies.

"I love this song too Sam. I didn't touch my smartphone; it's inside my pocket. I guess Granny Fic and Gan started playing the music for us. Granny Fic and Gan please take us back down to the museum!"

The lurching movement is disconcerting and my stomach drops painfully as the spacecraft continues to gain altitude. Hiccup! *Being trapped against my will inside a flying metal museum exhibit that is not supposed to be able to fly, is definitely not for me.*

The museum roof begins to emit metallic screeching sounds that are so loud we can hear them inside the command module. The replica flying saucer perched on the peak of the roof yawns open like a giant clam shell. The roof continues to open with a loud mechanical grinding and groaning. When the gap is large enough, command module *Columbia* wobbles as it shimmies through the roof opening and continues rising up toward the open sky.

"How is this possible? This exhibit doesn't have an engine or a jet thingy, whatever it's called!" I exclaim breathlessly.

I'm seriously regretting taking my grannies to the UFO museum. Sometimes I forget about the otherworldly abilities they can wield when they choose to do so. When they are sitting around in the Tumbleweed sipping coffee and munching on pastries, they almost seem like normal human grannies. *It's clearly a mistake to underestimate them.*

"Sedona, don't worry. We can fly anything at all, just by utilizing our coffee-fueled brain powers. We have been drinking so much of your homegrown coffee since we met you, that we can fly to the moon and back! No propulsion system is necessary. Just relax and enjoy touristing and we will cheer you up!" Granny Fic assures me confidently.

"Well, that may be so, but what about all of the humans in the museum? We can't let anyone see us flying off with a museum exhibit! It's theft by taking and that's a crime. The authorities will arrest us and then you'll lose your freedom to tourist around Earth! You'll be taken away from me and we'll never see each other again. Please, for your own safety, take us back into the museum and return this exhibit!" I hiccup loudly as I try to reason with my troublesome grannies.

"It is not possible for us to be detected. We are projecting a barrier around this antiquated space vessel and we are invisible to potential onlookers." Granny Gan replies smugly. "Do not fear the lawful authorities on Earth, we will keep you safe."

"Relax ladies, enjoy your touristing and be cheered up now!" Granny Fic shouts merrily.

I spy the bright flashing lights on the flying saucer replica as we pass through its open halves. We pick up speed as we clear the museum roof and its decorative flying saucer. In just a few minutes, we are rocketing into the clear blue sky. I can feel the command module shimmy alarmingly as it is buffeted by swirling air currents.

"I feel cheered up now. I'm finished touristing. I'm feeling very happy now. Let's go back to the museum and I will take you to a nice restaurant for lunch. I'm ready to eat lunch now. Please, just take us back down." I desperately implore our disobedient granny space pilots to behave.

I'm hoping my promise to visit a restaurant will convince the brothers to return us right away. Other than the greenhouses and coffee bar tents, they haven't really experienced a dine-in restaurant. Maybe promising a novel experience will change their minds about taking us on a space flight. My cajoling doesn't work on the WatSoGian brothers. Pretty soon we are zooming at a terrifying rate of speed. I can't move anymore due to the g-forces exerted on me. It's an unpleasant, painful feeling of being flattened into the flight seat. Sam and I are now gasping for breath, held captive to the incredible forces working against us. We are powerless to change our fate. I pray silently for our safety. *Be careful what you wish for. I deeply regret wishing upon a shooting star that I could travel to space. It was an ill-fated wish. Space travel is definitely not for me.*

My eyes are streaming tears of fright and I blink repeatedly, unable to lift my hands to wipe away my tears. After what feels like forever, command module *Columbia* gradually begins to slow its ascent. After a while, I'm pretty sure that we aren't ascending any longer. *Are we hovering or orbiting? I don't know.*

The interior of the module is dark and frigid. I'm painfully cold, but at least the intense weight is finally lifted from my chest. My harness jingles as I shiver in my seat. When I can finally lift my head, I look over at Sam and she gives me a weak thumbs up.

Curious, we begin to look at our surroundings. Outside the large viewing window in front of us, we gaze at the dark blue-black expanse pierced by pin-pricks of starry light in which the moon glows like a gigantic luminous white pearl.

"Sam, I think I can see the curvature of the Earth. Do you think so too?" I speak in a weak shaky voice, while my long hair is floating vertically above my head in a troll doll hairstyle.

"I guess so. It's very beautiful." Sam's voice trembles with the extreme cold.

"It's incredible, Grannies. I don't know exactly how you managed this, but thank you for this experience. I'm still terrified but it's amazing." I smile at Granny Fic and Gan who are surrounded by vertically floating clouds of pink fabric.

"I never imagined what it would look like this high up." Sam's teeth chatter as she weakly tries to raise her hands and clap.

"Fic and Gan?" I inquire. "How far above Earth are we?"

"Sedona, we are approximately fifty-two miles above the Earth. This makes you astronauts according to the current standards of your country." Granny Gan replies.

Granny Fic is grinning his charming, pointy green-fangs grin. "We must descend now. It is too cold for you humans to stay up here any longer."

"We are able to make enough oxygen for you and we are manipulating the pressure and temperature inside the module to keep you alive. It is an intense effort and we need to save some strength to pilot the command module back to Earth." Granny Gan explains.

My stomach rises painfully into my throat as command module *Columbia* drops forcefully. I am jolted hard against the seat back. Hiccup! Sam and I both cry out in surprise. *What is happening?*

We are descending rapidly back to Earth. I close my eyes and concentrate on not getting sick, since I don't have a sick bag handy. I keep telling myself we'll be back home soon. The module rocks violently as we pick up speed in a sickening free fall. Once again, Sam and I are squished painfully and pressed hard into our seats. Breathing becomes difficult and I can't move at all. In an attempt to comfort us, Granny Fic and Gan send a cool breeze of decadent coffee aroma that swirls around Sam and I during our return flight. It seems to offer us a little calm and comfort during the uncomfortable trip.

Finally, the descent of the command module slows noticeably. The module interior gradually becomes warmer and brighter as we descend closer to Earth. After a while, it is painfully bright and I blink rapidly as my eyes water.

Now that the g-forces have lessened considerably, I can look around the interior. I see condensation droplets clinging to the interior metal walls. I can also move again as the pressure fully lessens and I'm not pressed painfully against my seat. I take a deep breath of relief now that the worst is over. I give Sam's arm a gentle, reassuring squeeze.

"We are nearly home." I say to my friend.

"I never want to do that again." Sam replies.

"Me either."

Guided by our granny impersonating, insubordinate alien pilots, the module slowly sinks into the clam shell shaped opening of the flying saucer replica. The module continues to move down through the roof opening and into the interior space of the museum. Finally, we land with a loud scrape on the floor, back inside the exhibit space designated for command module *Columbia*.

The moment we're back on solid ground; we frantically wrestle with the old metal buckles on our flight seat harnesses. Still reeling from the wild space flight, we practically fall out of the astronaut's flight seats on our frail and wobbly legs. With trembling fingers, Sam and I help extricate each other from the sweaty flight suits.

"Sam, are you feeling alright? You look sickly and green." I ask as I struggle with the zippers and metal clamps on her flight suit. My fingers are clumsy as I try to help liberate my friend from the technical fabric.

"My head is spinning with a vertigo feeling. I feel as weak as a newborn foal whose long spindly legs are still unable to support it. How about you? Are you alright?" Sam begins tugging on the clamps and fasteners on my flight suit.

"Same. You described it exactly right. I hope the feeling wears off quickly. I'm afraid that the museum staff will call the police before we can escape. We need to get out of here as quickly as possible. I never should have brought our WatSoGian grannies here. I had no idea that they had the ability to fly a museum exhibit. It's unbelievable." I say as stress tears leak from my eyes.

Once we peel off the sticky flight suits, we arrange them carefully back into position on the astronauts' flight seats. The interior looks exactly the same as it did before the flight, so at least nothing is damaged. The condensation droplets should dry up pretty fast now that the module is back inside its exhibit space. I'm glad we didn't harm the museum exhibit. I exhale with relief.

Finally, we careen clumsily out through the capsule portal. Sam and I are extremely unsteady on our feet. We sway precariously from side to side. Luckily, there is no one near the command module *Columbia* exhibit and I look around for a quick escape route. I am still terrified that the police will come in and arrest us.

"Come on. We're leaving before anyone catches us. Follow me." I say urgently, as I gesture for our mutinous grannies to follow Sam and I.

I lead us to a nearby employee exit and we all clamber outside into the blazing desert heat. The bright sunlight is disorienting after our illicit space flight. I weave a little as Sam and I drunkenly stumble toward town. Our grannies serenely float along next to us, completely unaffected by our space travel. They both have satisfied grins on their unrepentant alien faces.

I lead us to the nearest diner and we walk around to the back. We step onto the covered patio and choose a table right in front of a large fan mister. Sam and I sink unsteadily onto the wooden chairs. We both glare at our grannies as they float down onto the chairs between us, still grinning.

When our server stops by our table, I order a round of extra-large iced coffees. For our appetizer, we choose the sweet potato fries. For our entrees, we all decide to get the grilled cheese sandwiches with sliced tomatoes. For dessert, I order the deep-fried molasses cookies to share with my friends. After our exhausting misadventures in space flight, we're settled in to relax with our meals and we all refuse to move any time soon.

Chapter 41

Theme song: "Truth be Told" by Carly Pearce and Matthew West from the album Brand New Deluxe Edition

"Hey Sedona!" Sam shouts loudly as she pounds on the door of my Tumbleweed before sunrise the next morning.

"Wait a minute, Sam. I'm on my way." I nearly trip over Rex and Patch as I try to get to the door.

I open the door for Sam and I smile with surprise when I see Missi and Murphy standing behind her. I step outside snuggled in my cozy long sweater. Rex and Patch hop down the steps and greet our early morning visitors.

"Good morning, everyone. Come sit down and relax. I'll bring out coffee and breakfast. I've been cooking and it smells delicious. I hope you're all hungry."

Our view this morning is a dramatic blood orange, peach, and lemon-yellow sunrise. The savory scent of pan-fried bacon wafts around us. I serve my friends plates of scrambled eggs with Old Croc extra sharp cheddar cheese, diced tomatoes, onions, and bell peppers. Each plate is garnished with sweet orange wedges and crispy bacon slices. I hand out mugs of caffé mocha.

This morning, I really need the warm comfort of my coffee. I'm ready to reveal the truth about Fic and Gan to Missi and Murphy. I hope I'm making the right decision, since the safety of Fic and Gan depends on their reaction. I believe that I can trust them, but I still feel very nervous as I sip my soothing caffé mocha.

We sit in camp chairs under the patio awning facing each other with our plates balanced on our knees. It's chilly this early in the morning, so we hold our steaming mugs of coffee nestled in our hands for added warmth. The dogs are nearby gobbling up their food from the bowls set out for them. Topaz is content in her corral munching on hay. Sometimes I like to hide a few carrots inside her hay bag as a healthy treat.

This morning, the Fragrant Bean parking lot campground feels like a ghost town. All of the visitors, vendors, and other campers packed up and left immediately after the coffee festival ended. *Since our group will be traveling long term together and we are preparing to visit an otherworldly sasquatch tribe, the time has come for me to tell the truth. I'm ready to reveal the intergalactic origins of our grannies. I can't put it off any longer.* I nervously clear my throat.

"Missi and Murphy." I clear my throat again and cough. "I have something important to share with you but it can't leave this circle of friends. This is top secret information. It's so secret in fact, that not even the government or the military knows about it."

I point to each one of us sitting together in my campsite. Missi and Murphy appear intrigued at my mysterious words. They look around at each of us and then they look at each other and lean in close. After a few moments of quiet discussion, they both nod their heads in agreement.

"I hope that we don't regret this. But we choose to trust you. Okay, we agree not to share this with anyone else. What's going on?" Missi asks.

"Great. First off, I am asking both of you to keep a very open mind, but also to take this knowledge to your graves. This is for your ears only." I begin my revelation. This is a lot to ask of new friends and I'm going to trust in God of Heaven that everything will work out just fine.

"I'm sure that you've noticed our grannies are a bit unusual. They are like family to me, but they are not related to me. Also, they are not from here originally." I pause trying to gather my thoughts.

"More specifically, they are not originally from Earth." I say with conviction.

Missi and Murphy lean in close to one another with their shoulders touching, they clasp hands tightly and their eyes widen in amazement at my news.

"What do you mean, exactly? This doesn't make sense." Missi speaks softly and leans forward a bit.

Granny Fic and Gan release an enticing warm breeze toward us. It carries the scent of oven baked cinnamon apple pie and hot cocoa. The delicious scent envelopes our campsite as it wafts soothingly around us. With a start, Murphy looks around excitedly.

"Sedona, do you have an apple pie baking in the oven?" Murphy asks hopefully.

"Uh, no. Sorry. The scented breeze? It's a gift from Granny Fic and Gan to help you relax. Just like aroma therapy to help manage stress."

I continue explaining my grannies' origins. "Granny Fic and Gan are in fact intergalactic aliens. Tourists visiting Earth. They are originally from planet WatSoG. I have no idea where it is located, except that it is in some far away galaxy named Wreximus Maximus. Their grandparents visited Earth as part of the WatSoGian expedition trips back in the 1940s and again in the 1960s. They are completely friendly visitors and they won't hurt anyone. Please believe me, they are safe and trustworthy."

"No way! Are you inventing a new role play game right now?" Murphy utters hopefully.

"This sounds like an intriguing game. I'm in." Missi says.

"Guys, this is not a game. I'm telling you the truth. They just want to drink coffee and eat lots of food. Unfortunately, they can't return home. Sam and I are taking care of them. We must keep them safe and that means that no one else can know about their true identities." I lean forward and I look directly into Missi and Murphy's faces, giving them my direct stare to show them that I'm completely serious. "I'm not joking, this is all true. You both have been around them for a while. Surely, you can see that they are gentle and harmless. They are my family now. If anyone outside our group finds out about them, then Fic and Gan will be in serious danger. The authorities would detain them. I will never see them again. Will you keep our secret and help us protect them?" I smile and look hopefully at Missi and Murphy.

"Sedona this is amazing!" Murphy exclaims excitedly and laughs loudly. "It's hard to believe that such a thing is possible. However, I can see that you are entirely serious and if you and Sam believe it is true, then I accept it as truth."

Missi smiles widely and looks at us. "Me too. It's incredible but I believe you, and yes, I will keep your secret. We trust you and we will help you."

Murphy kisses his wife on the cheek. "What an unexpected adventure this trip has turned into. Far out man!"

Missi smiles at Murphy. "This is turning into a great trip. Granny Fic and Gan, we love you just the way you are. Thank you for trusting us to be your friends."

"Count us in on your adventures." They both say at the same time, with their hands still firmly clasped together.

"Alrighty then. There is another important issue we need to discuss. First, let me pull some shots of espresso and make more caffé mochas for us. While I'm inside, can I bring anyone more bacon and eggs?"

"That's the ticket! Now you're speaking my language." Murphy says.

"The excitement of this adventure makes me really hungry. Or maybe it's just the cold morning air. Thank you." Sam replies.

I climb up into the Tumbleweed and prepare our coffee drinks. I gather the remaining eggs and bacon and our drinks, then step outside. After everyone is served, I happily settle into my camp chair.

"Yesterday, Granny Fic and Gan told me that they need to visit a group of friends from their home planet." I look over at my friends enjoying their coffee and meals and I smile at them. "Their friends live in the Channeled Scablands of Washington state. Will you two help us take our grannies to their friends after the funeral?" I look at Missi and her husband and await their answer.

"What? There are other aliens living here? This just keeps getting better and better! You do realize however, that the Channeled Scablands are a huge wilderness and they are very remote. We can lead you to the Scablands, but can Granny Fic and Gan find their friends in the wilderness?" Murphy asks.

"We have been in communication with our friends SasQueen and Sas-Tribe. They provided their exact coordinates to us. Once we arrive in the Channeled Scablands, finding our WatSoGian friends will not take too long."

Missi and Murphy chat quietly together for a few minutes. Afterward, Missi smiles brightly at us. "Of course we can help you find your way there. Let's plan a route from your husband's funeral in Sandy Town to the Channeled Scablands."

They ask me for my road atlas and I collect it from the Tumbleweed's cab. Missi and Murphy plot our route carefully. Together, they review the maps and jot down a few notes. Sam and I carry our utensils and plates inside. We work together to clean up the kitchen. After everything is clean, dried, and stored away, we check back in with Missi and Murphy. I lean out the door and grin at Missi and Murphy, who are just sitting silently and gazing at Fic and Gan. The happily married couple is looking quite starstruck with dreamy expressions of wonder on their faces. *Aw, they're seeing Fic and Gan in a new light and they're fascinated.*

"Please join us inside. We'll be more comfortable with the maps and notebooks if we sit in the dining booth while we discuss our travel plans." I call out to my friends.

Granny Fic and Gan, with their long dresses gracefully trailing below them, rise up into the air above their camp chairs and float back to the Tumbleweed to join us.

"Whoa! Far out! Granny Fic and Gan can fly?" Murphy shouts in surprise at our grannies' unique method of travel.

"What else haven't you told us about your grannies Sedona?" Missi asks as she and Murphy follow the floating brothers inside.

"I probably forgot to mention that they are identical twins and they are purple, gold, and glittery when they are not dressed in their granny disguises. Also, they have three legs and feet. Oh, and they have flashlight eyes when they take off their granny glasses. Otherwise, I think you're all up to date." I reply with a grin. Once we are crammed into the dining booth, we review the road atlas and the notes.

"Take a look at the map of Nevada. This is the highway that we can travel on when we leave Sandy Town, then this state route is where we drive until we reach the interstate and we take that into southern Washington. Then we take this interstate and follow it to the minor back roads into the Scablands." Missi points to the various maps with her pencil as she flips between the pages of the road atlas.

Without warning, Granny Fic and Gan project the internet through their bright flashlight eyeballs. Even though Sam and I have witnessed this phenomenon before, it's always a shock when they perform this otherworldly feat. Missi and Murphy are visibly frightened at the sight of the brothers' intensely bright glowing eyeballs. Their eyes are as blindingly brilliant as intense LED headlights set to high beams.

"That's a unique skill, Grannies." Murphy laughs nervously.

"It's safe to say that is the last thing that I expected to see today." Missi remarks while gazing up at the huge map illuminating my wall. She joins hands with her husband.

"Thank you, grannies, what a nice map." I grin at my grannies.

I review the route that Missi and Murphy outlined in my road atlas. I study Granny Fic and Gan's map on my wall. I check for the presence of any low, height restricted underpasses. I check that there are no tunnels along our route due to the presence of the LP tanks onboard our RVs.

"Missi and Murphy, thank you for planning our route. It looks good to me. Sam are you comfortable with our travel plans?"

Sam takes a closer look at the highlighted route in my road atlas and consults our notes and the large map illuminating my wall. "The Channeled Scablands sound very mysterious. I can't wait to experience the landscape with you guys. This looks good to me as well. Thanks very much for your help, Murphy and Missi."

Together we study the huge map glowing on my wall. Granny Fic and Gan float over to their map and they point out the location of the home territory of their friends. "This is the location of the SasTribe and if you will take us there in your cumbersome land vehicle then we will be much grateful. This is very acceptable to us! We approve this!"

"We will take you there after Lew's funeral. If you can be patient for a few more days, we will all take you to see your friends. I think it's safe to say that we are happy to help you, Grannies. Sam, are you ready to break down camp and hit the road?"

"As soon as I'm done appreciating your homegrown coffee, I'll be ready to get started. Then we can get this caravan on the road."

Satisfied with our tasty breakfast and our travel plans, we awkwardly slide out of the dining booth while accidentally bumping shoulders and elbows. Missi and her husband head back to their B&B to collect their belongings and to check out. Sam walks back to her Bambi with CJ and Rocky at her heels. After my friends leave, I get busy breaking camp.

I lead Topaz into her trailer and I load flakes of fresh grass hay into her hay bags and refill her water buckets. I stow away her portable corral panels, then pack up my camp chairs and galaxy shaped wind chimes. After retracting the patio awning and putting away the last of my supplies, I drive over to the dump station.

Sam and I meet there to empty our gray and black water tanks. The first task is to refill our fresh water tanks with our water filters secured to the potable water fill hoses. Afterward, we stow away our clean water filters and then we empty our gray water tanks. Next, we slide on our long rubber gloves, ready to perform our least favorite task. Using a long-handled tank wand, we flush and clean out our black water tanks. We perform a clean water rinse, being sure to wash down the pavement thoroughly and we also wash our rubber gloves thoroughly before stowing them away. After washing our hands, we do a safety check around our vehicles and also check our tire pressures and our trailer hitches.

"Ready to get rolling on the highway?" Sam asks. We smile and high five each other.

"I'm ready to continue this journey. This has turned into the most unforgettable coffee festival trip we've ever experienced. Thanks for traveling with me, Sam. I appreciate it so much." I'm feeling very blessed to have friends who are willing to stand by me during this stressful and exciting time. *Traveling together as a caravan through the desert is going to be memorable.*

We meet up with Missi and Murphy at Fragrant Beans N' Broccoli Fresh Food Market. Granny Fic and Gan are excited to push our shopping carts as we wander through the large store.

Sam and I fill our carts with groceries and supplies for our campers, while Missi and Murphy choose a few light snacks for their truck. They choose sparkling water, dark chocolate covered whole almonds, and tart green apples for snacking during the trip. After stocking up our RVs, we are finally ready to depart Fragrant Bean. Together we begin the drive to Sandy Town for Lew's funeral.

Chapter 42

Theme song: "From the Day" by I AM THEY from the album I Am They

I lead our caravan driving my Tumbleweed with Topaz's trailer in tow. Granny Fic and Gan, wrapped in cozy plaid shawls, sit in the dining booth with shortbread cookies clutched between the long claws of one hand. They have their *Star Trek* mugs of coffee nestled securely in cup holders. Patch and Rex lie under the table hoping for a few shortbread crumbs.

My grannies are engrossed in a pair of new books that we just bought at the market. They wear reading glasses perched delicately on their long pointy noses. They both chose to read the same novel *Aliens, Campers, and Coffee* by Karen Bruno. *I'm highly amused at their choice of reading material, since the novel seems to eerily echo their own personal experiences here on Earth. I can't wait to read it too, just as soon as they finish reading their paperback copies. Or, maybe I'll just purchase an electronic copy of the intriguing book for my e-reader, that way I don't have to wait for my grannies to finish reading it.*

Missi and Murphy, in their truck, follow directly behind me. Sam and her dogs bring up the rear in her station wagon towing her cheerful pink-painted Airstream Bambi. We drive straight through, with only a few necessary stops. Finally, we arrive in the undeveloped desert wilderness outside of Sandy Town with plenty of time left in the day before the funeral starts.

With a sigh of relief, I spy the familiar wide sandy plain flourishing with desert plants including scrub grasses, yucca, cholla, and an endless forest of spiky Joshua trees stretching far away into the distance. We park in an overflow gravel parking area not too far from the funeral parlor. Our vehicles are too large to fit in the lot that is situated next to the building. The smaller lot will be very crowded later this afternoon. I'm sure the entire town will come to say goodbye to Lew. My friends park their vehicles near the Tumbleweed and they step outside to stretch their legs.

I unbuckle my seat belt and slide out of the driver's seat. "Come on Grannies. Let's take Patch and Rex for a walk, since we have lots of time before the funeral starts." I fetch the dogs' leashes while Rex and Patch sit patiently by the door. "Are you boys ready for a hike?"

Granny Fic and Gan toddle over wearing their wide brimmed floppy sun hats and sunglasses. They take hold of the dogs' leashes. Today my grannies are wearing maxi dresses in a lovely lemon-yellow embellished with purple, blue, and pink lilac flowers. Lately, they have been dressing as twin grannies. *I think it's quite charming and they're adorable.*

Patch and Rex dance excitedly, their claws tapping on the floor. They're ready to hop out of the camper and go for a long walk. We step outside together, then I jog back to my trailer and open the door. Topaz greets me with a loud bray and then she promptly sneezes all over me. *Ew!* I clip the rope to her halter and then I wipe my shirt sleeve gently across her back, wiping off her green sneeze residue. I'll take some time to brush her coat later.

Sam, with CJ and Rocky, meets up with us and together we enjoy a few minutes of walking and stretching our legs. Well, Granny Fic and Gan are actually floating and hovering over the ground as my dogs pull them along. I notice this makes it easier for our grannies to keep pace with us. Missi and Murphy join us and share green apples with everyone to fortify us for our hike. We chat companionably together.

At this moment, I'm feeling a little emotional and unsettled. It's weird to be back in Sandy Town. Attending a funeral is always distressing. This particular one is just too personal, very painful, and plain awkward after the public and embarrassing death of my marriage.

I'm also still processing the shock of poor Lew's tragic accident. *He deserved better than to drown in the effluent-filled cab of his work truck. What a waste for him to leave this Earth so soon.* I feel sorrow for him, but I'm grateful that my friends are here to support me. The desert landscape surrounding the funeral parlor is beautiful and together my chosen family and I hike into the desert to enjoy the wind and sunshine.

"Sedona, how does it feel to be back home in Sandy Town?" Missi inquires.

"It's really strange to be here again. I'm scared to face all of my ex-neighbors. I embarrassed myself in the diner in front of the whole town. It was such an awkward spectacle and my behavior will go down in town history as a cringe-worthy moment. The townies love that kind of drama and they have a very long memory. There's nothing else to do in such a tiny town, except to be involved in all of your neighbors' personal dramas. Everyone here learned the sordid details about what happened between Lew and Louanne and I feel so ashamed."

I look down at my hiking boots as they scuff against a rock on the sandy desert floor. Little puffs of dust rise up from my footfalls. Topaz nudges me with her wet muzzle. I reach over and gently rub her forehead.

"I understand that this is very hard for you. We are here to support you. Just smile and hold your head up high. Everyone also knows that you did nothing wrong and in fact you're the innocent one in this fiasco. They know that it was Lew and Louanne who were the adulterous cheaters in a stealth romance. You don't have anything to be ashamed of Sedona." Sam smiles sadly at me while patting me gently on the shoulder.

I nod my head, feeling too choked up at the moment to say more on the subject. Back at the Tumbleweed, I spend a few minutes setting up the small portable corral and ensuring Topaz has plenty of fresh water and grass hay. I secure her shade tarp across one side of the corral. With my chores finished, it's time to clean up and face the town. We return our dogs to the air-conditioned comfort of my Tumbleweed. We refill water and food bowls for all of them. The four dogs can keep each other company while we're at the funeral.

I change clothes in the privacy of my bedroom, while Rex and Patch are snoozing on my bed. My elegant funeral outfit consists of a dressy pair of black slacks and a dark gray long sleeved feminine blouse with a high neckline. My blouse has an intricate pattern of shiny metallic silver flowers with long stems and leaves adorning it. I'm also wearing my best dress shoes. They are Doc Martens black ankle boots and they're artfully embroidered with beautiful blooming red roses, green leaves, and tied with green laces. *I love my fancy dress shoes.* My long hair is brushed and pulled back into a low ponytail with a green satin hair scrunchie.

Missi and Murphy change into their funeral clothes in the privacy of the bathroom. Missi is wearing a long gray skirt with a midnight blue blouse and a feminine gray blazer. I smile when I notice the large green coffee mug brooch pinned to her lapel.

She grins mischievously at me as she raises the hem of her long skirt slightly to reveal her signature Doc Martens white ankle boots decorated with glued on roasted coffee beans. Today they are tied with green laces. Murphy is wearing pleated gray slacks, a midnight blue button-down dress shirt with a gray blazer. A few minutes later we step outside to meet Sam and I'm surprised how windy the afternoon has become.

Sam is wearing one of her creations, as are Granny Fic and Gan. They are each attired in elegant maxi dresses and opera gloves. They feature an intricate geometric print. The beauty of the dresses is in the metallic sheen of the fabric. Each dress is a lighter shade of metallic gray. When seen together, the color tones of the three dresses shimmer from charcoal, to gray, then to silver. The effect is dramatic. Sam happily accessorizes with her dressy rhinestone embellished formal black flip flops. Granny Fic and Gan are wearing their pink cross trainers. They each carry a silver hand bag and a matching cane.

"You clean up real nice." We say at the same time and then laugh aloud.

"Sedona, are you ready to face the town?" Sam asks me and gives me an encouraging smile.

"Never." I say meekly. "Let's pay our respects to Lew."

Missi, Murphy, Sam, and my grannies all close ranks around me and somberly we walk over to the funeral parlor in the gusty wind.

Chapter 43

Theme song: "In the House" by Crowder from the album Milk & Honey Deluxe Edition

The Ashes to Ashes, Dust to Dust is the sole funeral parlor and church serving Sandy Town. The old church stands sentinel on the outskirts of the remote town. It's situated several miles outside of town along a forgotten stretch of the Extraterrestrial Highway.

The Dusty, as the townies call it, is housed in a cracked adobe and old parched wood beams and timber-framed building. It's one of the original town buildings, dating from the 19th century, when outlaws outnumbered peaceful and law-abiding citizens. Surrounding the church, and stretching out over several miles of wild desert, the town's only graveyard lies in wait. The forlorn graveyard is a dispiriting cluster of sun-bleached headstones, spiky Joshua Trees, thorny cacti, and endless cinnamon-colored sand as far as the eye can see.

The church interior retains its simple and quaint old frontier character, with the modern addition of electricity. It has a distressed boot heel and spur scarred uneven wooden floor with wide planks. Long wooden pews fill the warehouse-sized room. Unusual for its era, this original building was constructed by an optimistic preacher and town volunteers who expected Sandy Town to boom in years to come and so it's rather enormous in its proportions for such a tiny rural town.

The antique wooden stage has a pinyon pine lectern in the center and nearby is the small Baptismal pool. The back wall is adorned with a rough-hewn, white fir cross which is outlined by incongruous, modern white LED lights that illuminate the dim interior of the Dusty. The entire town is packed inside and the church is buzzing with loudly whispered conversations.

Heads turn as the heavy, carved wood, double doors slam with an echoing boom behind me. The explosion of sound travels around the cavernous room announcing my return to the heartless person who ruined my life. The blast of scorching wind and dust that rushes inside causes me to duck my head and squeeze my eyes tightly closed. The unexpected burst of wind causes a few strands of hair to loosen from the scrunchie and the flying strands swing around and lash my face. I sneeze forcefully at the dust that blows in with my entrance. My neck twinges with pain from the strength of my sneeze. *Why can't I ever go unnoticed in this dusty town? My presence here will definitely stir up a few souls.*

I raise my head and swipe my unruly hair from my face. Blinking my watering sea-green eyes, I feel my face getting hot and turning red. As I walk in with Sam and my posse of new friends, I'm feeling decidedly unwelcome due to the judgmental stares from a few of my ex-neighbors. The dusty chapel feels gloomy compared to the brilliant sunlit afternoon I left behind. I pause to let my eyes adjust to the dimness.

I spy my cousin Louanne Pooey. She is surrounded by her large girl squad gracing the front pew, which is supposed to be reserved only for the family of the deceased. *It is definitely not reserved for his sinful mistress and her disrespectful, gossipy entourage.*

Gathered around the fashionably dressed women are a large crowd of Lew's rowdy high school friends. His brother Stew and his lawyer John are sitting on either side of my cousin. Some of Lew's friends are gossiping loudly and laughing obnoxiously as if they were attending a high school reunion, instead of a funeral. *Louanne clearly relishes being the star of the show. Poor Lew, upstaged at his own funeral.*

I shake my head and sigh loudly in disappointment. My cousin, who has antagonized me since we were children, turns to stare at me, as I search for a seat at the back of the crowded room. Again, my eyes are drawn irresistibly to the front pew. I'm shocked when I get a good look at her dress. Louanne is encased in an antique, over-the-top, black widow's weeds floor length dress, as if she were mourning a husband in the Victorian era. *Unbelievable. Her outlandish widow's weeds mourning dress is very inappropriate and downright disrespectful to Lew's family because they were not even married.*

"Vintage couture!" Sam hisses in my ear and grabs my arm in her excitement. "Her dress appears to be an authentic Victorian crape gown. Ooh, I love the shiny jet beads embroidered along the bodice. Oh, and just look at the exquisite floor-length veil. It's beautiful. Although, I'm pretty sure that kind of veil should be worn only when the widow is outdoors. She's committing a serious fashion faux pas. Instead, I think the fashion etiquette of the day dictates that she should be wearing a little black hat with a tiny veil when indoors. I wonder if she found her outfit in an antique store? Maybe she had it custom made? Oh no. Sedona, it looks like she is committing another serious social blunder, she is wearing a lot of sparkly bridal diamonds on her left hand."

Sam doesn't normally gossip, but in this case, the seamstress in her is both fascinated and repelled by my theatrical cousin and the Victorian haute couture funeral costume. My friend's enthusiastic fashion commentary nearly causes me to burst into emotionally unhinged stress laughter. *Keep it together, Sedona. Maintain your Christian dignity.*

I'm relieved when I find two pews with a few open spots. Sam and I squish together with Granny Fic and Gan in one. Missi and Murphy squeeze into the pew directly behind us.

"Thank you for coming to Lew's funeral. I'm grateful you are here with me. It's an unbelievable and devastating tragedy. I'm so sorry for Lew's suffering. I still can't believe that he is really gone from this world." I utter with a feeling of overwhelming despair.

Sam wraps her arm around my shoulder to offer comfort. Miserable tears escape my eyes as I try desperately to hold onto my overwhelming emotions. This entire situation is still hard to accept.

As Missi takes her seat, she gently pats my back and whispers. "There's no way that we would let you attend this funeral without us. I'm so sorry for what you are going through. Be strong, my friend. We've got your back."

Chapter 44

Theme song: "Almost Home" by MercyMe from the album inhale (exhale)

Reverend Peter walks out onto the stage. He stands tall and imposing at the lectern, underneath the bright LED lights anchored to the old wood beams. His shoulder length, wavy black hair and waist length, curly black beard shine brightly under the lighting. He taps the microphone gently and then looks out over the crowded pews packed with mourners. He silently studies the crowd, his deep brown eyes searching, casting around like a fishing net into the crowded sea of people, seeking a bountiful harvest. Under the preacher's gaze, the crowd falls silent, even the rowdy group in the front pew finally quiets down. After a few minutes, he nods his head satisfied that peace has descended upon the house of the Lord.

"Welcome and peace be with you. Thank you for gathering here in the house of the Lord to celebrate the life of Lew Dung. While we all feel sorrow at his untimely and tragic loss, we should be celebrating instead, because God offers His children life everlasting. Because of God's saving grace and mercy through our Savior Jesus Christ, it is impossible for the grave to hold onto God's children. Let us take comfort in God's words in the *Holy Bible* New International Version. Today, I will start by reading from 1 Thessalonians 4:14-18, NIV."

Reverend Peter's deep voice commands our attention as he reads aloud. "1 Thessalonians 4:14-18, NIV states, 'For we believe that Jesus died and rose again, and so we believe that God will bring with Jesus those who have fallen asleep in him. According to the Lord's word, we tell you that we who are still alive, who are left until the coming of the Lord, will certainly not precede those who have fallen asleep. For the Lord himself will come down from heaven, with a loud command, with the voice of the archangel and with the trumpet call of God, and the dead in Christ will rise first. After that, we who are still alive and are left will be caught up together with them in the clouds to meet the Lord in the air. And so, we will be with the Lord forever. Therefore encourage one another with these words.'"

I follow along, reading silently in the *Holy Bible* from the pew. I find the reverend's sermon comforting. Reverend Peter stops speaking, clears his throat, and takes a drink of water from the tall beveled glass on the lectern. As he tilts the glass up, LED light reflects off the shining surface of the glass and a brilliant burst of color flashes across the church and illuminates Lew's casket with a tiny rainbow. A chorus of hallelujahs echo around the room.

Chapter 45

Theme song: "One Awkward Moment" by Casting Crowns from the album Only Jesus Deluxe Edition

Reverend Peter begins speaking again. "At this time, I invite the bereaved widow Sedona to come up here and say a few words in remembrance of Lew. Sedona, please join me." Reverend Peter looks directly at me from across the room and I feel trapped in his piercing gaze.

Reluctantly, I rise and slowly make my way up to the front of the church. I feel the weight of hundreds of curious stares upon me as I trudge to the stage. I'm very nervous and I have no idea what to say. I want nothing more at this moment, than to remain quietly in the back of the room surrounded by the love and support of my sweet grannies and my close friends.

Awkwardly, I trip over my own uncooperative feet as I ascend the uneven wooden steps. With a quick push up, I barely manage to save myself from a painful face-plant on the stairs. I hear someone in the crowd shriek in surprise. Self-consciously, I hold my breath and clench my teeth as I hear contemptuous laughter explode from Louanne and her rowdy friends. I feel my face burning with shame. There's no doubt in my mind that it's turning a festive shade of cranberry as I climb to my feet and slowly cross the wooden floor on unsteady legs.

Reverend Peter waves a hand at me to hurry over to the lectern. He smiles encouragingly and adjusts the microphone lower for me.

He hands me his *Holy Bible* and whispers to me. "For strength and guidance."

I nod at him and turn toward the sea of people staring up at me with scrutinizing expressions on their faces. I open the *Holy Bible* to the Gospels. Looking out into the crowd there is a seemingly endless and embarrassing silence as I gather my thoughts. I hope the right words will flow from my lips after my ignominious arrival on the stage. *Heavenly Father, please provide me with benevolent words to eulogize my husband. In Jesus' name, amen.*

Chapter 46

Theme song: "Ain't no Grave" by Crowder from the album Neon Steeple Deluxe Edition

"Faithful friends and neighbors, thank you for being here today in remembrance of Lew. I will read from the Gospel of John, chapter 11, verses 23-27 NIV. Please open your pew Bibles and follow along." I pause for several minutes while people open up their Bibles. "'Jesus said to her, "Your brother will rise again." Martha answered, "I know he will rise again in the resurrection at the last day." Jesus said to her, "I am the resurrection and the life. The one who believes in me will live, even though they die; and whoever lives by believing in me will never die. Do you believe this?" "Yes, Lord," she replied, "I believe that you are the Messiah, the Son of God, who is to come into the world."' This is the truth that we are seeking in this tragic moment and this comforting Scripture assures me that Lew is in Heaven. Please remember that God loves us no matter what we have done. If we believe in Him, God faithfully keeps His promises and He promises us eternal life in Heaven." I pause to gather my thoughts.

"What more can I say about Lew? We all knew him well. Many of us grew up together and attended school with Lew. He was a decent and hardworking man. As you know, he was the owner of Dung's Doody Thrones, which ultimately caused his tragic demise. He faithfully contributed many volunteer hours to our town. Lew was always willing to lend a hand to his friends and neighbors. I hope that you will choose to remember him for the good works that he did, and forget about the recent embarrassing events that caused the death of our marriage. I forgive him completely and I will remember him as the best version of the person he was for so many years here in Sandy Town." Suddenly, I stop speaking as Louanne's rude laughter thunders across the room.

She unleashes a tirade to her friends criticizing my words about Lew. I stare at Louanne in horrified fascination while she continues ranting. I clear my throat, and the noise echoes across the church, amplified by the microphone.

"Louanne." I say firmly, as I continue staring directly at her. "Cousin, I truly forgive you for having an affair with my husband and for your part in the demise of my marriage to Lew. I genuinely forgive you and I wish you peace, love, and blessings. However, please stop criticizing me. I haven't done anything to you to deserve it."

Ungraciously and full of angry resentment, Louanne screams at me. "How dare you! Sedona, you're a pathetic bleeding heart! I don't need your forgiveness for anything! You got exactly what you deserved! You are just a ridiculous, self-righteous Bible-thumper!" Louanne rises up, standing tall over the seated mourners surrounding her, rudely pointing her finger at me.

I'm stunned speechless as I stand frozen in place behind the lectern. I'm completely humiliated in front of the entire town, again. Triumphantly, Louanne sits down in a voluminous cloud of Victorian black crape fabric, her floor length weeping veil completely shrouding her body.

With a shocked look on his face, Reverend Peter rushes back to the lectern and takes the microphone into his hand. He sympathetically pats me on the shoulder with the other hand as I finally step away. Mortified, I make a hasty retreat from the stage as I hear the reverend resume speaking to the mourners. I stare at the floor boards as I scamper to the back of the church. Relieved, I slide into the pew next to Granny Fic and Gan. They look up at me in concern and flash green-fanged smiles of encouragement. Sam grabs my hand and squeezes it tightly.

"Are you okay? Louanne is unbelievable. Her behavior is so mean spirited. Do you want to leave early? We can high-tail it out of here right now."

"I'm okay Sam. Thanks for your concern. Let's see this thing through to the end. I'm grateful to be off that stage and back here with you and our grannies. Public speaking is definitely not for me."

"Well, you did great. You showed true grace under pressure. I like that you kept your eulogy positive and you only said kind words about Lew. I especially loved that you said you completely forgive Lew and Louanne." Sam takes my hand; pats it affectionately and then releases it.

"Sedona, you really held it together and you displayed dignity and grace. Good job." Missi whispers as she and Murphy both lean forward and pat me on the back.

"Yeah, you said exactly the right thing. Just ignore your cousin's rude outburst." Murphy advises with a quiet and gentle voice.

Chapter 47

Theme song: "Forgiven" by Crowder from the album American Prodigal Deluxe Edition

Reverend Peter speaks with humble authority to the crowded room. "Thank you, Sedona. Well said. We are truly children of God when we offer forgiveness, grace, and mercy to people that mistreat us. Your display of spiritual maturity shines like a light and is a good Christian example for the entire town. In the Gospel of Matthew, chapter 5, verses 14-16 NIV, Jesus encourages us by saying, 'You are the light of the world. A town built on a hill cannot be hidden. Neither do people light a lamp and put it under a bowl. Instead they put it on its stand, and it gives light to everyone in the house. In the same way, let your light shine before others, that they may see your good deeds and glorify your Father in heaven.' Friends, do you understand? In the Gospel of Matthew, chapter 4, verse 17, NIV it reads, 'From that time on Jesus began to preach, 'Repent, for the kingdom of heaven has come near.' Please take comfort in this next Scripture and hear this. Are you listening? In the Gospel of John, chapter 5, verse 24, NIV Jesus also tells us, 'Very truly I tell you, whoever hears my word and believes him who sent me has eternal life and will not be judged but has crossed over from death to life.'"

Reverend Peter smiles warmly at his listeners and begins speaking again. "Friends, don't you see? It's not too late to change your ways. God loves you. In the Gospel of Luke, chapter 15, verse 7, NIV, Jesus says to each and every one of us, 'I tell you that in the same way there will be more rejoicing in heaven over one sinner who repents than over ninety-nine righteous persons who do not need to repent.' Those words are the proof to show each and every one of us that our Heavenly Father always welcomes back His children. Return to God each and every one of you. It is time for you to begin attending our church services again. We have all missed you these past few years. I personally invite you to join us here Sunday morning at 11 a.m. You are always welcome in the house of God."

Finally, Reverend Peter wraps up the funeral service. "Friends." He intones in a strong and commanding deep voice. "I want to send you out into the world with one final verse. If you remember nothing else from this day, please, for your own good, remember these words from the Gospel of John, chapter 14, verse 6, NIV, 'Jesus answered, "I am the way and the truth and the life. No one comes to the Father except through me.' God bless each and every one of you. Jesus Christ is Lord and Messiah. Hallelujah. Peace, love, and blessings to everyone."

Chapter 48

Theme song: "Old Church Choir" by Zach Williams from the album Chain Breaker Deluxe Edition

Reverend Peter shifts his gaze to the back of the room and directs a kind smile toward me, then he picks up his *Holy Bible* and takes a seat in the chair placed next to the lectern. The church choir stands and begins singing a cappella John Newton's famous song "Amazing Grace."

After the choir concludes their song, Reverend Peter stands and returns to the lectern. "Friends, I invite you all to please stay with us a little longer this afternoon for a brief celebration of life service for Lew. As you probably already know, we're a Baptizing church. I invite you to join the family of God today, right here and now. If any of you are ready to accept God and Jesus Christ and to receive the gift of eternal life, I invite you to join me at the Baptismal pool and to receive your Holy Baptism. According to the Gospel of Matthew chapter three we believe in a Baptism of repentance for those who need to come back to God and to repent for their sins."

Reverend Peter stands quietly for several minutes observing the crowd of people seated in the pews. Apparently satisfied that everyone is paying attention, he continues his sermon.

"During this time, I will also perform the solemn ritual of Holy Communion next to the Baptismal pool. Please form an orderly line up the center aisle and everyone come to the stage and let's save souls today. I'm right here to help you and this is your chance to be Born Again into the Body of Christ and to receive forgiveness and eternal salvation. God is calling you right now. Will you answer His call? All you have to do is be brave enough to take the first step and simply join me at the pool during the musical performances. If you were Baptized as an infant, I invite you to come renew your Baptism with a Baptism of repentance. I believe it's crucial and more meaningful for each adult to actively choose Baptism for yourself, since as infants we don't understand this decision. My belief is based on the fact that as an adult, Jesus Christ chose to be baptized by John the Baptist. When Jesus arose from the Jordan river the Holy Spirit descended upon Him. This is your opportunity to start anew on your journey with God of Heaven and Jesus Christ, our Lord and Savior. Now, I'll turn this part of our service over to our talented church band, The Angelic Holy Rollers, and our wonderful choir who is singing with them today." Reverend Peter smiles excitedly at the crowd, as he steps away from the lectern and walks across the stage over to the Baptismal pool, which is set farther back.

The Angelic Holy Rollers step up onto the stage. The band members are dedicated members of the church who love to praise God with Christian rock music. They stroll confidently to their instruments.

Logan strides over to the keyboards and begins playing a tuneful melody while his bandmates reach for their musical instruments. Wayne, the tall bearded choral singer reveals his deep baritone singing voice through a mesmerizing Gregorian chant.

The talented lead guitarist Buddy picks up a Fender Player Telecaster and unleashes a riff that resonates across the crowded church. Brenda and Luna-Maria are leading a team of interpretive dancers wearing angel costumes. Together they are dancing gracefully on the stage. The dancers are swaying, twirling, and shaking tambourines decorated with colorful ribbons and long glittery streamers that are swirling in the air around them. Their angel wings and halos sparkle under the stage lights.

The rhythm guitarist Karen smiles and picks up an acoustic-electric guitar. It's a Taylor 414-ce grand auditorium. She pushes her long silver hair out of the way and settles the guitar strap over her shoulder. She strums a few powerful chords and the musical notes sing out like a clear ringing bell and resonate across the room.

The bass player Eric takes hold of a Fender Player Mustang Bass PJ and pulls the guitar strap over his head. He plucks the strings and a roll of thunderous beats boom across the stage. The drummer Diane takes her place on the drum throne at the metallic gray Pearl drum kit. She joins in and taps out a quick rhythm. Diane smiles charmingly and twirls her drumsticks and then continues unleashing a tattoo of drum rolls and cymbal crashes.

The lead singer Rachael grasps a hand-held microphone and waves hello to the people seated in the pews. "Hi everyone. Our heartfelt condolences on the loss of our friend and neighbor Lew. Let's send our dearly departed brother in Christ off to Heaven with love and some of our favorite music. Sing along with us during our performances. Come up front to Rev. Peter at the Baptismal pool and get your Holy Baptism and accept Holy Communion. Eternal life is God's gift to all people. You don't have to earn it; you only have to believe it. Accept Jesus Christ and come up here and claim your free gift of eternal life. Please pray with me now. Heavenly Father, we love you, we worship you, and we praise your Almighty name. We give thanks to you for every blessing. Father, we ask for forgiveness and eternal life in Heaven with you. Please bless us with the Holy Spirit and let Him guide us to do your will. Please work within our church today to change lives and to call your children back to you. We ask for this in Jesus' name. Amen. Now we're ready to perform covers of songs from some of our favorite Christian musicians in celebration of our brother Lew returning home to God. Okay, let's praise the Lord together." Rachael smiles and nods her head to her band members.

The Angelic Holy Rollers unleash a rousing rendition of Crowder's song "Grave Robber" from the album The Exile. It's the perfect Christian rock song to start Lew's celebration of life service, especially with Reverend Peter standing at the Baptismal pool ready to perform Holy Baptisms.

The next song The Angelic Holy Rollers unleash is Anne Wilson's "Hey Girl" from the album My Jesus Anniversary Deluxe Edition. The church is thumping with joyful music and everyone is singing along with their hands raised up toward Heaven.

I feel a sudden overpowering urge to get up and go speak with Louanne. I truly want to hide in my seat next to my friends, where I feel safe and comfortable. Except this strong feeling won't let me go, and it's compelling me to seek out my cousin and try to set things right between us. I don't know if it's even possible to set our relationship back on the right track, but this is my last chance to try.

"Sam, I need to go up front and talk with Louanne. Granny Fic and Gan please stay here in the pew with Sam."

"What? Are you serious? After everything she put you through?" Sam is flabbergasted at my dubious plan.

"It's a leap of faith." I reply and I pat her hand to reassure her. "Don't worry. I'll be fine and I'll meet you all outside after this is over." I smile at Sam and then I turn around to smile at Missi and Murphy.

"Okay, Sedona. We'll see you later. Godspeed." Missi replies. Murphy, holding his wife's hand smiles encouragingly.

I rise from the safety of my seat. I march resolutely toward the family section where Louanne is still sitting with her girl squad. It's hard to approach this group of people who clearly don't like me. I feel uncomfortable and at a loss for words. *What should I say to Louanne? What can possibly repair this broken relationship?*

I raise my head and look toward the front pew. I notice Reverend Peter is smiling encouragingly at me from the stage. It feels as if he understands my mission to repair my relationship with my cousin. It's encouraging to know that he is supportive.

As I arrive at the pew where Louanne is sitting, I reach out and gently tap her on the shoulder. I can barely see her face shrouded inside the enormous black weeping veil. The Angelic Holy Rollers begin performing the song "Crazy People" by the band Casting Crowns from the album Healer Deluxe Edition. I smile joyfully and a nervous giggle escapes my lips. I try to control my emotions but the song is so perfect for my situation right now. It's one of my favorite songs and I'm happy to be one of God's crazy people who put all of our faith, hope, and trust in the Holy Trinity. *Perhaps the world thinks we're crazy for following God of Heaven and trusting Him to guide our path and every choice we make and every action we take.*

"Hi Louanne. Cousin, we need to talk." I gently bite down on my bottom lip so I don't laugh again as I silently sing the lyrics of "Crazy People." I notice that all of her friends are glaring at me with annoyance for interrupting their time with their ringleader.

"What do you want, Sedona? You have some nerve coming up here to bother me!"

Chapter 49

Theme song: "What if I Gave Everything" by Casting Crowns from the album The Very Next Thing

"Louanne, despite everything that has happened, you and I are still family. Why don't we start acting like it? I want you to know that I found out what you and Lew planned together. I know everything that you did. How would you feel if someone treated you the way that you and Lew treated me?"

Louanne stubbornly stares at me in silence. Through her veil, I can barely see her face, but it's definitely wearing a stony-eyed expression. Finally, she softens her features and then she shrugs her shoulders at me.

"That's it? There's nothing that you want to say to me?" I shake my head at her stubborn refusal to own up to her actions. However, I'm not ready to give up yet.

"What you and Lew did to me was immoral, harmful, and very painful to me. Essentially, you stole my husband and my home. You chose to participate with Lew to ruin my marriage, my home, and my personal finances. Your actions with Lew were cruel but they can't be undone. So that being said, even though it's the hardest thing for me to do, I choose to forgive you. Even so, you still need to make amends for your actions. I'm asking you to share some of your millions with the food bank charity Feeding America. You now have the wealth and ability to change lives for the better, instead of causing harm. You have the opportunity to use your abundant wealth to help people. Make sure that you donate generously and give a portion of the money to charity. Choose to be a force for good in the world and help people when you can. I don't want there to be any lingering bad feelings between us. So, I want to say that I'm sorry for the way that our relationship has been so unhealthy in the past. Let's leave it behind us. I want us to start over and to become friends."

The Angelic Holy Rollers start playing an emotionally charged cover of Crowder's song "Somebody Prayed" from the album The Exile. The loud music and truthful lyrics wash over me while I wait for Louanne to make up her mind.

"Well, since you scurried up here to grovel at my feet, I guess I can forgive you, Sedona."

I can tell that Louanne is smirking at me from behind her weeping veil and her friends laugh loudly right to my face.

Hmm, forgive me for what exactly? It should be the other way around. *Okay, Heavenly Father I choose to forgive Louanne for mistreating me and for stealing my husband and for conspiring with him. I also choose to forgive Lew for perpetrating this deception against me. I pray that you will forgive them. I ask for this in Jesus' name, amen.* After my heartfelt prayer, I feel an immediate rush of peace wash over me and my emotional pain is soothed.

"Well, Sedona I can give some money as a donation to Feeding America. I will do it in memory of Lew, and for the tax write-off and financial benefits to me. I'm certainly not doing it for you or because you asked me to. I'm very curious about your personal motives. Why are you asking me to donate money? What do you get out of it, Sedona?" Louanne responds vehemently with a harsh, criticizing tone in her voice.

"Louanne, in the *Holy Bible* Gospels, Jesus advises his followers to sell our belongings and to give the money to help others. So, since you willingly participated with Lew's plans to deceive me, which ultimately enabled Lew to sell my home without my consent, the least that you can do is to use some of the money to help other people. I always try to follow Jesus' teachings. That is what I get out of it, following Jesus' teachings faithfully. It's the most important thing to me. It should be important to you as well, since you were raised up in the church your whole life." I patiently explain to my difficult cousin. If I can show her a better way, and lead her into following Jesus, maybe it will help bring healing and much needed peace to her life.

In the next moment, The Angelic Holy Rollers switch songs and the crowded room is filled with an enthusiastic version of Zach Williams's song "Baptized" from the album Rescue Story. As the meaningful lyrics take root in my soul, I suddenly realize that this is the only solution to our relationship problems. *With God of Heaven all things are possible. Thank you, Heavenly Fa-*

ther. I give thanks to you for making a way forward for us. Of course this is what you wanted all along, for peace to be restored and for broken relationships to be healed. Heavenly Father thank you for leading me. I will faithfully follow you. In Jesus' name I pray, amen.

Chapter 50

Theme song: "No Matter What" by Ryan Stevenson featuring Bart Millard from the album No Matter What

"Louanne, if you are ready to be friends, stand up and drop your black shroud. I want to give you a hug cousin." I smile at my cousin with a playful challenge and I hope that she chooses to cooperate with me.

Louanne shrugs her shoulders at her friends as she stands up and takes off her floor length weeping veil. Carelessly, she tosses it on the pew bench. The shiny and slinky fabric flows like a waterfall and slides off the smooth wooden pew and puddles onto the floor boards at her feet. I gently enfold her in a hug of reconciliation.

"Come on then, Louanne. I dare you to come up here and get baptized with me. Louanne, the *Holy Bible* teaches us that the Kingdom of God has come upon us and we need to repent for our sins now. Don't delay. We also have to stop our sinful behavior. God of Heaven is calling us to believe in Him and His only Son, Jesus Christ."

Louanne silently stares at me with a moody gleam in her eyes. She turns to her rowdy friends and they laugh aloud again.

"Louanne, if you want eternal salvation, then you need to accept God in your life and to place your trust in God, Jesus, and the Holy Spirit. Louanne, are you bold enough to love and to serve God? Are you feeling courageous enough to follow Jesus? Are you brave enough to repent for your sins and to begin following Jesus today? It's the best decision that you will ever make in your entire life. If you believe in God and Jesus Christ, you will receive eternal life in Heaven. Trust me, salvation from God of Heaven is more valuable than anything on Earth. Please understand that I acknowledge and I agree that each person has free will and every person should make their own choices in life and especially about the religion they choose to follow. I sincerely respect human cultures and religions. I sincerely respect your right to make your own personal choices about your own individual lifestyle. I also believe in the rights to freedom of speech, the freedom to choose your own religion and to practice religion, and the freedom of expression. I sincerely respect all people and their own personal choices about living their own lifestyles. Travel your own unique path in life. Whatever you choose to believe in: I wish you peace, love, and blessings."

"I'm not sure and I'm feeling conflicted right now. I grew up in this church and I'm from a Christian family but I turned away a long time ago. As an adult, I've lived my own life by making decisions on a whim of selfish emotions for so long now. I don't know if God will welcome me back and I don't know if I can do all the work of following Jesus' teachings in the Gospels. To me, being a Christian seems like a lot of requirements to fulfill."

This is probably the first time that I have ever heard my cousin speak from the heart. It's progress and I'm grateful for her willingness to speak honestly with me. Entrenched self-destructive habits have held her captive for much of her adult life and she has chosen to follow a selfish and unhealthy path that has only caused her to be desperately unhappy. I sincerely want to see her set free and to be truly happy.

"Louanne, have you been content and do you feel that you are living with peace and joy in your soul, especially considering the choices and the path you have been following in recent years? Has turning away from God of Heaven brought you closer to salvation? Do you honestly think that your life choices will lead to eternal life?"

"No, probably not. Honestly, I haven't been happy in decades and I've been struggling with an endless desire to buy more things and to try to live a more lavish lifestyle than my friends. I've been focused on chasing relationships in an effort to be loved and to feel special. I've been focused on selfish desires and collecting worldly wealth and luxury possessions that I thought would make me feel special and successful. I only managed to fill up my house and my garage with a lot of expensive items that I don't actually want. They do not bring me happiness, peace, or joy at all. My personal relationships keep failing and I still end up unloved and all alone. Everyone eventually walks away from me and so I keep pursuing new relationships. I don't understand why they keep failing. Collecting money and objects doesn't seem to fill up the dark empty space inside my soul. I thought that winning against you by stealing Lew away and having all of his attention would make me feel special and much happier. Right in this moment, I can see that it only brought me heartache and shame. Why would God want me back after everything I've done?" Louanne's eyes are shining with tears and she looks miserable as she stares at me.

I feel a pang of sympathy and compassion for my cousin. Life is really hard and we all make mistakes and often we choose the wrong path. I believe that it is never too late to make positive changes and to reverse unhealthy choices.

"Louanne, God wants you back no matter what because He created you and He loves you. The kind of love that God offers is everlasting, it's not like the kind of love that humans share. Human love is fragile and fleeting but that's not the case with God. His love is unbreakable and His love is eternal. I understand the struggles that you have been going through. I'm sorry that you have been experiencing failed relationships. I know exactly how that feels and how devastating it is. The truth is all of us have experienced what you're going through at one time or another. You are not alone in your struggles. Don't give up hope. Your life can get better but it's completely up to you to make the necessary changes in your behavior and your choices."

"I know it. I just don't know how to get started."

"Professional counseling and therapy are great tools to help you make changes in your life. It's not easy starting over but it's entirely possible. The crucial truth that you're missing is that God of Heaven and Jesus Christ love you, no matter what you have done. Jesus teaches us in the Gospels that all kinds of sin and slander can be forgiven, except for one sin. Jesus calls it the eternal sin, which He explained is speaking out against the Holy Spirit. So, doesn't that mean that 99% of sins can be forgiven? That's very generous! It sure makes it easier to get into Heaven. I believe we are always welcome and it's not too late, if we sincerely want to return to God. I believe He is the God of second chances. That's why He sent Jesus Christ to the cross to be the atoning sacrifice for the forgiveness of our sins. I want you to know that God helps us to believe and to grow our faith, all we have to do is to answer His call. Louanne, if you choose to accept God and Jesus Christ, then God will heal you and faithfully guide you along His chosen path for you. God of Heaven gives the Holy Spirit to everyone who believes in Him. The Holy Spirit is a precious gift and once you receive it, you can never lose it. I believe that with the Holy Spirit living within our souls, belonging to God of Heaven is the most joyful and fulfilling experience of our existence on Earth and also in Heaven, for eternity. This is your chance to receive eternal salvation and to have life everlasting in Heaven. Will you make a fresh start by accepting God's invitation today? You have to choose for yourself what happens to your soul. It is the burden of free will that all of humanity carries. What do you choose to believe in?"

As I pose my questions to my cousin, The Angelic Holy Rollers launch into a new song. It's my favorite song by I AM THEY featuring Matthew West "Found my Freedom" from the album Faithful God. The inspirational message and music are rocking the church. I'm swaying and tapping my foot in time with the music. I suddenly clasp hands with my cousin and I twirl us in a circle, right in the middle of the aisle. Heads are turning in our direction. Our neighbors are curious to see what happens between us after Lew and Louanne's ill-fated love affair.

"Louanne, the *Holy Bible* teaches that Jesus Christ gives you living water when you accept God as your Heavenly Father and Jesus Christ as your personal Lord and Savior. It means that God will immediately bless you with the gift of the Holy Spirit. In time, with healing and counseling, you will be overflowing with love and joy that never leaves you."

"I would like to have lasting joy and love. Being blessed sounds like a much better way to live my life." Louanne mulls over these new ideas and possibilities for her future.

"Louanne, I truly want you to have peace, love, and blessings. The gift of eternal life is within your reach; it's right here just waiting for you to choose it. The Holy Spirit will become your guide and He will never leave you. He will faithfully guide you to follow God's will and His plan for your life. Your soul will be saved for all of eternity. Your life will be filled with God's promise from now on."

"Louanne to be clear, it doesn't mean that your life will suddenly be completely perfect because we live in a fallen world of sin, but it does mean that you will be walking with the most powerful force in the universe: The Holy Trinity. When things go wrong as they often do, you can lean on the promises of God with blessed assurance that your soul is safe within His care. I'm still able to find peace and joy through my close and personal relationship with God, even in the worst of times. I want that for you too. With God, all things are possible. Eternal life from God of Heaven is the only gift we really need and it's the only gift we never want to return. It's all that truly matters in our entire existence and I sincerely hope that no one misses their chance to receive it. Don't miss your chance."

Chapter 51

Theme song: "Amen" by Matthew West from the album All In

"I choose God! I want to return to God. I believe in God of Heaven and Jesus Christ. I accept God as my Heavenly Father and I accept Jesus Christ as my personal Lord and Savior. I choose to repent for my sins and I want to get baptized so that I can be forgiven and saved for eternity. I want eternal life in Heaven with God and Jesus!" Louanne asserts joyously.

The Angelic Holy Rollers enthusiastically perform a rousing cover of Zach Williams's song "Everything Changed" from the album Chain Breaker Deluxe Edition. The powerful song is filling the church with hope and I smile at Louanne and hold out my hand in invitation to her.

"Louanne, I'm happy for you. I'm grateful that we repaired our relationship. Welcome back to the family of Christ. How do you feel?"

"I feel a little different. Like maybe everything is possible for me now. The ability to receive healing and the chance to make healthy changes in my life are possible now that I belong to God. Hopeful for my future, yes that's how I feel."

Relief floods my soul. In helping my wayward and troubled cousin come back to God and Jesus, I am also overcoming the soul crushing obstacles of anger, betrayal, and deep emotional pain. I choose to forgive everything and to repair a badly damaged relationship. *It's not easy following God, but it's so worth it. Obeying God of Heaven and His will repairs my heart and soul. Life everlasting and receiving the eternal peace and joy in Heaven triumphs over the trauma within the human condition here on Earth.*

"Good, now let's go get baptized together. Are you ready?"

Louanne nods at me, suddenly speechless with her overwhelming and lifesaving decision. Silently, she grabs my hand and holds onto my arm with her other hand as we walk up onto the stage together. With peace and harmony restored, we approach Reverend Peter and the Baptismal pool.

Chapter 52

Theme song: "Washed Clean" by Zach Williams from the album Chain Breaker Deluxe Edition

"Ladies, I'm delighted that you have reconciled with one another. The saints and angels are singing in Heaven right now. Come to the living water." Reverend Peter smiles the most beatific smile that I have ever seen. The radiance of his smile expresses pure joy for our repaired relationship and for our acceptance of God's will and His plan for our lives. With reverence, the reverend performs the Holy Baptism ceremonies for my cousin and I. Immediately afterward we partake in Holy Communion.

When Louanne steps out of the Baptismal pool, I wrap her in a dry towel. I give my cousin a hug of gratitude and I feel happy that we have finally put our differences behind us. Louanne stands as witness for me, smiling with peace and glowing with joy as I receive my Baptism for the repentance of my sins.

As I rise up from the Holy Water, a huge sense of relief overwhelms me because all of my sins are washed away. I feel renewed and at peace with God. With forgiveness, contentment settles deep inside my soul. Even though I was Baptized when I first accepted Jesus Christ, I feel grateful for the opportunity to repent for my sins and to renew my Baptism and my covenant with my Heavenly Father. *Hallelujah!*

As we step down from the stage, we are handed fresh dry towels. We dry off as much as we can and then we each drape a dry towel around our shoulders. With harmony and peace restored in our relationship, my cousin and I smile as we walk back to our places in the pews together.

"Louanne, promise me that you will call me soon. Let's not waste this second chance. I promise to stay in contact with you as well. Would it be okay if I come to visit you for Christmas?"

"Sedona that's a fantastic idea. I will try to call you at least once a month and we can get to know each other truly and sincerely. I'm very sorry for my reprehensible and selfish actions, please forgive me. I'm sorry for the wasted years and I promise to make up for it. A Christmas visit sounds lovely. I'm a great cook and I love serving holiday meals. I'm looking forward to seeing you for Christmas. Please bring your friends if they would like to join us. It would be nice to get to know them too. Our last Christmas together was when we were still kids, right?" Louanne smiles playfully at me.

"Oh, goodness gracious. I nearly forgot about that Christmas argument we had when we were kids. I'm so glad that we have finally grown up. I'll see you at Christmas. This one will be peaceful and joyful for sure." I grin sheepishly at the painful memory of our childish and angry disagreements. I'm very glad that those days are in the past.

Now that the first couple of Baptisms are accomplished, more people are willing to come forward. The line down the center aisle is quite long and I notice with surprise that Sam, Missi, and Murphy are in line as well. I stop by to chat briefly and I hug my friends, then I return to my pew to sit with Granny Fic and Gan. We're joyful witnesses as our friends are baptized into the family of God and Jesus Christ. I'm so grateful that many souls are being saved today. I know in my heart that there is rejoicing right now in Heaven over all of the newly saved souls.

After all of the Holy Baptisms are conducted and the last Holy Communion is concluded, everyone returns to their seats in the pews. Together as a peaceful and united church congregation, we sing along to the last song covered by The Angelic Holy Rollers. It's the hauntingly beautiful song "Gratitude" by the band I AM THEY, featuring Cheyenne Mitchell from the album Chapel Sessions. The ethereal music flows throughout the church and the blending harmonies of all the voices in God's house bring healing and peace to the mourners.

After the conclusion of the funeral, I chat briefly with a few people who kindly offer me condolences. Finally, I cautiously make my way over to visit with Lew's brother Stew for a short conversation.

"Hello, Stew. I am sincerely sorry for your loss. I want you to know that I loved your brother sincerely and faithfully in the best way that I could. I still love him and I forgive him. I'm sorry how things turned out between Lew and I. I hope you will take comfort in the knowledge that I truly believe that Lew is welcomed into Heaven. I believe that God is loving and merciful. I believe through the grace of our Lord Jesus Christ that God forgives His disobedient children. I will continue to pray for you and your family."

"I'm sorry too, Sedona. Thanks for saying that. I believe he is welcomed into Heaven too. I'm sorry that my brother let you down. He didn't appreciate you and love you in the way that he should have. I know that he wasn't good at handling relationships and quite frankly I always thought that he didn't deserve a good woman like you, but I know that he was very lucky to have you in his life." Stew blinks his watery eyes as he gazes sadly at me. He reaches out and gives me a comforting hug.

"Peace be with you." As I speak Jesus' comforting words to Stew, I feel peace descend upon me as well. Once and for all, I feel that this emotional chapter in my life is closed. I slowly make my way through the crowded church. Without looking back, I step through the heavy, carved-wood doors out of The Dusty and into the light.

Chapter 53

Theme song: "We Believe" by Newsboys from the album Restart Deluxe Edition

My companions are waiting patiently outside in the bright desert sunlight. They envelop me in a compassionate group hug. We laugh a little because our clothes are still damp from our immersion Baptisms. As my friends step back, Granny Fic and Gan stay close to me, standing on either side of me, they gently take hold of my hands. I inhale a delicious tiramisu scented breeze sent by my intergalactic grannies. I sigh audibly. As the translation of the word tiramisu implies, the scent is a real pick me up and I truly feel cheered up now. My grannies walk by my side as we slowly return to our campers. As we're walking, I feel my damp clothes drying out in the sunshine and wind.

"Missi and Murphy, I was thrilled to see you standing with Sam in the Baptism and Communion line. It's a momentous occasion. Each of you just received the gift of eternal life. It's wonderful. How do you feel now that you are Baptized and Born-Again Christians?"

"Sedona, I'm very relieved and excited. It feels like a lost part of my soul has been restored and healed. Thank you for bringing us to Lew's funeral. We wanted to be here as supportive friends for you, but it turned into an amazing life-changing blessing. What do you think Murphy? Do you feel the same way?"

"Indeed, I do. Even though we believe in God, Missi and I don't attend church back home. I'm glad that we met you Sedona. Otherwise, we never would have visited the Ashes to Ashes and Dust to Dust church. This trip turned out to be an incredible experience for Missi and I. I think it was the right time and place for us to make a new start in life."

"Sam, how about you? Do you feel any different now that you are Baptized?"

"I feel like a new creation. Like Missi and Murphy, I always believed in God as well. When I was growing up, I was taught to believe in God but my family never went to church. So, I never got into the habit of going to church either. Until today, I didn't even realize that getting Baptized was so important. Being here and listening to Reverend Peter's sermon was enlightening and I'm delighted that I got Baptized today. I don't think that I would've been brave enough to ever just randomly walk into a church and ask to get Baptized. It just felt right in this moment, here in this place, and especially after you forgave Lew and Louanne for their cruel betrayal. It really showed me how deeply your Christian values guide your life and I want that for myself as well."

"That's fantastic, I'm really pleased. Well, it has been an emotional and special day. While it was a sad occasion, I'm glad that something wonderful has arisen from the sorrow of Lew's tragedy. I don't know how you guys feel, but I'm too worn out to drive anymore today." I yawn hugely. "Is it okay if we boondock out here tonight? Missi and Murphy, you are welcome to stay in the Tumbleweed. I have a comfortable guest bed for you to use if you would like to stay with my grannies and I. It will save you the trouble of having to drive all the way back into Sandy Town to stay at the motel."

Missi nods her head in agreement. "I think that's just the thing we need right now, a quiet and restful night. It has been a momentous day. A beautiful, life-changing day."

"What a good idea. Since we're not driving tonight, I think it would be fun if we have dinner and a game night." Sam enthuses.

"I love the idea of dinner and gaming, Sam."

"Yeah, it's not spooky to camp next to a funeral parlor and an old graveyard in the desert wilderness. Not spooky at all." Murphy laughs with a playful smirk.

Missi grins and kisses her husband on the cheek. "Well, at least you're here to keep us safe." She looks fondly at her husband and gently runs her nails through his long beard.

When we reach our campers, I unlock the door of my Tumbleweed, where our four dogs have been napping during the funeral. They crowd the doorway in their excitement to greet us.

"Hello, puppies. Back up please." I gently flutter my hands toward Rex and Patch using the signal that I taught them when they were puppies. Immediately, my dogs take several steps backward, making enough room for us to climb the steps and enter the camper.

"Neat trick." Murphy smiles with amusement.

CJ and Rocky look perplexed and they continue standing in the doorway wagging their tails enthusiastically. Sam steps up first and her dogs follow her away from the entryway. They affectionately rub themselves against her legs as she leans down to scratch their backs and pet them.

Once everyone is settled comfortably inside, I walk back to my bedroom and change into my hiking clothes. Sam changes her clothes in the bathroom. Once I finish dressing, I slide into my hiking boots and collect my backpack. I toss in a bunch of baby carrots and refill my large water bottle and fetch our dogs' leashes. Now Sam and I are ready to enjoy a short hike with our dogs.

"Missi and Murphy, make yourselves at home. Please help yourselves to anything you need. There are plenty of snacks and drinks in the kitchen. There are cards and board games in this cabinet. I have Star Trek Galactic Enterprises, Star Trek Monopoly, and another card game called Yes, Yes Yeti Risk-Taking Card Game! Here's a deck of playing cards as well. Granny Fic and Gan will you please make sure our guests have everything they need? You are the hostesses while we are out walking the dogs." I set a plate of sliced Honeycrisp apples and cheddar cheese on the dining table, a bowl of pistachios, and then I pour everyone a glass of sparkling water.

Chapter 54

Theme song: "Walk with You" by Zach Williams from the album Rescue Story Deluxe Edition

As we step outside, I notice that the afternoon has become increasingly windy. At the corral, I smile when I see Topaz peacefully napping under her shade tarp. Above her head, the tarp flutters with the breeze and she snores loudly and twitches her ears. My smile widens when I notice that she is sleeping with a mouthful of hay and several long stalks of hay are sticking out on either side of her mouth. Topaz begins chewing her hay as she awakens at my approach.

"Hi Topaz. Let's go for a walk with Sam and the boys." I smile and scratch her gently under the jaw, then I clip a rope onto her halter.

We walk slowly, as the dogs stop and sniff the desert scrub plants and then eagerly follow every scent trail. It's a hot, sunny afternoon. I'm glad that I brought lots of water and baby carrots to share. I tighten the chin strap on my pink sunhat as the wind gusts a little harder.

"Sam, do you mind if I play music while we're walking the dogs?"

"Oh, that sounds good, Sedona. I love listening to music. What kind of music are you listening to these days?"

"I prefer Christian rock. Is that alright with you?"

"Of course. That sounds heavenly."

I pull my smartphone from my back pocket and open Pandora. I choose the Brandon Lake station and hit play. The first song that plays is Brandon Lake's song "That's Who I Praise" from the album King of Hearts.

"Sedona, I noticed that you stayed in control of your emotions and your behavior was calm and patient during the funeral. I think your cousin Louanne behaved rudely. It seemed like she was trying to goad you into making an embarrassing scene. Maybe she wanted to cause you to have a breakdown in front of the entire town? Her behavior was mean and yet you were respectful to her and then you told her that you forgive her. I could tell that you were completely sincere in your forgiveness. How do you do that? I don't think that I could have done the same."

I smile at Sam sauntering along in her stylish outfit. She looks relaxed in a pair of hiking boots, casual khaki slacks, and an adorable long sleeved, pale green linen blouse. She embroidered it with colorful flowers, butterflies, and hummingbirds. She peers at me from under a huge straw sunhat.

"Thank you for saying that, Sam. I was struggling to maintain my Christian dignity." I smile sadly at my friend. "It was devastating to see Lew's casket sitting in the church and that's such a terrible and final farewell. Such a sad ending and then I saw Lew's brother Stew sitting with Louanne. He looked so depressed and hopeless and so I knew that I had to be compassionate and keep my own emotions under control. It was the respectful thing to do but it wasn't easy." I glance over my shoulder and see a huge, shaggy gray dog following us at a distance. "Oh, look over there Sam. It looks like there's a stray dog following us."

"Oh, my word. That's not a wolf, is it? It's enormous and has a menacing appearance. I wonder what it's doing out here all alone? Is it wild?"

"Sam, I don't think there are wolves living in the deserts of Nevada. I think they're usually forest and mountain animals. We do have coyotes here but that's no coyote. I wonder if it's a wolf hybrid? Well, it hasn't tried to attack us. Maybe it's just a rather enormous stray dog. Let's stop here and I'll set out the water bowl for it. Poor thing, I wonder how long it has been wandering alone in the desert?"

I open my backpack and retrieve the pet bowl and water bottle. I fill it with cool water and then I place handfuls of fresh baby carrots next to the bowl. Sam and I move away with our leashed dogs and Topaz to give the stray some space and a chance to come over and get lifesaving sustenance. The next song that plays on my smartphone is "Lookin' for You" by Zach Williams from the album A Hundred Highways.

Chapter 55

Theme song: "God is in this Story" by Katy Nichole and Big Daddy Weave from the album Jesus Changed my Life Deluxe Edition

"By the way Sedona, what do you mean by your Christian dignity? I've never heard that expression before."

"Well, it's because I believe that God of Heaven is paying attention to my words and my behavior. It's unacceptable for anyone to claim to be a Christian but to behave sinfully, unlawfully, and inappropriately. So, I think to myself 'Remember your Christian dignity.' This thought reminds me not to sin and to give people as much grace as I'm able to give. So, I ask myself: Am I loving unconditionally and forgiving unconditionally? As a Christian, I make every effort to follow Jesus' teachings in the Gospels. God's standard is what I want to live up to and that is essentially what my Christian dignity means to me. I'm trying to make up for missed opportunities and to make up for all of the times that I didn't follow Jesus. I'm trying to be faithful but sometimes I fail. I'm still a work in progress but I'm sincerely trying to become the person God created me to be. I notice the more time I spend studying the *Holy Bible* and praying and asking God to help me change, the easier it gets."

I pause to take a drink of water from my water bottle and Pandora starts playing "I Need Jesus" by Matthew West from the album My Story Your Glory Expanded Edition.

"Oh, I thought that maybe you never struggled with your faith like I do. You have always seemed so devoted to God and to Jesus. It makes me feel encouraged to know that you are also a work in progress, like me. We can help each other as we practice our faith. So, what did you and Louanne talk about before you got Baptized together? I was surprised when you both went up to Reverend Peter at the Baptismal pool."

"Well, I tried to be kind, but I told her that I knew everything she did to help Lew ruin my happiness and to deceive me. I also asked her to make amends for their sins by sharing money from the sale of my home with the Feeding America food bank charity to help people. That way something good can come from the bad deeds that she and Lew did together. It makes me feel better and it helps me to be able to forgive them. Forgiving them helps me heal too. The amazing thing is that right then and there, she decided to change her life for the better and to return to God. So naturally, I invited her to get Baptized with me and we repaired our broken relationship through following God and Jesus. Remember Sam, with God all things are possible."

"Sedona, thanks for sharing your story with me. It gives me hope to know that it's never too late to return to God of Heaven, no matter what we have done. I guess that's the true meaning of grace and forgiveness. I'm thankful to be Baptized and to be a Born-Again Christian. I'm also completely amazed that you and Louanne are suddenly on friendly terms again. It didn't seem possible but I'm happy to hear it. It's hard to believe that she would just suddenly decide to be nice again."

"With God all things are possible, Sam. Although, I do understand how you feel, it's like whiplash. Maybe she needed someone to listen to her struggles and to encourage her. It's possible that she was acting out because of emotional trauma and it was a cry for help. I've been through it myself. We all need help in times of trouble. I'm sorry that she was struggling and no one else helped her. I sympathize and understand that she is wrestling with the challenges in life. All the unfairness, and the trauma, and heartbreak that we all endure. Louanne lost Lew as well. I'm trying to be compassionate, patient, and kind. I call it "managing personalities" we all have a personality to manage and it's not easy. I'm always struggling to manage my personality. I was very surprised myself that she accepted my offer of reconciliation and friendship. I'm grateful that she was willing to get Baptized with me and start our relationship over. I'm genuinely happy for her. She and I are going to spend Christmas together this year. Believe it or not Sam, she also invited you and Missi and Murphy to join us. She said that she loves to cook holiday meals and she would like to host us at her home here in Sandy Town."

"That is remarkable. I suppose that it would be an interesting holiday get together. Well, why not? Forgive and forget and follow Jesus to joy. It sounds like a good plan to me." As we're chatting, my Pandora app starts playing the song "All Joy no Stress" by Rhett Walker from the album Gospel Song.

Chapter 56

Theme song: "Redeemed" by Big Daddy Weave from the album Love Come to Life: The Redeemed Edition

As we're waiting for the stray dog to approach the food and water, the next song starts playing on Pandora. It's "Less Like Me" by Zach Williams from the album Rescue Story Deluxe Edition. As we stand listening to the music, we shift our feet and our hiking boots create tiny dust clouds as we stand patiently with our animal companions.

I slide my sunglasses down Mount Everest. I peer at the stray as it comes closer to us. Sam and I watch as the stray dog comes over to get a drink. After he empties the water bowl and gobbles up all of the baby carrots, the shaggy gray dog finally comes over to inspect us. He politely greets my dogs, wagging his tail in a flurry of grateful enthusiasm and then inquisitively sniffs around our boots and legs. Our dogs happily wag their tails and make friends with the newcomer. They sniff noses with the stray and then they sink into a bow, inviting him to play.

"Aw, these guys are cute together, Sedona. I'm surprised how quickly our dogs accept him into the pack. I think they understand that this guy needs our help. Will you adopt him?"

"Maybe. I need to be sure he's really all alone out here and hasn't just wandered away from his person."

"Sedona, I think that I'm ready to get a better understanding of God and Jesus but I haven't read much of the Bible yet. Have you read the whole Bible? Can I join you later when you do your Bible study?"

"Sam, I think that's a great idea. Let's do some Bible study together. At church in my Bible study classes, I've read the *Holy Bible* cover to cover twice. Now I spend more time studying the Gospels because as a follower of Jesus, I feel that it's very important for me to understand His teachings and to faithfully follow them. I'm happy that you want to join my study time. Believe it or not, it's really wonderful and fun." I push my sunglasses back up the high ridgeline of Mount Everest, my distinctive Roman nose. I smile at Sam, feeling quite cheered up now.

"Really Sedona? How can studying the *Holy Bible* be fun?"

"Oh, look Sam, this poor dog is really thin and he is not wearing a collar. I wonder if someone just dropped him off along the highway to fend for himself out here in the desert? That's just cruel. Let's see if he continues to follow us back to the Tumbleweed. To answer your question, I always play my favorite Christian praise and worship music before Bible study. I dance around singing along and joyfully praising and worshipping God. Then I study a few chapters in the Gospels and pray. Afterward, I make coffee and play my favorite video game, *Star Stable Online*."

"Mercy me, you're right. Your particular style of Bible study sounds fun. I can honestly say I'm looking forward to joining your class tonight. By the way, our new shaggy friend is still following us."

"Aw, poor lonely dog. I was hoping that he would run back to his person if they were out hiking together. Since he isn't wearing a collar, I'm guessing that he is indeed a lost stray. Well, I'll be happy to adopt him if he wants to come with me back to the Tumbleweed. He seems gentle and friendly enough. I can't leave him out here in the desert all alone."

I walk faster and adjust my grip on my dogs' leashes as they speed up a little. Sam lengthens her stride to keep up with us. Topaz trots along with us on her long lead rope. The big shaggy stray is trotting next to my dogs as we hike back to my camper. It looks like we're officially adopted by the homeless dog. Pandora is now playing the song "I got You" by Zach Williams from the album A Hundred Highways. As we're strolling along with our dogs and Topaz, I hold up my smartphone and show Sam my YouVersion Bible app.

"Sam, I use YouVersion every day to read or listen to the *Holy Bible*. You should use it too. One of the many features that I like is the audio Bible. YouVersion will read the entire *Holy Bible* to you. I use *The Listener's Bible: NIV Edition* but there are many different versions of the Bible to choose from. I listen to the Bible while playing *Star Stable Online* and when doing chores, cooking, and even when I'm flossing and brushing my teeth. I pay attention and listen carefully. I'm sincerely trying to learn Jesus' message in the Gospels and I want to keep my focus on God. I think YouVersion will be helpful to you as well because they also have hundreds of educational guided Bible study plans included in the app. These study plans are written by reverends and other qualified experts in theology to help you develop a deep understanding of God's word and how to apply it to your daily life. I use the guided Bible study plans every week."

"It sounds like a good idea. I will try it. I think our game night will be much more meaningful if we all do Bible study together first."

"Amen to that. Well, would you look at that, it appears I have just adopted a new furry family member." The lonely stray follows me to the door of my Tumbleweed. "Sam, would you please bring Patch and Rex inside with you and your dogs? I'll turn out Topaz in her corral and then I'm going to give my new friend here a good flea combing, brushing, and a thorough shampooing right here at the Tumbleweed's outdoor shower before I invite him inside."

Chapter 57

Theme song: "No Other Name" by Casting Crowns from the album The Very Next Thing

As Sam steps inside the Tumbleweed, she sees Murphy and Missi working in the kitchen. Murphy is making mocktails. He mixes sparkling water and cranberry juice over ice and garnishes the glasses with a slice of lime and a sprig of mint. Missi prepares celery sticks filled with cream cheese, along with Havarti, and Cheddar cheeses served with multigrain crackers and sliced fruit.

I finally climb inside the Tumbleweed, bringing my freshly groomed shaggy dog with me. Everyone welcomes him with gentle petting and a few tidbits from the bowl of baby carrots on the counter. Sam and I feed our dogs. With full bellies, they pile into the pet beds for a snooze. Murphy hands each of us a drink.

"Mocktails and appetizers, Murphy and Missi this is a nice surprise. You're so thoughtful, thanks."

Sam tastes her drink and smiles. "Ah, this is so good after a long hike."

"Sedona, where did you find this handsome young fellow?" Missi asks while petting my new canine companion.

"This sweet guy was wandering all by himself out in the desert. He started following us on our hike and he made friends with our dogs. I'm calling him Windy because we met him on a very windy day. Before we leave tomorrow, I'll take him to the town vet for a health checkup. Maybe the vet will know who his person is and can reunite them. If not, he's welcome to stay with me."

"That's a cute name for him. I like it and I guess you didn't want to call him Sandy even though you found him in the desert, because Old Judge Sandy caused you so much grief with his antiquated laws. I'm glad you rescued him before he expired of thirst or had a deadly encounter with a rattlesnake." Missi smiles and offers me the plate of sliced fruit with cheese and crackers.

"What breed do you think he is? He's huge and very shaggy." Murphy comments as he gently scratches Windy's neck.

"I'm not sure but he kind of resembles a deer hound or maybe a wolf hound. I wonder how much he weighs? He is giant."

"Yeah, I was thinking the same thing. I guess close to a hundred pounds, even though he is pretty lean." Sam responds.

While enjoying our mocktails, we work together in the kitchen gathering ingredients and setting out a healthy meal. On the table, we arrange the appetizers and platters of romaine lettuce, shaved Parmesan cheese, Rosso Sicilian tomatoes, Tropea onions, capers, and sliced oven-roasted chicken breast. For the dressing, there is olive oil and pepper with freshly chopped rosemary, basil, and oregano.

We slide carefully into the u-shaped dining booth. We laugh at our awkward seating squeezed shoulder to shoulder, with Granny Fic and Gan hovering at the edges of the booth. I say the blessing for us and we enjoy the delicious meal.

After we finish eating, Sam and I volunteer to wash the dishes. While we're chatting together, I remind Missi and Murphy they are more than welcome to bunk in the Tumbleweed. Even with myself and my grannies and three large dogs, there is still more sleeping room here than in Sam's cozy Bambi.

Chapter 58

Theme song: "That's what we Need" by Anne Wilson from the album My Jesus Anniversary Deluxe Edition

"Hey Missi and Murphy, Sam and I had an idea for this evening's entertainment. Would you like to join our Bible study and afterward play *Star Stable Online* with us?"

"Oh, well we haven't really read the *Holy Bible* yet. Um, what do you think Murphy?" Missi turns to Murphy, kisses him and gently runs her nails through his thick beard.

"It's always a yes to playing video games, my sweet. I'll fetch our laptops from the truck. Missi, I think we should join the ladies' Bible study. Now that we are Baptized, it's time to learn more about what it means to be Christians. Together we are on a new journey in life and I'm happy to travel on this path with you, my love." Murphy takes his wife's hand and places a kiss in her palm.

On my laptop, I navigate to YouTube and go to Crowder's channel where I choose a great song for our Bible study time. I turn up my sound system and press play on Crowder's song "Milk & Honey" from the album Milk & Honey. *It's a song that's delicious to my ears and also nutritious to my soul.* Tonight, I skip my usual habit of dancing and singing to spare my friends, I don't want to scare them away. While I do have good rhythm thanks to years of playing guitar, I'm a clumsy dancer and I can't carry a tune.

The next song I choose is "a lil Church (nobody's too lost)" by TobyMac from the album Heaven on my Mind. When the music is finished, I cue up the Gospel of Matthew in my YouVersion Bible app. From the nearby cabinet, I fetch my hardback copy of the *Holy Bible* New International Version. I smile as I pass it to Sam so she can share it with Missi and Murphy. I think the Gospel of Matthew is a good place to introduce Sam, Missi, and Murphy to Jesus' ministry.

We take turns reading aloud in the first seven chapters and then we pray together. After the conclusion of our prayer and to wrap up our Bible study, I play a few more songs for us on YouTube. First, I play Matthew West's song "Don't Stop Praying" from the album Don't Stop Praying. Next, I select "Holy Rollin'" by Zach Williams from the album A Hundred Highways. I love this song and it feels rather appropriate considering we're sitting inside a wheeled transport vehicle. I also play "King" by Crowder featuring Maverick City Gospel Choir from the album Milk & Honey Deluxe Edition.

"I'm surprised that the *Holy Bible* is way more exciting than I realized. It's full of action and adventure, drama, and it introduces the world to the original supernatural hero, Jesus. All those famous comic book heroes are just fictional copycats. Although, I always liked Superman, he's dreamy. I did enjoy the music as well. I wanted to get up and dance a little but I didn't want to disrupt our class." Missi says.

"Hey, I love comic books and I still read them all the time. Hmm, should I be worried about your secret crush on Superman? I thought I was your dreamy hero. Missi you can dance anytime you want, sweetheart. I love that you enjoyed the *Holy Bible*. I found the chapters pretty easy to understand. I really liked the part in Matthew chapter three where John the Baptist lived alone in the desert wilderness subsisting on locusts and wild honey. He was the original wilderness survivalist but much better because he was a prophet and serving God by preparing the way for Jesus. I wonder if the popular TV shows *Survivor* and *Naked and Afraid* were inspired by his lifestyle? Except that John wore clothing made of camel's hair so he wasn't naked and he definitely wasn't afraid because God was looking after him, so never mind." Murphy answers with humor twinkling in his eyes.

"I like comic books too. When I was a little kid, I read the *Archie* comics and I watched the TV show *Wonder Woman* which was based on DC Comics. I also watched *Star Trek* as a kid and I still do as an adult. I've seen all of the various *Star Trek* TV series and movies. But I digress. I'm glad that everyone enjoyed our Bible study as much as I did. I thought that starting in the Gospel of Matthew would be easier. To me, it has a clear message and it gets right to the heart of what we need to believe in order to receive life everlasting." I comment.

"I love that we can praise God through music. It's meaningful to me to have Christian music in Bible study. It makes it feel more like a church service." Sam responds while she steps over to the cabinet and places the hardback copy of the *Holy Bible* inside.

"Me too, Sam. Christian music enhances my sense of blessedness. I use *The Listener's Bible: NIV Edition* on the YouVersion Bible app and also listening to Christian music on Pandora is my daily habit. It makes me happy. Whether I'm driving, hiking, or sky watching I'm always listening to the Gospels and to my favorite Christian music. There are a lot of talented Christian musicians that are working hard to share God's message and Jesus' ministry. In case you're curious, these are the musical artists that I enjoy listening to: Anne Wilson, Carly Pearce, Cheyenne Mitchell, Katy Nichole, Zach Williams, Crowder, Maverick City Gospel Choir, Bart Millard and MercyMe, Sam Wesley, Walker Hayes, Casting Crowns, Matthew West, TobyMac, Rhett Walker, Jeremy Camp, I AM THEY, Big Daddy Weave, Third Day, Chris Tomlin, Ryan Stevenson, Gabe Real, Newsboys, Mac Powell, Brandon Lake, Pastor Steven Furtick, and Elevation Worship among many others. Oh, do you mind if I play one more song for us? You need to hear "Truth be Told" from the album The Exile by Crowder. This fellowship gathering was a nice change for me. It's enjoyable to have a group of friends to study with. Most nights, it's just me listening to music and reading the Gospels aloud to Granny Fic and Gan. Now, is everyone ready to play *Star Stable Online* together?"

Several hours later, Sam wishes us a good night and returns to her Bambi with CJ and Rocky. I convert the dining booth into a queen-size bed for Missi and Murphy. Then I make it cozy with soft sheets, pillows, and blankets. Granny Fic and Gan are dressed in the long white nightgowns that Sam created for them. The gowns are covered in ribbons, lace, ruffles, and embroidery. They are charmingly old fashioned and their style is Victorian era with a high neckline, long sleeves, and a hem line that grazes the floor. My prim and proper grannies are also wearing white bonnets over their wigs, with long ribbons tied under their chins. With their elegant nightgowns trailing below them, my intergalactic grannies float gracefully up into the cab over bunk. They glide under the colorful patchwork quilts to get their nightly rest. I smile as I notice they don't actually lie on the bunk cushions. Instead, they levitate a few inches above them with the quilts draped over them.

Like me, they enjoy reading before going to sleep. Both of my grannies are clutching their copies of *Aliens, Campers, and Coffee* by Karen Bruno. I blow a kiss good night to my grannies. Granny Gan catches the kiss and his long claws make a loud clacking noise as he closes his hand around the airborne kiss. Granny Fic blows me a return kiss good night. Soon, the Tumbleweed is peaceful and quiet and we all settle in for a well-earned rest.

At the back of the Tumbleweed, sequestered in my bedroom, I lie comfortably on my back, in my cozy bed snuggled up with Rex and Patch lying on either side of me. Windy is sleeping contentedly in a pet bed at the foot of my bed. Poor Windy is just too enormous to fit in my bed with Patch, Rex, and I. I gave him a few plush dog toys and one of my towels to sleep with so he will feel cozy. I'm confident that he is safer and much more comfortable here with us than being alone in the desert. I'm buried under my fuzzy blue and green plaid blanket with my e-reader perched on my knees. I spend a few hours reading my new novel *Aliens, Campers, and Coffee* by Karen Bruno. Afterward, I pray silently and then I cry myself to sleep, finally releasing the last of my sorrow for my husband Lew.

Chapter 59

Theme song: "My Feet are on the Rock" by I AM THEY from the album Trial & Triumph

In the morning, we rise early. Sam arrives with her dogs so we can all eat breakfast together. I prepare caffé mocha for my friends. I serve cinnamon toast, yogurt, and large bowls of whole grain oatmeal topped with blueberries, raspberries, and blackberries. I hand out travel mugs of fresh coffee for everyone to enjoy during our expedition to the scarred landscape known as the Channeled Scablands.

After breakfast, I borrow Missi and Murphy's truck to take Windy in for a health checkup at Sandy Town's sole veterinarian. Rex and Patch's vet, Dr. Sneezie, tries scanning Windy with a microchip reader to identify an owner but unfortunately no microchip is detected. Dr. Sneezie has no record of Windy being a patient at her practice, so Windy will remain in my care. After a physical exam, vaccinations, and a complete lab work up, the kindly Dr. Sneezie declares that my new companion is fit and healthy.

The day is clear and bright with a blazing sun hanging in the blue sky. Unfortunately, it's another windy day. Our vehicles are traveling at a snail's pace due to the unruly winds. Missi and Murphy, riding in their pickup truck, lead our caravan through the desert. I follow behind them carefully driving my Tumbleweed. Last in our caravan, is Sam driving her vintage station wagon and expertly towing her Airstream Bambi despite the windy conditions.

Since we will be far away from settlements and towns, Fic and Gan no longer need to disguise themselves as grannies. However, they are so enamored with Sam and her fashionable outfits, they choose to continue impersonating grannies. Today, they're wearing matching purple maxi dresses decorated with pink flowers. They accessorized the outfits with pink flip flops, purple turbans, and pink opera gloves with large bangle bracelets.

My intergalactic grannies are accustomed to traveling in my Tumble-weed. They are happily lounging in the dining booth with *Star Trek* mugs of coffee. On the dining table are bowls filled with chocolate covered almonds and cranberries. They are both reading copies of *Aliens, Campers, and Coffee* by Karen Bruno. On the table are the games Star Trek Galactic Enterprises and Yes, Yes Yeti Risk-Taking Card Game!

The drive turns out to be uneventful and we make it to Washington state in just one day. We take the opportunity to stop at the last big town to stock up on groceries and supplies for our stay in the wilderness. Granny Fic and Gan provide the coordinates for the final leg of our trip. From here on out, we will be boondocking in the SasTribe territory.

When we leave the last town and paved roads behind us, we journey into the Channeled Scablands wildlife refuge wilderness. Granny Fic and Gan give me directions for the last bit of travel. Now the Tumbleweed takes the lead in our caravan to seek out the SasTribe. After living in the sandy deserts of southern Nevada, I find it curious that this desert has very little sand and soil.

It's essentially a flood scarred landscape of bare rock as far as the eye can see. Much of the bedrock is exposed and it has an odd, undulating texture. I spy towering rock formations, formidable cliffs, steps, and buttes. There are weird stacks of small rocks piled up into triangular spires and strange scooped out channels in the bedrock. *Rather than rock stars there are rock scars.* It takes us awhile to find a suitable area that is reasonably level to park our campers. Granny Fic and Gan are beyond excited and they begin flying around the interior air space of the Tumbleweed with their long dresses fluttering in their wake.

"Hold on, dear grannies. It takes me a few minutes to get the Tumbleweed safely parked and level."

The moment I shut down the motor, Granny Fic and Gan fly out the door with Windy, Patch, and Rex following close on their heels. Gleefully, my grannies are flitting around and exploring the new landscape. The dogs are following my grannies and marking their new territory. I unbuckle my seat belt and slide out of the driver's seat. I tuck my flying saucer key chain into the front pocket of my blue jeans and climb down the steps. My feet are on the rock and it's actually quite pretty with wavy lines and swirls of different colors. I wave when I see Sam walking over with CJ and Rocky.

"This is breathtaking." Sam looks around in awe of the dramatic landscape.

I join my friend and together we gaze in wonder at the Channeled Scablands. The ancient flood-sculpted land surrounding us is vast and beautiful. The only sound I hear is the sighing of the wind as it swirls around the rock formations. The land appears empty at first glance and yet it isn't. High overhead I spy birds of prey circling and gliding effortlessly on the thermal air currents. What really captures my interest are the many color variations and patterns in the rocks. This place is hauntingly beautiful.

"What do we do now?" Murphy asks as he and Missi take a seat in the camp chairs arranged under the Tumbleweed's patio awning.

"Good question." I shrug my shoulders as Sam and I join them, taking a seat in the shade. "Granny Fic and Gan are in charge of this expedition. Heaven help us. I'll go inside and prepare food for us. There's no point in starting our new adventure on empty stomachs."

I hop up from my chair and climb the steps into the Tumbleweed. I prepare fresh spinach and spring mix salads. I grate fresh Parmesan cheese over the salads and top them with grape tomatoes, baby carrots, chopped walnuts, cashews, sliced almonds, sliced avocados, dried cranberries and yellow raisins. I add a drizzle of balsamic vinaigrette dressing. I pull shots of espresso and make large iced mocha lattes for everyone. In a few minutes, I call my friends to come inside and collect their meals.

We gather in the kitchen to collect our travel mugs of iced mocha and our plates heaped with delicious vegetables, fruits, and nuts. We slowly move toward the doorway and one by one step down. On the bottom step, Sam suddenly stops behind Missi and Murphy. I accidentally bump into Sam as I'm climbing down. They are all frozen in place, blocking the doorway and my exit.

"Oops, I'm sorry Sam. Are you okay? Hey, what's wrong?" I ask while trying to peer around the three of them. Suddenly I shriek in fright, nearly dropping my plate.

Chapter 60

Theme song: "Face to Face" by Zach Williams from the album Rescue Story Deluxe Edition

Standing in our campsite are two towering visitors who seem to have stepped out of a 1960s era hippie commune. Except for the fact that they're WatSoGian sasquatch dressed in hippie fashion. They must be at least eight or nine feet tall. Our visitors are decked out in multicolored woven cloth vests worn over short sleeved peasant blouses and groovy bell-bottom jeans. They're wearing very long carved wood bead necklaces that hang down the front of their blouses. I notice that their clothing is embroidered with the same WatSoGian geometric patterns and symbols that I saw inside Granny Fic and Gan's crochet needle. Their oversized feet are bare and very hairy. They are completely covered in lustrous, russet-brown hair that is very long and wavy. They both have light caramel-colored beards that reach down past their waists.

Even though I thought Sam and I were prepared to meet our new WatSoGian friends, we are both suddenly speechless in their towering presence. Granny Fic and Gan fly over to graciously welcome our visitors.

I'm surprised that my grannies didn't mention that their friends are very fashionably dressed hippies who drive off-road vehicles. I'm completely captivated by our new friends. *It's hard to believe I'm meeting more aliens living right here on Earth.*

It turns out that Granny Fic and Gan have been in constant communication with SasQueen during our travels. She was informed of our arrival and her two emissaries were already on standby to welcome us the moment that we arrived in the Scablands. *I'm relieved that we didn't have to embark on a long trek to find the WatSoGian sasquatch.*

"Fellow WatSoGians, welcome to our cumbersome land vehicle encampment." Our grannies speak at the same time. "It will be a moment before our humans regain their ability to speak." My grannies float gracefully higher up into the air so they can shake hands with our new friends.

One of the emissaries steps forward. "Hello everyone. Welcome to the SasTribe commune. My name is Bill and this is Leonard."

"Hello, it's nice to meet you all. Peace, love, and blessings to you." Leonard flashes us a peace sign with his enormous hairy hand and the long hair on his arm undulates with his movements.

Murphy steps forward and shakes hands with the sasquatch gentlemen. "Hi, I'm Murphy. This is my beautiful wife, Missi. Nice to meet you as well. Impressive 4x4 off-roaders. Just look at the size of those rock-crawling tires. I bet these Jeeps travel boldly where no other vehicles have gone before. Sorry, I couldn't resist a little *Star Trek* humor. But seriously, these are the perfect vehicles for this challenging terrain. Do you mind if I take a closer look at them?" Murphy sets his plate of salad down on one of the camp chairs and walks with big bouncy strides over to the Jeeps.

"Of course. I'm glad you like the electric Jeeps. They are quite a lot of fun to drive, especially in this unique terrain. We have endless routes through the Scablands to experience the thrill of rock crawling. Trust me, you will get to experience some wild thrill rides here in the Channeled Scablands in these 4x4s." Bill replies pleasantly with a terrifying fang-toothed grin.

Murphy seems to be more excited about the Jeeps with the enormous knobby tires than about our incredible visitors. Sam, Missi, and I grin with amusement at his enthusiasm for the off-roaders. Missi shakes her head fondly at her husband and walks over to Murphy who is practically drooling over the Jeeps.

Murphy speaks imploringly to Missi. "Honey, sweetie, my one true love. Can I get a Jeep 4x4? Wouldn't it be fun to drive one of these?"

Missi smiles at her husband and pats his arm affectionately. "We'll see, sweetheart." Missi rises up onto her tiptoes and sweetly kisses her husband and then gently combs her fingers through his full beard.

Sam and I finally step forward to greet our visitors. "Hi, I'm Sedona. Thank you for inviting us to visit. You live in an incredibly mysterious land and it's stunningly beautiful. It's nice to meet you. This is my friend Sam."

Sam smiles flirtatiously up at our giant visitors. She boldly steps closer to them and shakes hands with Bill and Leonard. They smile down at her from their lofty height.

I'm trying hard not to stare, but I'm having a hard time dragging my eyes away from Bill and Leonard. Together, they exude charisma that is hard to ignore. They have a dynamic presence. After a few minutes, I remember my manners.

"Leonard and Bill, we were just about to eat. Would you like to join us? I have plenty of salad and coffee left." I inquire with a friendly smile while holding up my plate of salad.

"I could eat!" Bill states with enthusiasm.

"Leonard, how about you?"

"Do you have any fresh road kill or warm bloody meat? One of your dogs will do just fine. Kidding! I love dogs. I'm just kidding. I really prefer vegetables. Salad is great, thank you."

I set my plate on an empty camp chair. I catch Sam's eye and I point to my eyes and then to our dogs and then to her. Sam nods in understanding and I climb back inside the Tumbleweed. I emerge a few minutes later and serve Leonard and Bill their meals. My friends help me arrange our camp chairs into a large circle and we all settle in to relax together. Bill and Leonard are too enormous to fit into my human-sized chairs, so they settle themselves on the rocks at our feet, sitting cross legged. I say a quiet blessing over our meal. I'm thrilled to see that Leonard and Bill bow their heads and pray with us.

Granny Fic and Gan are holding their salad plates while serenely floating above their chairs with their iced coffees resting in the cup holders. "Do you like living here on Earth? What about WatSoG, do you miss home as much as we do? When you traveled to Earth did all of your family come with you? Do you like coffee? Coffee is very acceptable to us!"

Bill answers between bites. "I live on coffee. My entire family and all of their friends traveled together with the WatSoGian expedition to help carve out the SasTribe commune here in the Scablands. I like living here but I was born here. I've never visited WatSoG. I often hear my parents speaking about WatSoG and though they love living here on Earth, I think that sometimes they miss WatSoG."

Leonard nods his head in understanding. "I was born on WatSoG. I was old enough to remember the long trip to Earth with my family. I was only a half-grown cub at the time. My family and I like living here on Earth. I think it probably took them many years to adapt to life on Earth but our kind has carved out a comfortable home and we enjoy a great life here."

I finish my salad quickly and politely excuse myself for a few minutes to feed our dogs and to check on Topaz. I return to my chair and listen to the rest of the conversation.

"We are instructed to bring you as soon as possible to SasQueen. Our gracious leader extends her invitation to visit our fortress. We will drive you across the Scablands when you finish your meals." Leonard explains.

"This is very acceptable to us! It is pleasurable to have the company of WatSoGians again and we are happy to join your commune for a visit. We approve this! Before leaving WatSoG, we promised our grandparents Tti and Unee that we would visit SasQueen. We must fulfill our promise. Our thanks, Leonard and Bill for extending the peace, love, and blessings of Wat-

SoG upon us. We are saddened that our family are still home on WatSoG and we are not allowed to go home ever again. We miss our family greatly, but our human and animal companions are very acceptable to us and they have helped us to feel less alone on Earth." Granny Fic and Gan speak at the same time.

I smile at my dear grannies. I understand the depth of their despair and loneliness over their separation from their family. I feel a pang of sympathy for them and I know how they feel since I'm mired in regret about my mom and my husband.

"I have a few concerns about visiting the SasTribe fortress. What about our animal companions and my coffee plants? I won't leave them here all alone at the campsite. I don't mind staying here to care for them while the rest of you go with Bill and Leonard."

"That won't be necessary, Sedona. Please bring your animals and plants. We respect and welcome all forms of life at the SasTribe commune. There is room for everyone to journey with us. Fic and Gan informed us about the size of your family. We traveled here with two off-road Jeeps plus the small livestock trailers that you see here. We are able to accommodate your needs." Leonard kindly reassures me.

I glance over at the Jeeps again. I notice that each vehicle has wide, all-terrain tires with aggressive tread patterns to cope with the rocks and channels of the Scablands wilderness. Even the small trailers have been adapted to handle the extreme and rocky terrain. They have a higher-than-normal ground clearance and they're also equipped with off-road tires and suspension.

"Alright I can see that you came prepared to transport all of us. Thank you. How long will we be staying? Should I pack clothing and pet food for the journey?"

"SasQueen has approved a visit of two weeks duration. It is SasQueen's honor and her pleasure to host all of you and there will be plenty of food for everyone. However, we wish for you to be as comfortable as possible during your stay with us. Please bring any personal belongings that you wish and whatever will make you the most content during your visit. Leonard and I will help you load your animal companions and supplies into the trailers."

I'm worried about the extreme rocky landscape and I hope the bumpy ride won't be too uncomfortable for my animals. I'm glad to help Granny Fic and Gan visit their WatSoGian friends and I hope they all have a wonderful visit together. *As long as we are all together as a family group, I'm content no matter where this journey leads me.*

"Sedona I'll help you gather your supplies and pack up. Then you can help me get my things from the Bambi. Together we will take good care of our little family."

"Thanks Sam. I'll clean up the dishes and then we can get started."

Sam jumps up to help me and in thirty minutes we are ready to venture into the unknown. We lock up our campers and rejoin our company. Sam and I carry my coffee plants over to the Jeep. Bill helps me load our companion animals into the stock trailer where they will safely travel together. I'm pleased when I notice that the trailer has thick rubber floor mats, wood shavings, and well-padded interior panels. He secures the trailer door and we're ready to depart. I watch with interest as Bill contorts himself to fit into the driver's seat. It appears to be a very tight space for such a large being. I notice that the Jeeps don't have roofs and that allows enough head room for our guides.

Sam, Granny Fic and Gan, and I climb into the back seat. There is just enough room in the small cargo bay behind our seat for my potted coffee plants. We arranged them carefully to prevent them from falling over during our off-road adventure. In the second Jeep, Missi and Murphy accompany Leonard.

"Please buckle up it's going to be a rough journey." Bill advises.

"Aye aye, captain. By the way, I'm a Trekker and I noticed that you and your friend have famous names. Is it just a coincidence or is there something more I should know?"

Bill roars and then laughs loudly. "So, you noticed, did you? That's groovy. My parents love *Star Trek* and so do Leonard's parents. Leonard and I grew up watching the original series and we're Trekkers too."

"Oh, Bill now you've done it. You and Leonard will be treated to Sedona's endless monologues about all of the episodes from all the *Star Trek* series. Brace yourself." Sam laughs with amusement.

We start our journey, moving slowly across the bumpy terrain. I look back and watch as our campers disappear from view. We drive across a flat rocky expanse bordered by rock towers and outcrops. Suddenly our Jeep pitches alarmingly at a terrifying angle as the off-roader rolls slowly in a controlled crawl down into an enormous bedrock channel. It lurches from side to side as it crosses over the sculpted basalt bedrock. Leonard expertly pilots the second Jeep down the same path following in our wake.

Sam and I are buckled in securely but we are still bouncing so fiercely that we both grab onto the seats in front of us to steady ourselves. I look over at Granny Fic and Gan and they are calmly floating above the seat with their long dresses hanging below them. *What a great way to avoid the hard, bumpy ride. I'm just a tiny bit envious of their smooth-as-air ride.*

I'm also feeling unpleasantly queasy from the incessant lurching of the Jeep. This ride feels like being on an airplane during severe turbulence. I wish I had a sick bag for my motion sickness. I swallow the feeling and I will myself to contain it. Eventually, we begin to gain elevation and the Jeep climbs slowly up out of the bumpy channel. At this point, I'm desperately missing my steady Tumbleweed and the smooth, paved highways that we normally travel on. *Rock crawling is definitely not for me.*

I've completely sweated through my clothes after a couple of hours of rough riding through the bone-jarring terrain and a few vomit pit stops. I notice that Sam's face is delicately dotted with ladylike perspiration while I'm drenched in a puddle. Even so, she is likely as uncomfortable as I am. We are both so frazzled from the trip that we don't speak. We sit in miserable silence, clinging tightly to the seats.

Finally, we pull into yet another long rock channel carved by ancient flood waters. It has a towering butte looming at the far end. Our drivers navigate straight down the length of the dry channel and when we reach the end, they take us around to the back side of the massive rock formation. The Jeeps stop suddenly right in front of the steep rock wall. In a few moments, a camouflaged faux-stone garage door grinds slowly open and the Jeeps drive into the darkness of the gaping maw. Sam and I are clutching each other nervously and peering into the darkness.

"What's happening? Where are we going?" Sam barely manages to squeak out her words through a fear-tightened throat.

"There's no reason to worry. We are entering the SasTribe subterranean fortress. We're home. We will be joining the commune in a few minutes."

Leaving our familiar world behind, our convoy drives single file into a deep, dark tunnel. As the door closes behind the vehicles, complete darkness envelopes us. The headlights engage and by their reflected glow, I can make out chiseled rock walls on either side of the off-roader. The going is much smoother and I can finally relax back into my seat. After a few minutes of driving, the tunnel is angling steeply downward and we begin descending into the earth. Eventually, we pull into a wide, brightly lit cavern. There are many electric Jeeps parked along the outer wall. Bill drives over to the charging station and parks. Leonard pulls in next to us. They plug the Jeeps in to recharge the batteries.

Sam and I slide out of the Jeep's back seat and stand on shaky legs. We share a sweaty hug, relieved that our wild ride is finally over. Our clothes and hair are a little disorderly and tangled from the windy and extremely bumpy ride.

"We made it. I'm so happy to be stationary again. Bill thank you for driving us safely over the intense terrain."

I wave at Missi and Murphy as they climb out of their off-roader on unsteady legs. I clip a rope to Topaz's halter and gently coax her out of the trailer. She doesn't look too frazzled from the trip and I breathe a sigh of relief. Our five dogs follow us out of the trailer and eagerly explore the area around the parked vehicles. Sam calls them back and clips leashes onto each one.

Granny Fic and Gan, with not a single wrinkle in their dresses and looking well rested despite the hard ride, float serenely out of the Jeep and join us. Noticing our sweaty and disheveled appearances, they send Sam and I a frosty breeze that carries the delicious scent of peppermint ice cream. Sam and I smile appreciatively and sigh contentedly.

"Ah, that's a refreshing breeze. Thank you, Grannies." I say while taking my dogs' leashes into my shaking hands. I smile at my uncharacteristically messy friend. "Thanks Sam. I wonder where this unusual journey will lead us?"

"Let's go find out." Sam smiles confidently.

Chapter 61

Theme song: "Home" by Zach Williams from the album Chain Breaker Deluxe Edition

"Sedona, this is very acceptable to us! We approve this! This experience will lead to good things for each of us. This is where you must have faith. Let us help you. We will take the leashes for you. We love to float alongside your canine companions."

"Thank you, Grannies. You're right of course. I will rely on my faith in God that only good things are on the horizon. Lead on my friends."

"Sedona, I will ask some of the SasTribe members to collect Topaz's hay for you. For now, please follow us and we will guide you and your friends into the cavern system." Leonard says.

Leonard and Bill help Missi and Murphy gather our belongings from the trailer and then they lead our group toward a lighted passageway. We enter another narrow rock tunnel and after a short hike we emerge into an immense cavern dwelling. *Whoa, it's a stunningly beautiful abode.*

Towering multihued rock walls and ceilings are striking shades of cream, nutmeg, and cinnamon enhanced with a darker ribbon of coffee-colored rock. The colors smoothly blend together like a river flowing throughout the stone. The patterns and colors contained within this cavern home are a natural art form.

Bill gives me a closed-lip smile. "Sedona, if you bring Topaz this way, I will lead you to a pasture where we have a herd of donkeys. I'm sure that she will be comfortable living with our herd during your stay with us."

"I was worried about where Topaz would be kept during our visit. I just didn't know what to expect. I'm so relieved to know that you also keep companion animals. Are they Earth donkeys or are they originally from WatSoG? If they're alien donkeys, will they cause any harm to my girl? Will she contract some unknown disease or infection from WatSoG? She's family and I'm responsible for keeping her safe."

This time Bill reveals a ferocious-looking smile, he's so amused that he can't hold it back. "SasTribe is very fond of keeping a donkey herd. They are indeed Earth donkeys. Their ancestors were living here in the area and we started feeding them during the winters and eventually they kind of became family to us. That's why we carved out a beautiful pasture for them to enjoy. Why don't you and Topaz follow me into the cavern system and you can see for yourselves?"

Suddenly I'm undecided on my course of action. This seems entirely too coincidental and what if Bill is leading me away from my group for nefarious reasons? What should I do? My anxiety ramps up and sweat is starting to roll down my torso soaking my shirt. Being separated from my party of friends while among alien sasquatch seems dicey to me. However, where else can I keep Topaz during our stay in a cave? Undecided, I stand rooted to the spot.

"Granny Fic and Gan! Will you please come with Topaz and I to meet the donkey herd?"

"Sedona, you are turning an alarming shade of eggplant. Is everything alright?" Bill inquires mildly.

Granny Fic and Gan float over to me. They take one look at my face and gently take hold of my hands. "Let us go touristing together into the caverns with your sweet Topaz. This is very acceptable to us! We approve this!"

Suddenly, I feel a cool breeze waft around me and I inhale the soothing scent of peppermint and eucalyptus oil. I feel much better. *Although, what good can my 39 1/2 inches tall grannies do to protect us from a 108 inches tall alien sasquatch if things get hairy down there in the deep dark cavern?*

We follow Bill down a new tunnel that twists and turns away from the main abode. After a long hike in the darkness, we emerge into a high-walled enclosure. I spy chisel marks all over the cavern walls indicating that the Sas-Tribe carved out the enclosure by hand from the natural stone. This part of the rocky domain has no roof and sunlight pours down nourishing several vegetable fields and one large pasture. There is a stream running through the fields. I notice that the grassy meadow has a few trees and is occupied by a very large herd of peacefully grazing donkeys. The open-air cavern is filled with warm sunshine and a gently blowing breeze.

Bill holds the pasture gate open for us. After pressing a kiss to her fuzzy forehead, I set Topaz free with her new herd. Topaz is surrounded by the inquisitive donkeys and they greet her and inspect her carefully. After all of the curious donkeys have finally decided that Topaz really is a donkey despite her miniature size, they all move off together to graze.

We spend a few minutes watching the herd and Bill points to each of the donkeys and tells us their names. I laugh with delight when I realize they are all named after characters from the various *Star Trek* television series and movies. We all chat companionably as Bill guides us back through the long tunnel to rejoin our friends.

I'm amazed at the rustic luxury on display in this beautifully decorated rock dwelling. Sam and I look at each other with delight. *The SasTribe are living an unexpectedly luxe lifestyle.*

"This is not what I was expecting. Look at this unique home. It's sumptuous." Sam exclaims with the joy of a person who loves elegant decor. "I feel like I'm at an exclusive resort. I love the furnishings."

There are stalactites clinging to the cave ceiling and placed among them are luminous crystal chandeliers sparkling above our heads. They display rainbows of dancing light upon the cavern ceiling. Elegant silver floor lamps illuminate the artistic patterns and beautiful colors in the curved stone walls.

We walk across deep plush carpeting in a stark arctic white. There is an army of Roombas charging like a company of tanks to a battlefield, valiantly grooming the floors. I smile at the sight of them ranging across the fields of carpeting seemingly in tactical formation.

A battery of beautiful sofas and club chairs are arranged all around the vast room. The handmade furniture is carved from exotic woods and the cushions are covered in handwoven dyed burlap fabric. Elegant coffee-colored sofas and wide cream colored club chairs are adorned with brass studs and carved wood accents.

Massive stone fireplaces add glowing warmth and comfort to the cool stone rooms. A stunning collection of marble sculptures of trees, flowering plants, butterflies, hummingbirds, and wildlife are scattered among the seating area.

There are several ornately carved mahogany dining tables stained a dark chocolate hue. The tables look as if they can comfortably accommodate a hundred diners each. Placed at intervals along the length of each table are centerpieces that illuminate the dining area. They are arranged in enormous green marble bowls filled with white pebbles and strands of twisted LED mini lights are entwined around wide silver flameless candles. The dining chairs are oversize club chairs with white fabric and silver studs. Wood framed color photographs of the magnificent Scablands adorn the rock walls.

Chapter 62

Theme song: "Hello Beautiful" by MercyMe from the album Lifer

Before us, the entire SasTribe is gathered in the vast space. There must be hundreds of loyal members protectively surrounding their leader.

SasQueen steps forward and welcomes us. She is imposing and stands out among the russet-brown haired members of SasTribe with her lovely caramel-colored hair. *Ooh, she's a beautiful caramel queen.* Like SasTribe, she is also barefoot and attired in hippie-style clothing handmade from natural fibers. SasQueen is dressed in a colorful cloth vest over a peasant blouse and she also wears bell bottom blue jeans. The fabric she wears is also embroidered with the same WatSoGian geometric patterns that I saw in Granny Fic and Gan's crochet needle.

"I am SasQueen, leader of this Earthly WatSoGian colony. Welcome fellow WatSoGians. Welcome humans. You have the honor of being the first of your species to be invited into our peaceful commune. We are pleased that you have agreed to stay with us. Fic and Gan, your grandparents are dear friends and trusted allies. We thank you for joining us. We wish to honor your historic visit with a feast later this evening."

SasQueen gestures grandly with both of her long hairy arms. The long caramel hair on her arms sways with her movements. "In the meantime, please join me for a cup of coffee and scones so that we may become properly acquainted." SasQueen displays a fierce fang-toothed grin that she probably intends to be welcoming, unfortunately it's terrifying.

SasQueen lumbers over to one of the oversize dining tables and claims the ornately carved throne at the head of the table. The tables and chairs are very tall and the attendants place mounting blocks in front of the chairs that we will sit in. We wait politely until the WatSoGian queen is seated. She graciously gestures to the club chairs arranged around the tables and as SasTribe settles in, we climb up into our chairs. We humans look very silly in the giant chairs with our legs and feet dangling above the floor. Once I'm seated, the table top is nearly level with my chin, which will make it so much easier to shovel in the delicious meal. When SasQueen bows her head, the SasTribe members follow suit and my friends and I quickly comply. SasQueen utters a blessing in WatSoGian and then repeats her words in English. Afterward, Sam and I share a startled look of astonishment with Missi and Murphy. *What is happening? The SasTribe are Christians? Christian alien sasquatch friends are definitely for me.*

SasQueen looks at us with amusement. Her fierce visage is transformed by a toothy grin of mirth and bright amber colored twinkling eyes. "Are you surprised humans? Didn't Fic and Gan tell you about us? The SasTribe is a self-sufficient Christian commune. We produce everything that we need right here in the cavern system. Including our own food, clothing, and solar power. We also produce Bible study guides and we have several social media accounts that we use to share the Gospels. We also maintain a website that has Bible study plans and also shares *Holy Bible* Scriptures to help spread the Good News about the Kingdom of God far beyond our little corner of the Scablands. Through countless generations, the SasTribe has always lived a lifestyle that the modern world labels as Jesus freaks."

After the blessing, the queen's personal attendants silently move to the table on bare hairy feet. One carefully pours steaming coffee into her tall tankard and then adds milk and honey. Others present the queen with serving platters of sliced apples, strawberries, cantaloupes, grapes, bananas, and an assortment of dried fruits and whole nuts. Another platter holds fresh picked broccoli, baby carrots, grape tomatoes, cauliflower, and sliced cheese. Other attendants present serving platters piled with fruit scones and clotted cream and honey.

I gladly inhale the invigorating scent of coffee rising from my mug, which is conveniently sitting directly under my nose. When the platters of food are finally presented to me, I gather some trail mix, carrots, broccoli florets, and a cranberry and orange scone. *Dining in a luxurious cavern enclave with a mythical alien sasquatch queen and her shaggy hippie tribe is definitely for me.*

I collect a few carrots and sneakily stretch my arm down under the table sharing the bounty with Patch, Windy, and Rex. SasQueen catches sight of my movements and she smiles knowingly at me. My face reddens with embarrassment and I hope that I haven't offended the queen. I'm still unsure of the customs here and I want to be a polite guest.

"Since this is your first visit with us, I assigned Peace and Eden to be your personal assistants during your stay. They will take wonderful care of you. Fic and Gan, they will help you and your humans adjust to life with the SasTribe. They will also escort you everywhere so that we will not lose you in the bowels of the cavern system. After our repast they will take you to your quarters and help you to settle in." SasQueen gestures and two of her attendants step forward.

The attendants appear to be teenagers. They smile shyly at us. "It is nice to make your acquaintance."

Granny Fic and Gan float over and greet them with a fist bump. "It is very acceptable to make your acquaintance as well. We approve this!"

I smile and wave cheerily. "Hello, it's nice to meet you."

"Peace and Eden, your help is much appreciated. I would not want to get lost down in the bowels." Sam smiles broadly at our new assistants.

"Now that we are all cozy and caffeinated, Sedona you must share with me how you became acquainted with Fic and Gan. It is quite rare for other WatSoGians to visit Earth and even more so for them to befriend humans. You must have a particular appeal for this to be so. Enlighten me, please." SasQueen looks directly at me with her amber eyes shining with unabashed curiosity.

I place my scone back on my plate and I sit straighter in my chair. I take a large gulp of coffee and share my unusual tale with the queen. "Well, I grow potted coffee plants in my shower using grow lights and I started brewing my own homegrown coffee beans and..."

As I tell my outlandish story, I'm still amazed at the unexpected direction my life has taken. As I speak to the queen, I feel deeply grateful and satisfied with the incredible experiences that have popped up so unexpectedly in my life. *Adventure is definitely for me.*

SasQueen nods her head as she listens attentively to my words. The enormous hirsute queen howls with laughter as I share with her how terrified I was when Granny Fic and Gan first materialized uninvited inside my securely locked Tumbleweed. With an embarrassed smile, I explain how I tried to exorcise them by shaking the metal crucifixes that dangle from my blessed olive wood bracelets. The queen howls even louder and pretty soon most of the SasTribe join in. The dining room is filled with the deafening sound of roaring WatSoGian sasquatch. With a start, I notice that most of the SasTribe are staring at me with fascination as they listen closely to my bizarre tale. SasQueen grins with amusement as I tell her how the sound of their long knife-like toenails screeching and scraping across my floor still haunts my dreams occasionally.

"It is obvious Sedona, that you choose to wander down the road less traveled. I believe that you and your amiable companions are a fine example of your species. I can see why Fic and Gan chose to befriend you. It is entirely possible that your unique coffee is just a bonus that you bring to the relationship. Now, it is time for me to take my leave. I am in need of a long rest. We will reconvene here tonight for the evening meal." SasQueen nods regally at us as she rises from her throne. SasTribe respectfully stands. I nearly fall off my chair as I try to climb down and Murphy kindly grabs my arm to steady me. The queen leans down and bestows a kiss upon Granny Fic and Gan before she exits the dining hall with her gaggle of attendants following in her wake.

Chapter 63

Theme song: "My Story" by Big Daddy Weave from the album Beautiful Offerings Deluxe Edition

My little family and I follow Peace and Eden down yet another seemingly endless stone passageway to a warren of rock carved bedrooms. Bill and Leonard help several SasTribe teenagers carry our backpacks, dog food, and my coffee plants. Sam and I are assigned to a large room that we are sharing with Granny Fic and Gan. Missi and Murphy are escorted to the room next door. *Good heavens, the sleeping quarters do not disappoint.*

We sink into soft, snowy faux fur area rugs that decorate the natural stone floors. The space is lit by several brass floor lamps. Our cavernous room has three king size adjustable beds. The headboards are covered with hand-woven silver fabric painted with gold WatSoGian geometric print. The beds are draped with plush white comforters. They are adorned with numerous plump pillows encased in handwoven silver pillowcases decorated with gold WatSoGian geometric print.

Huge carved blackwood bookshelves cling to the stone walls. The shelves are overflowing with every type of literature that you could ever wish for. Il-luminated in the glow of more brass floor lamps are elegant white club chairs accented with blackwood legs. The chairs are arranged in front of the enormous stone fireplace to take advantage of its glowing warmth.

Draped over the club chairs are fluffy silver blankets embellished with gold WatSoGian geometric print. More snowy faux fur area rugs lie at the feet of the club chairs.

The en suite bathroom has a crystal chandelier hanging from the stone ceiling. Its glowing light radiates across the ceiling, accentuating the rough surface and highlighting the veins of color in the stone. Plush silver rugs add warmth to the natural stone floor. There is a huge soaker tub with multicol-ored LED lighting and heated jets. Hand-carved blackwood candle stands with silver candles grace the wide rim of the tub. I spy a ridiculously massive and very tall toilet. When we enter the bathroom, the enormous toilet seat illuminates. *I hope that I don't fall into the sasquatch-sized toilet. Use with caution.*

"Sedona, we are never ever leaving this amazing place." Sam smirks playfully and gently bumps me with her elbow.

"We live here now and we will forever be known as cavern dwellers from this day forward." I agree wholeheartedly. "This is the most stunning home I have ever seen. I love the curious mix of natural stone caverns and highly elegant furnishings. Plus, I'm enjoying the company of its unique inhabitants." *It turns out that alien roommates are definitely for me.*

After our tour of the suite, Sam and I set out several food and water bowls for our dogs. Since we had to leave the pet beds in our campers, we borrow several spare blankets from the closet. I fold a few and place them on the stone floor for my dogs. Sam does the same thing next to her bed and she creates a cozy nest for Rocky and CJ.

"I can't wait until bedtime because I'm going to borrow a book and curl up in one of the reading chairs for a bedtime story." I comment while inspecting the collection of hardback books stacked in the beautiful carved-wood bookshelves.

"Oh, I love story time. I'll join you. These cozy reading chairs next to the fireplace are so inviting." Sam remarks. "Between the heated soaker tub and the library with the cozy fireplace, I kind of never want to leave this room."

Granny Fic and Gan fly over and join us in the reading nook to help us examine the bookshelves. They float up toward the ceiling to get a closer look at some of the books.

"Sedona, there is a hardcover copy of the novel that we are all reading. Look there, it is shelved on the left. *Aliens, Campers, and Coffee* written by Karen Bruno. Fascinating. It is a limited edition with photos and pastel artwork and it is hand-signed by the author." Granny Gan floats down to me carefully holding the rare signed edition.

My granny gently passes me the hardback book. I carefully open the cover and there is indeed a hand written inscription by the reclusive author. I read the message aloud to my little family. "To my dear friend and mentor, SasQueen. I truly appreciate your assistance with regards to the details of the WatSoGian expeditions to Earth. I'm enchanted by your colorful stories of WatSoGian myths and legends. I greatly enjoyed the tour through your fantastical gardens. Best of luck with your exotic blooms. Your friend, Karen."

"It is a lovely inscription. Friendships are to be treasured. This is very acceptable. We approve this." Granny Gan says while dabbing at his eyes with a handkerchief.

"I wonder how SasQueen got this hand-signed limited edition? Could she know the socially awkward and shy writer? Do you think maybe they are close friends?" Sam asks.

"From the inscription, it sounds like they are indeed friends and that the writer visited here. What if she stayed in this very guest room? Maybe she wrote some chapters right here in this cozy reading nook." I say, looking around the room.

"Sedona, will you read us a bedtime story this evening?" Granny Fic and Gan ask together. Granny Gan levitates up into the air and returns the signed limited edition of *Aliens, Campers, and Coffee* to its place on the bookshelf.

"Good idea. For a bedtime story, I will read from *The Lost World* by Sir Arthur Conan Doyle." I say while pulling a copy from the bookshelf. "It's a great book for those who love adventure. How about I read some chapters from Lewis Carroll's book *Alice in Wonderland* while we await the SasQueen's return this afternoon? Here's a modern reprint of the original 1865 edition. This copy features the illustrations by Sir John Tenniel." I retrieve *Alice in Wonderland* from the bookshelf and gesture to the reading chairs.

"Wait a moment and I'll run next door and see if Missi and Murphy want to join us for the reading. I'll be right back." Sam scurries out of the room to retrieve our friends.

In a few minutes, Sam returns with Missi and Murphy. Finally, we are all seated in the cozy club chairs near the toasty warmth of the flickering stone fireplace. We happily settle in for story time. Hours later, Peace and Eden come to our room and escort us to dinner.

Chapter 64

Theme song: "To the Table" by Zach Williams from the album Survivor: Live from Harding Prison - EP

The dining room is aglow from numerous candles and stone fireplaces. Soft, flickering candlelight pulses from the chunky silver candles nestled in beds of white pebbles pooled inside green marble bowls that are scattered along the length of the carved mahogany tables. The warmth and glowing light emanating from several rustic stone fireplaces envelopes the diners in a soothing embrace.

We are invited to dine at SasQueen's table. She holds court seated in her throne at the head of one of the long tables. Granny Fic and Gan are asked to sit next to each other on one side of SasQueen. Sam and I are seated across from our grannies. Murphy and Missi are seated next to us. SasQueen's most trusted advisors and assistants are also seated close by at the queen's table. The rest of the SasTribe are dining with their families seated at the other ornately carved tables. SasQueen raises her huge hairy paw. The candlelight gleams menacingly on her long sharp claws. The dining room falls into respectful silence. The queen bows her head and offers a blessing over our meal.

Bountiful platters of fresh spinach, spring mix greens, cherry tomatoes, sliced carrots, sliced avocados, dried fruit, whole nuts, sliced apples, sliced bananas, oranges, apricots, and herb seasoned roasted vegetables are carried by an army of the queen's attendants. They surround the queen and wait patiently until she fills her plate.

Afterward, they silently swarm all of the tables patiently bearing their burdens until each diner fills their plate. I happily select fresh fruit and vegetables, trail mix, and finally I take a spoonful of the herb seasoned roasted vegetables. My mouth begins to water at the delicious aroma of warm herbs and spices wafting up from the oven roasted gold, red, and purple baby potatoes, caramelized onions, and sliced carrots that are drizzled with olive oil.

SasQueen clears her throat with a loud growl. Conversation ceases and heads swivel toward the queen. She raises her tankard of iced coffee and takes a large swig. "Fic and Gan, I invited you and your Earth friends here for a very specific reason. SasTribe needs your help with a troubling situation that has been plaguing us for the last year. Essentially, we have a serious public relations problem."

I share a look with Sam, Missi, and Murphy. They look as surprised as I feel at the moment. What could possibly be troubling the SasTribe and their imposing leader way out here in the remote wilderness? From what I have seen so far, they appear to live a comfortable life entirely on their own terms.

Granny Fic and Gan levitate slowly up into the air until they are at eye level with SasQueen. They float serenely above their chairs as they address our benefactress. "SasQueen and SasTribe, we are happy to be reunited with you, our fellow WatSoGians. This is very acceptable to us! We approve this! We are honored to be here in your fortress. Tti and Unee sent us here to be of assistance in any way that we can." The WatSoGian brothers speak at the same time in perfect unison, as they spread their arms to encompass all beings seated at the massive dining tables. Several SasTribe members raise their tankards of iced coffee in acknowledgment.

"Excuse me, SasQueen. Would you please explain the type of problem that you are encountering? If we understand the situation, perhaps we can formulate a plan together to resolve it." I speak respectfully and then I smile at my friends encouragingly. I sincerely hope there is something that we can do to help SasTribe.

"The SasTribe are being tracked and hunted by large groups of humans that trespass on our lands. Apparently, they belong to bigfoot hunters and cryptozoology research teams. Perhaps you have heard of this type of thing? These groups of enthusiastic yet misguided cryptozoologists are of course attempting to collect evidence of our existence. Many large groups of humans come here to film a television series. They camp on our lands for many weeks. They conduct exhaustive searches and they run around the Scablands with television cameras yodeling fictional sasquatch mating calls. They also set up field cameras and bring various types of disgusting meat. Often, they leave "sasquatch bait" on boulders and rock formations. Perhaps with the hope of luring one of us in for a photo op. This behavior is repugnant and completely uncivilized! This silly activity of the humans only manages to feed the birds of prey in the area. These misinformed humans seem to believe that we are wild animals and carnivores. It's really quite disturbing to watch these humans carry on." SasQueen pauses her monologue to catch her breath.

"It appears that some of the humans are TV explorers, researchers, biologists, or are contestants on reality television shows. Perhaps some of them are hosts of podcasts and websites promising to reveal the "truth" of the myths and legends surrounding bigfoot or sasquatch. Sadly, they know nothing of our true nature." SasQueen reveals the scope of the problem facing SasTribe.

"How unfortunate. It sounds like your community is being systematically harassed by trespassers." I remark.

"How can we help you?" Sam inquires.

"We have been working on an extensive project for quite some time. I believe it will be instrumental in tackling this issue. After you finish your meals, I will show you." SasQueen smiles mysteriously at us.

Intrigued, my friends and I continue to enjoy our meals while listening to SasQueen's explanation. Steaming platters of whole-grain oatmeal seasoned with cinnamon and cardamom are served for dessert. The spiced oatmeal is accompanied by bowls of sliced walnuts, whole cashews, almonds, dried cranberries, and yellow raisins. I add a spoonful of nuts and fruit to my oatmeal, then pass the bowl to Granny Fic and Gan. The brothers grin at me in delight. The nutritious food is delicious and when we finally fill our bellies, we are completely content.

"Come walk with me. I will lead you through the cavern system." SasQueen commands us as she rises majestically from the table. The SasTribe rise from their chairs with their leader. My friends and I quickly stand in respectful silence as we await the guidance of the queen.

"Fic and Gan please journey at my side. We have much to discuss. Your human companions will be escorted by my assistants Peace and Eden."

Chapter 65

Theme song: "Back to the Garden" by Crowder from the album American Prodigal Deluxe Edition

My little family and I follow Peace and Eden who are guiding us with flashlights down into the cold, dark subterranean tunnels. Murphy and Missi are walking close to each other holding hands and chatting companionably. As I walk along next to Sam in the glow of the flashlights, I admire the raw beauty of the rough stone. Eventually, the passage begins to get much darker and descends gradually. The air temperature drops noticeably as we continue to descend into the secret depths of the cavern.

As we progress further through the passages, the stone beneath our feet is slick in places from the gently weeping ceiling. I feel a cave kiss land on my head. The icy droplet of water melts into my hair. I shiver at the weird sensation.

"Sedona, where do you think the SasTribe is taking us? Should we be worried about our safety following them down into the unknown bowels of the Earth?" Sam whispers to me as we walk side by side, carefully navigating the slippery stone pathways.

"Don't worry Sam. I felt that way the first time I ventured into the tunnels with Bill but everything was fine. I trust Granny Fic and Gan completely and by association, I trust their friends SasQueen and SasTribe. We're on an authentic adventure and I'm sure that it's going to be fun. Have a little faith, Sam."

The passage through the cavern gradually widens as we hike along. We are navigating carefully around the ancient sentinels of the caves; stalagmites growing up out of the cavern floor. Above our heads, stalactites hang tenaciously from the ceiling occasionally dripping a kiss into our hair. In places, the stone floor is gritty with eroded bits of rock that grinds into powder under our boots. Surprisingly, we begin to feel a breeze wafting through the passage and we gaze around us as we follow far behind SasQueen, Granny Fic and Gan, and the members of SasTribe.

Peace and Eden continue to lead us through several more subterranean levels of twisting passages. Eventually the stone floor beneath our feet gradually begins to rise higher and higher as we walk. After another thirty minutes of hiking, we emerge into a vast open cavern cloaked in swirling mist. As the mist recedes, it reveals an immense tropical rainforest. We stand in awe of the splendor displayed before us, blinking our watering eyes to adjust to the sudden brilliant sunlight.

The melodious sound of birdsong fills the forest. Many strange-looking birds dart between various nests cradled in the tree branches. The towering rock walls of the cavern loom high above us. Immediately, I notice the cavern has no ceiling and it's wide open to the blue sky above us. The forest is filled with rays of sunlight slanting through the mist and fresh air circulates through the vast space.

Countless species of unusual and never-before-seen birds and butterflies inhabit the forest. Bird calls echo off the towering stone walls. The tropical trees and flowering plants radiate outward to fill the cavern with gently swaying green leaves and brilliant multicolored flowers.

There is a stream gurgling musically as it flows through the protected nature preserve. Its pristine waters, that begin as an underground river, rise up to flow through the cavern system. The fresh water is naturally filtered by its passage over the rocks. The stream nourishes a meadow of colorful wildflowers, plants, shrubs, and trees.

I'm enthralled by the weird varieties of plants, insects, and birds. In this haven of botanical beauty, I spy a few gigantic butterfly species thriving as they dine on the nectar of enormous flowers. I can't believe what my eyes are seeing. *How is this possible? What kind of an otherworldly garden is this?*

I spy unusual hummingbirds, butterflies, bees, and moths flying from flower to flower. The feathers of the eagle-sized hummingbirds shine in the sunlight revealing metallic silver and purple polka dots. Covering their bodies are yellow feathers with orange and green zigzag patterns. There are enormous and vividly patterned butterflies the size of hang gliders. They are erratically flitting among the blooming trees and plants. The butterflies display various colors ranging from palest pink and soft luminous yellow to deep metallic bronze, copper, silver, and gold.

SasQueen turns toward us and smiles broadly displaying her fearsome fangs. She spreads her hairy arms wide to encompass the view before us. Sunlight glints off her lovely caramel hair which is glowing and swaying in the breeze.

"Welcome to our extraterrestrial gardens. We are WatSoGian botanists and conservationists." SasQueen proudly announces to her captivated human audience. "I believe the time has come for us to come out to the Earthlings. To live openly among the Earth citizens. To boldly show them the value of intergalactic diversity. Over many generations here, SasTribe has carefully studied and nurtured extensive cavern gardens. What you see here is only one of the gardens."

Granny Fic and Gan start humming loudly and then they suddenly levitate up into the air. They zoom across the rainforest to peer at the WatSoGian wildlife, trees, and flowers. They are consumed by energetic flying zoomies for several long minutes as they speed around the nature preserve. Finally, they wear themselves out and fly back to us.

"This is very acceptable to us! We approve this! It is enchanting to see a proper WatSoGian garden hidden here on Earth and this makes us feel more at home than ever before." My intergalactic grannies dab at their misty eyes with their handkerchiefs.

"This hidden forest is unbelievably beautiful. What are your plans for your gardens?" I ask the queen curiously, without taking my eyes off the incredible sight. *Beautiful extraterrestrial gardens are definitely for me.*

"Most of our gardens have grown into large tropical forests like this one. We conserve rare trees, flowering plants, birds, and butterflies from WatSoG. We transported many native species with us on our expedition to Earth. Now many decades later, they are flourishing here in our fortress. We wish to open our caverns and botanical gardens to ecotourism for the delight and education of the Earth citizens. Perhaps we can encourage all beings to value the beauty and peace of our wild nature. We wish to educate visitors about Sas-Tribe and WatSoG. Our goal is to encourage humans to appreciate and to peacefully accept all beings that live here. I believe that educating our visitors about the flora and fauna of WatSoG is a pathway to peace and acceptance. Perhaps we can encourage humans to care more about living in harmony with each other and the Earth. I believe that we can change the minds of humanity through ecotourism. With compassionate acceptance and respect, we can encourage all beings to love and to accept each other for who we really are. Let's cease judging other beings' preferred lifestyles and simply coexist in unity and acceptance with one another. We will no longer tolerate the practice of forcing others to become who and what we think they should be. It is better to love our neighbors as much as we love ourselves." SasQueen smiles beatifically at her entranced listeners as she reveals the heart of her campaign to bring lasting peace, love, and blessings to all beings.

If you enjoyed *Aliens, Campers, and Coffee* please take a moment to rate and review it. Reader ratings and reviews help people discover books to read. Sedona, Sam, and I are very grateful for your help. Sedona and Sam are such good dogs; don't you think that their story deserves five stars? For each positive rating and/or review left by a generous reader like you, my dogs will receive delicious treats. Please leave a review, so these sweet pups can be rewarded for your kindness. Thanks very much for your help.

The author's faithful companions, Sam and Sedona. Photo by Karen Bruno.

The author's pal Patch. Photo by Karen Bruno.

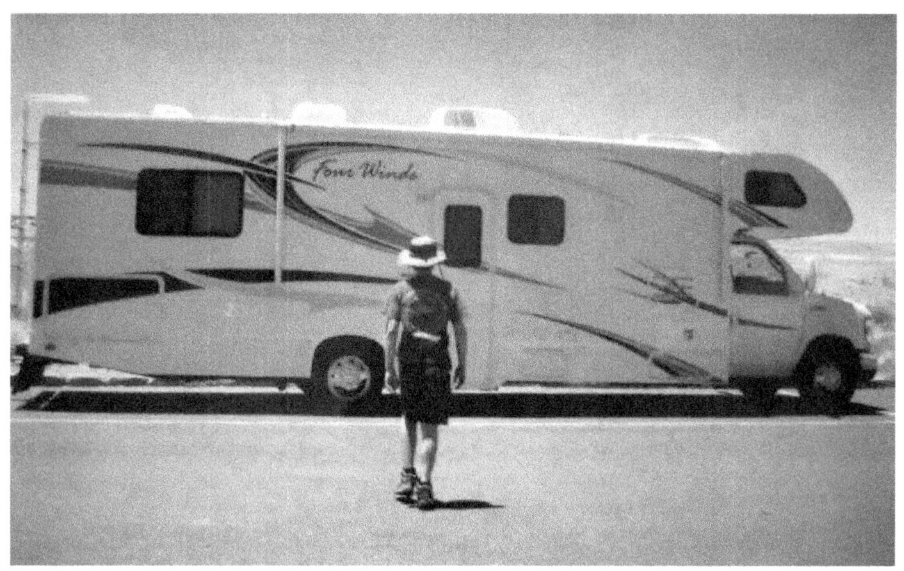

The author's Tumbleweed at Petrified Forest National Park, Arizona. Photo by Karen Bruno.

Karen Bruno and Rocky learning training level dressage. Photo by dressage instructor Andrea.
Jesus answered, "I am the way and the truth and the life. No one comes to the Father except through me." The Gospel of John, chapter 14, verse 6. *Holy Bible* New International Version.

"Very truly I tell you, the one who believes has eternal life." The Gospel of John, chapter 6, verse 47. *Holy Bible* New International Version.

Don't miss out!

Visit the website below and you can sign up to receive emails whenever Karen Bruno publishes a new book. There's no charge and no obligation.

https://books2read.com/r/B-A-SWMMC-PIPDF

BOOKS 2 READ

Connecting independent readers to independent writers.

About the Author

Karen Bruno enjoys intertwining elements of science fiction, humor, and the drama of complicated relationships that define our existence into her inspirational tales. Traveling with her family in their RV across America has inspired her writing. She is retired from working in the fields of: Aircraft maintenance on jet aircraft as an FAA-certificated aircraft maintenance technician utilizing both her airframe and powerplant licenses, working in a city government public relations office, and operating her own horse ranch with her family.

www.ingramcontent.com/pod-product-compliance
Lightning Source LLC
Chambersburg PA
CBHW050318160726
48002CB00001B/81